SEPARATED

BEE DAVIS

For permission requests, send an email to support@beedavis.art
Published by Honey Bee Publishing

First Edition
ISBN: 979-8-218-66628-6

Printed in United States
Editing by Kara Aisenbrey
Characters, symbol and map by Shayla Hammer
Format and cover design by Miblart

SUPPORTERS

Captain Mike's Dolphin Tours ~ ***Tybeedophins.com***
LeeAnn Marsh ~ ***tybeeproperties.com***
Stacy Horner ~ ***Islandstravel.net***
Ian Anderson
Mark Benevides ~ ***Segwayofsavannah.com***

If you would like to become a supporter with financial contributions, recognized on this page, contact support@beedavis.art

DEDICATION

This book is dedicated to those of you who lost a loved one and grieve, to those of you who carry the heavy weight of sorrow for any reason.

This book is dedicated to those of you who refuse to accept limited possibilities. To you, the reader, who take refuge in escaping the norm.

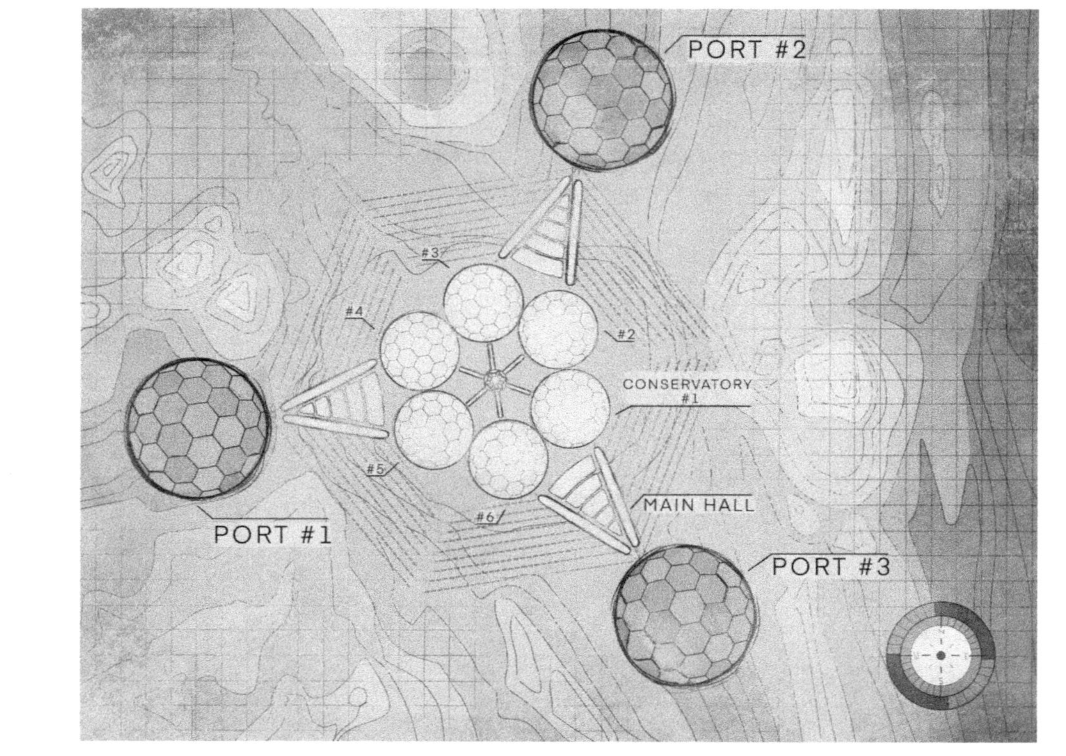
PORT #2
#3
#4
#2
CONSERVATORY
#1
PORT #1
#5
#6
MAIN HALL
PORT #3

The image is an ariel view of one of the 8 cities on Mars. Each are built the same.

- Three massive ports covered by dome shaped glass that host all transportation vehicles.
- There are two main underground hallways, covered by a curved glass roof that leads out of each Port.
- Nine residential extensions extend from the side of each hallway. Each extension hosts 88 apartments
- In between the main hallways is a galleria where there are schools, health centers, food preparation, eateries, and various public service shops.
- Each hallway connects to a massive conservatory or dome shaped greenhouse, in which food is grown either in the ground or from hundreds of layers of hydroponic growing trays. Some conservatories host special and seasonal classes.
- Only 1 conservatory, Conservatory #6 (or the Main Conservatory), hosts the Unity Festival and public cafeterias and private eateries.
- There are six Upper End hallways that extend from each conservatory, with three residential extensions on each hallway and 22 apartments on each extension.
- A small dome conservatory is at the end of each of the 6 Upper End hallways, creating the center of the city.

CHAPTER 1

A day on Mars is called a sol, which represents a solar day. Each sol is about 24 Earth hours and 39 minutes. And a year on Mars is 669.6 sols or 687 Earth days.

This was the sol it all began for the high school seniors who got to Unite with the one they loved. But it was the beginning of a dreadful existence for Virginia, who had no choice but to Unite with someone, anyone—or be sent to live on a different planet with her only living relative.

There was nothing more important to the people of Mars than Uniting—it was, after all, how their civilization had come to be, when centuries ago, a native Martian helped the founding fathers and mothers by giving them powers that contributed to their survival. Powers only given to those who United, who touched the Unity Stone together.

The power of healing helped the early settlers with any injuries or illness so that they could build without interruption. The power of creating joy, which was coupled with the ability to teleport to nearby areas, kept their spirits high and work got done faster. The power of creating peace ensured the harmony they needed to create life accommodations on such a desolate planet. The power of truth gave the United pair the ability to see into the future, to see things that were hidden and know the unknown; this power also came with the ability to make things magically appear and disappear. Even greater powers were given: Royal powers, whose magic was as unique as the few humans who received them.

Every winter, for sixteen weeks, all eight cities on Mars celebrated Unions with the Unity Festival, which included dinners, dances, and Spaceball games. It was the only time each year that couples had the chance to Unite by touching the Unity Stone and receiving their powers. Virginia had looked forward to the festival her whole life—until Charles died.

She hurried home from her early-morning work in her laboratory, where she toiled to finish her final plant genetics engineering project for graduation. Paden would be over soon to hype her up for tonight's opening ceremony.

As she waited for her best friend to arrive and heated water for tea, the first memory she had of Charles began playing like a movie in her head. She'd shown up late for her first sol at her new school. The teacher fell silent when she walked into the second-grade class. As the kids pointed and laughed, the teacher directed her to the only open seat, next to a messy boy with pale skin.

As she sat next to him, all the snickers and sneers became silent, and every bit of loneliness and fear disappeared when the boy quietly said, "Don't be scared, they're just afraid of your hair. It has nothing to do with your poor clothes." She looked up to see an inquisitive bend in his brow and one finger aiming to inspect a creamy-colored ringlet dangling at the side of her face.

Virginia slowly backed her head away from the boy's encroaching finger.

He smiled gently, revealing a gaping divide between his two front teeth, then lowered his inspection finger. "See?" the boy whispered, looking around the room. "You're different." He became oddly distracted, staring into her bronze eyes. He put a large synthetic smile on and moved his head dramatically from side to side. "Do you see your reflection in my eyes too?" he asked with sincerity.

Virginia looked into his eyes. "N-no."

"Your eyes..." he said, "look like little mirrors. I can see myself in them!"

As she stared back into the windows of his soul, an ocean of waves swirled around her head. She sensed safety as deep as the sea when he whispered, "My name's Charles, and you don't have to worry, I'll be your friend. You and me will go on tons of space adventures and spend forever together."

Neither Virginia nor Charles noticed the teacher's disapproval until she clapped her hands in front of their faces.

Clap, clap, clap.

Virginia regained consciousness as her water began to boil over. She turned off the burner and held her face in her hands, remembering that he was gone. Grief swooped in to comfort her, warming up the empty cavity in her chest and heating the blood in her head and limbs until it too seemed to boil, and she wept.

The pair should have never met. Charles and his family lived in the Upper End, along with the city's governor, cabinet members, administrators, and Planet Protectors, just north of the large glass-domed Main Conservatory, where crops were grown and the Unity Festival was held. Virginia lived in the Lower End, south of the Main Conservatory, with the families who cooked food for the city, worked as aids and teachers, and labored to grow crops, working through natural disasters and all hours of the night to keep the city of Alcetra safe and comfortable. The city leaders had thought sending Virginia to a school in the Upper End would honor her parents' sacrifice: they'd died when she was only in first grade, on a mission collecting soil from Earth, leaving her to grow up with her Grandmother Blane.

And now that Charles was gone, she would have to Unite with someone before the last sol of the Unity Festival.

The door opened to reveal the eager grin of her best friend. "Big sol and big news! Have you seen it?" Paden said as soon as she was a few steps inside the apartment. Her face was bright as she continued to question Virginia's clueless expression. "On Amos News? The Ananta—magically appearing in the Main Conservatory?"

The Ananta was the purple symbol of perpetual love, of endless union. A love with a beginning but no end. A symbol of the extraordinary magic of Royal Unions.

Only the souls who had loved each other unconditionally in a previous life and found each other in this one were granted Royal powers, which included all of the powers of the Peace Makers, Joy Givers, Healers, and Truth Bearers. But they also had some special powers of their own, powers that were said to have the ability to make anything happen. Powers that were rumored to be limitless.

Virginia was a master at disguising emotion. She raised an eyebrow, which Paden accepted as an invitation to turn on the entertainment hologram. Virginia emptied herself onto the sofa and sighed as a tall, lanky overdressed bald guy appeared on the hologram. Amos was like a brother to Paden and Charles, like the grandson her grandmother had never had, so she always kept her mouth shut about him and watched his news show—and tolerated it when he made her the news for the sol.

"Do you have an idea what this phenomenon that appeared overnight may be?" Amos asked a band of girls who were staring up and pointing at the glowing purple Ananta suspended high in the center of the Main Conservatory's dome.

"See," one girl said, tracing the seamless line of the large figure eight with her pointing finger. "It's alive. The glow flickers. Like there's specks of purple light moving through it, keeping it connected."

"It certainly does look like there's some movement up there," Amos reported. "Do you think this could be an act of the Royals?"

Another girl from the group stepped toward Amos to answer the question. "Of course it is. It's purple like the symbol on the Royal flag, isn't it? And the Royals have the power to make something like this happen. Besides, I've read about them making extravagant displays like this long ago... before the curse."

Royal Unions had always been rare, as unusual as the unconditional love that made them so powerful, but they had become even more rare in the last fifty years. Some called it a curse. Many believed that Royals had become a fairy tale, a staple of the history books. This morning, along with the magical appearance of the Ananta, the belief in the greatest power between two human souls had come back to life.

After the commercial break, Amos appeared in the Upper End Hall, the only place where news from the other seven cities was available. "It looks like this mysterious Ananta has shown up in Morphus, too," he confirmed and walked to another information hologram that was reporting the news from another city. "And Erbos."

But Virginia was sad to face this sol, and all the sols of Unity Festival, and wasn't too concerned with anything but feeling better. "I don't see what's so exciting about this. People die whether they are Royals or not," she mumbled as she rubbed her dog's warm belly.

No, the Ananta was by no means her favorite symbol. The last time she'd seen a slightly different version of the Ananta, representing life forever, it was in a horizontal position, painted on the embarkment door at her grandmother's funeral only a few months ago. And not even a full year ago, only sols after last year's Unity Festival, she'd seen it when her heart was launched out the embarkment door with the ashes of her childhood sweetheart.

"Gin," Paden began gently, "whatever is going on out there is exciting. And you will meet someone to Unite with within the next few weeks, and we can begin our adult lives together. Maybe live on the same extension, start families at the same time. Things we always knew we would do."

"I should be Uniting for love, not out of necessity..." Virginia replied, annoyed.

Living space inside the Martian cities was limited. No one lived alone. Singles lived with family or they weren't allowed to remain on Mars. Because Virginia had no family left here, she had to Unite or leave the planet.

"Come on, Gin. This is the year we've been waiting for since we were little girls!" She gently rubbed Virginia's stocking feet and continued. "Charles is gone. It's been nearly a year. This is your one chance..."

Virginia had a hard time hiding her anger. She abruptly got up and walked across the room, replying in an irritated tone, "Until you lose someone who loved you for nearly your entire life, the one person you couldn't wait to spend every sol with, someone who never let you down and made an exciting life safe for you, don't tell me what I should do."

"I didn't mean to upset you. I grew up with Charles too. I know how much he meant to you," Paden argued humbly. "It's just... you know... although Singles here are just as important as a United pair, they must live with family, and your only relative lives..." She was silenced by Virginia's piercing cold stare.

Paden bounced up, her long silky black hair swaying behind her soft shoulders. "I've always seen us as being best friends forever. You know, even when we're little old ladies. I just want to Unite, get my powers, and spend my life with my bestie, that's all." She quietly put her empty cup in the sink, and when she returned to the living room, she finally asked, "Could you please just try to be happy this Unity Festival and give Uniting with someone your best?"

"Sure." Virginia sighed. "As long as it's a boy who knows I'm Uniting for the sake of convenience," she added.

Paden snickered. "Actually, I have some great news for you about that. But first, tell me you love this and that you'll wear it to the opening ceremony tonight." She held up Virginia's old skirt and top that she'd altered with decorative ribbon up the sides and around the trim. "The violet color was a bit of an accident, but it will show off the gold in your eyes."

Virginia chuckled in surprise. "It looks brand-new. Thank you." A hopeful grin curled up the side of her mouth.

"I added trim to make the top a little longer. If you weren't so tall and thin, you'd be able to find tops that didn't show so much of your pasty white skin."

"I thought it was a trend," Virginia replied with a smirk.

"Yeah!" Paden laughed. "Because Amos made you famous, following you and Charles around, recording your every move for the whole city to see."

Virginia rolled her eyes. "Right... a trend!"

When Amos was only thirteen and Virginia and Charles only ten, he began recording the moments they spent together and loading it onto the entertainment holograms. As he recorded and uploaded more content, it quickly became the local news for young teenagers. Charles and Virginia's adventures and non-adventures were often the highlight of his show.

"Well, clearly no one likes your hair, or there would be a bunch of girls with cream-colored ringlets with crop tops running around," Paden teased.

Virginia wasn't amused. She was always a little put off that her life was never private so that Amos could have his news show. "So... what's the great news you have for me?"

Paden smiled proudly. "Brothers. Twins, actually. Coming from the city of Diony to meet you and me at the opening Spaceball game."

"Why?"

"Because they heard what a catch we are!"

Virginia looked at Paden with wide eyes, waiting for the details.

"Okay... Mrs. Lox arranged it, and she asked me to ask you about courting one of the brothers," Paden explained.

"So I can say no?"

"Why would you want to do that? This would be perfect! They want Mrs. Lox's job, which means they would come here and neither you nor I would have to leave Alcetra. And we would be United sisters—if our Unions were favored by the Unity Stone, of course."

The Unity Stone was hosted in the Unity Booth, and when a pair touched it, the color of their new power glowed through their hands and bodies only for the seconds that their hands were touching the stone. Once they had their power, they carried it to their deaths.

Virginia's countenance dropped. "So they're horticulture nerds like me. Which means they don't fly in space. Which means they will be completely boring," she complained.

"Gin, I would love to meet some science nerd from the grand city of Nos who discovers freakishly strange life forms, but I am a student nurse. My father is a mechanic; my mother is an almond picker. No one is going to invite me to Nos. You and me? We just have to accept whatever we get. And although these guys aren't our dream, a Union with them would be a pretty fair deal," Paden lectured.

Virginia rolled her eyes. It was a heavy responsibility to bear along with the sadness of so much loss. "Yep. Gotta take the deal."

There were strange sounds at her door. She pressed the square button and the door slid open. She wasn't surprised to see the little pile of brightly decorated boxes. She had received gifts from Amos News fans on a few occasions. Uninterested, she set them on the kitchen counter.

Paden was hasty to open the packages. "Sweets! Bread! Soaps!" she yelled into the living room, where Virginia had returned to her melancholy state on the sofa with her fluffy little dog Ridgley. Paden read the printed cards aloud. "Graybell from Extension 220 sent the sweets, and she says, 'Sometimes love comes again.' The bread is from a group of girls from Extension 320. 'Believe' is their message to you."

With a bottle of soap under her nose and a hologram card attached to a small box in the other hand, Paden walked over to Virginia. "This box of candies is from Amos. He says, 'Keep your chin up, kid.'"

"Mmmm... That's nice."

"You see, Amos isn't such a bad guy. A lot of people really enjoyed watching you on his news show and want to see you happy. Your adventures with Charles were exciting. People in our city don't just up and fly around Mars or into space for the fun of it. But you two risked the wrath of Charles's dad just for an adventure! You two were more than news—you inspired people to be adventurous," Paden said with a smile.

Virginia's frown broke as she remembered the calm that swept over her body once she and Charles made it into space—after he'd fooled Old Man Willie into thinking his International Space Vehicle was an administrative ship. As they sat among the dark star-speckled space, catching their breath, Charles had looked at her, grinned devilishly, and sang a tune that really had no meaningful words, but echoed so majestically inside the cabin of the ISV.

With that memory, she knew she had to get her head right, because she couldn't go on without another one of her favorite people in life. She assured her best friend, "Don't worry. I'll be there. I don't want to lose you too."

Inside the Main Conservatory, Virginia and Paden stood silent, in awe of the magnificent grandeur of the Unity Festival: the massive Unity flags that draped the sides of the conservatory's dome; the Ananta that had magically appeared overnight, shining as brilliantly as a sun-kissed artichoke flower; and the tables overflowing with elegantly displayed food, decorated in the colors of the United powers, red representing the Truth Bearers, yellow representing the Joy Givers, green representing the Healers, blue representing the Peace Makers, and purple representing the color of the Royals.

Throughout the year, Alcetra's six conservatories were massive greenhouses for growing food, some also hosting classrooms and cafeterias. Every year, they cleared out all of the plants and classrooms of Conservatory 6, commonly called the Main Conservatory, to make space for the events of the sixteen weeks of the Unity Festival, only leaving the cafeterias open throughout the week.

Virginia and Paden walked around the round grassy center of the dome, where a classroom would normally be during growing season, with hydroponic growing trays hanging in the light of the sun, searching for a table filled with Paden's friends from the aid station. It was customary to sit at a table that was decorated the color of the United power you wished to have or that you thought your family was. A green table, the United color of healing, was exactly where they found Paden's friends from the aid station.

Although Virginia sat with the most caring nurses in the city, who many times during the last year had treated her grief with compassion and a warm bed and oxygen when needed, she felt alone and misplaced. She looked around at the tables and noticed her classmates, the ever-unoriginal Singles of the Upper End, all wearing the same newest-style suits in various shades of the same dark, drab colors and sporting similar slicked-back short haircuts—and all sitting at tables decorated purple, where the Singles of the Upper End traditionally sat every year.

Virginia's people-watching was interrupted when she heard her name with a question attached. "Can you repeat that?" she asked.

"If the Unity Stone could give you a power without being United, what would it be?" Nurse Dylan asked.

"Hmmmm..." Virginia stalled, fighting back the pressure behind her eyes that she knew would turn into tears if she didn't control herself.

Paden was excited to answer for her friend. "Oh, Virginia has a sixth sense. It's nearly scary the things she knows, the things she senses. She would certainly be given the red power of the Truth Bearers."

Virginia nodded in agreement.

"I think my mother is a Truth Bearer. She knows everything that I never tell her," one aid at the table added.

"How about Charles?" Dylan carefully directed the question at Virginia. "What power do you think he would have had?"

Virginia's face finally lightened as she replied, "Charles was so peaceful, calm, and kind. He would have definitely been a blue. A Peace Maker."

"Ooooh… blue and red makes purple!" another girl at the table blurted out, rubbing her two pointing fingers together to make a kissing gesture.

The nurses laughed and ate and gossiped, but Virginia was only interested in the heart of the Unity Festival. She excused herself from the table to get a closer look at the small crowd on the north side of the conservatory, just opposite the entrance to the Upper End where the Unity Booth was.

As she strolled through the crowds, she was warmed by a happiness in the air from the Singles and Uniteds, who wore easy smiles and moved about with grace, as if they were listening to the song of their souls.

Virginia came to the little square tent where a handful of couples stood in line, waiting to touch the Unity Stone and become United with their power. She watched one very happy couple come out and pose for the wall of families cheering and taking photos. The next anxious couple entered the booth, and as she waited for them, she mindlessly gazed at the colorful reflections on the white tent walls from the five holographic United flags that flashed around the top of the Unity Booth. The couple soon exited, screaming and bouncing toward their family, and Virginia hurried away into the crowds, attempting to silence the grief that rose inside her body, as furious as a Martian windstorm.

Suddenly, in front of her was a table full of all of Charles's Spaceball teammates, surrounded by doting Planet Protectors—the table she and Charles would have returned to with their United powers.

Why are they all so happy? Don't they know he's gone? she wondered while she stared at everyone at the table, noticing her head fill up with anger—or was it grief?

Escaping sadness, she walked into the blissful crowd, who flaunted new kitschy merchandise in all of the United colors. The vendors, stationed at the entrance to the Lower End, were flailing around hand-clappers and tossing balls and waving flags above their heads. Purple was the hot color this season, no doubt because the symbol of the Royals had shown up in the conservatory.

Virginia squeezed through the crowd to the row of vendors and stopped in front of the Love Counseling Booth, where the line of nervous couples was already much longer than the line to the Unity Booth. With only one chance during the season for official Union, couples paid to get advice about their love choice from the unseen but ever-so-famous character inside.

In front of the line, a woman with giant round eyes and glistening tea-colored skin spoke from an information hologram. There wasn't a single person watching it. "...there were seventy-seven red Unions, twenty-eight yellow Unions, fifty-four blue Unions, forty-one green Unions, and zero purple Unions. We always recommend that you follow the voice of your soul when choosing a partner to Unite with." She stopped, then started from the beginning with an even bigger smile. "The advice of the Love Counselor has not been approved by the Unity Festival Administration. You are free to enjoy the fun of this mysterious hologram at your own discretion. The Unity Festival Administration offices have tested—"

"Virginia, you're not thinking of...?" She turned around to see a tall overdressed bald guy backing away from her ear.

Her shoulders drew back and her eyes narrowed—he was likely recording her from the little camera pinned on his jacket pocket next to an oregano flower. "You know that I believe in following the sense of my own soul." Virginia crossed her arms. "Not to mention that this 'Love Counselor' hides behind a curtain and has yet to show his face."

"Yeah, seems shady to me too," Amos agreed.

Making her way back to the table with the aids, she noticed a familiar helmet of reddish-brown hair atop a petite woman moving toward her—her grandmother's interesting best friend, whom she loved dearly.

Virginia walked to meet her. "Ms. West! What are you doing here?" she asked, examining her never-before-seen exceptionally tidy attire.

"Meet my friends," Ms. West said, looking at the jolly-cheeked man with oily skin and the tall, refined woman standing next to him. "Farro, Professor in Plant Genomics, and his wife, Food Science Administrator, are here visiting from Nos and will be helping serve dinner to you young whippersnappers tonight."

Nos was the first city built on Mars, the city that all seven others had been designed after. The original city was home to the smartest Martian humans and hosted all the great science programs—including Martian Plant Genomics and Physiological Mechanisms of Plant Adaptation to Temperature Stress, the program that would have propelled Virginia forward in her independent studies if she'd had the opportunity.

She was shocked that simple ole Ms. West knew anyone from Nos, or that they would care enough to visit her.

"Come to my place after dinner and tell Professor Farro about the bean cultivar you've been working on," Ms. West said, flailing her hand around and walking away.

Virginia didn't know what to think. As exciting as the opportunity to talk about plant genetics engineering with a professor from Nos was, the heavy weight of having to give up her passion if she didn't Unite this season was a heavy opponent.

The violinists on the stage had started playing, and all the Singles took their seats, the magical mood of the evening setting in as the overhead lights dimmed and the colored lights in the center of their tables shot up through the conservatory's dome, dancing in synchronicity with the tune of the violin.

Lights lit up the center stage to reveal Mayor Max, who was responsible for the safety of everyone inside the city of Alcetra. He started with a little joke, which everyone politely laughed at, and then gave reports on the city's population growth and the success of their agriculture trade. He finished by introducing Mr. Clemata, the Unity Festival Administrator. The crowd whistled, clapped, and waved their new kitschy merchandise in the air. Mr. Clemata smiled humbly and bowed to the cheering crowd, until they were finally quiet. He began by sharing the total number of Unions that were registered with each power in Alcetra.

The crowd began to yell in unison, "Speech! Speech! Speech!"

It was the same speech he gave every year for the opening of the Unity Festival: the creed of Martian humanity that every student memorized in first grade, because there was nothing more important among the eight cities on Mars than Unity and the United powers.

Mr. Clemata motioned for the crowd to hush and began. "Every Union of love is made powerful with the magic of the Unity Stone. It is because of these magical powers of Union that we have a peaceful and healthy Martian civilization. You must allow your soul to lead you to true love, and choose love without expecting in return. It is our duty to love unconditionally and create the one Union that can never be destroyed—a Royal Union that only changes in form lifetime to lifetime and holds unlimited powers to do the most good for our planet." The excited crowd of Singles interrupted him with whistles and shouts and claps and stomps. Mr. Clemata waited until they quieted to finish the speech. "Heed the call of your soul to find this joyous Union of perpetual love this season, kids!"

Virginia sat quietly while the nurses around her clapped and whistled, taking the green laser light off their table and shining it around the conservatory along with everyone else. She loved her city, the people here, who were informal and rowdy at every given opportunity, but the heavy sadness of loss kept her seated and quiet.

She noticed the emptiness in her body, a great void deeper than the depths of her bones. Charles wasn't there. And he wasn't off on some adventure with his father. *He's gone. He's dead. He's not coming back.* She looked at Paden next to her, who was dancing and cheering in front of her chair, and forced a mini smile at her. *I may not ever have the soul connection I had with Charles, but this is my best friend, who is brilliant and loving and kind. And this is my city, with all its rowdy food-growing citizens. And that's enough reason for me to Unite with someone this season.*

"Grief is a heavy sadness that never really lightens. It's only us who become stronger under the weight."

~ Bee Davis

CHAPTER 2

Mars is about half the size of Earth. The diameter at the equator is 6,794 kilometers or 4,222 miles.

Early the next morning, Virginia walked her dog in the small underground solar-lit park between Conservatories 1 and 2. She didn't expect to see anyone and certainly didn't want to see the Spaceball coach who had been trying to get her to acquire her interplanetary license. She shuddered as the garden's exit sign gained space behind him with each step he took toward her. Coach Yung was just another memory of Charles that it felt better to avoid.

I could start walking toward the exit now. But I would have to pass him. I need to come up with a brilliant excuse for leaving in such a hurry.

Before she could think up the perfect lie, Coach Yung was standing in front of her with a warmth that invited her to smile as easily as if she hadn't spent the past year avoiding him. "Virginia. It's great to see you. And this little guy." He bent down to give little Ridgley a scratch behind the ear. "I haven't seen you in this garden for a long time," he said with a concerned bend in his brow.

She looked down at the plush green grass under her feet and picked up the ball that Ridgley had abandoned for Coach Yung's friendly tall black dog. "Right. Did I thank you for the platters of food you sent me... both of them?" She swallowed her pain at the acknowledgment of her two favorite people being dead.

"Of course. Of course you did," Coach Yung interrupted, freeing her from reliving the memory. "I figured feeding you would be better than pressuring you into taking your interplanetary license exam." He laughed.

Virginia laughed with him. *Aaaand here it comes! The reason I've been avoiding him for nearly a year.* "Coach, I'm graduating in sixteen weeks. It's too late for me to join the Spaceball team."

"Oh, but if you took your test, you could be..."

She fervently shook her head back and forth. Getting her IL meant she would have to fly in space, and she just couldn't fly without Charles.

"Oh, come on now," he coaxed. "You have more space flight experience than you should. You're as good as—if not better than—any of the pilots on our Spaceball team. At least get your license for the Planet Protector Reserves. They need you to be available to go out and fight foreign intruders and natural disasters."

Virginia stared into Coach Yung's eyes as he continued to gently convince her. She noticed her shoulders relax and peace and calm wash over her. *Could this be the magic of a Peace Maker?* She imagined the recognition she would receive throughout her life even as just a reservist for the Planet Protectors—and then imagined her future life in Alcetra without the ability to fly in space. Without the ability to escape the lie of her Union of necessity. "Yeah. Okay," she finally agreed.

Coach Yung lifted his brows and without hesitation pulled her into a reassuring embrace. "Don't worry, Virginia. You'll be okay up there without him," he whispered.

"Mmmmmm," she grunted.

"This Wednesol it is, then?"

"Okay," she confirmed with as much of a smile as she could muster.

Virginia returned to her apartment to find Paden sitting cross-legged on her sofa, shaking her dangling foot as if it had fleas on it, holding the skirt and top that she'd updated for Virginia to wear to the Unity Festival on her lap.

Paden was an only child and had lived at Door 2304 on Extension 220 since she was born. The two girls became friends during the Unity Festival of second grade, when

Virginia moved to Paden's extension at Door 23019 with her grandmother, after her parents died.

Paden huffed. "Why is this ripped?"

Virginia couldn't tell her that she'd slept in it. She shook her head. "I don't know. I love it. You did a great job. I was going to wear it to every Unity Dance this season."

"Gin. If you look a mess, or you're sad and no fun… or get sidetracked and show up late or not at all, your date may not be interested in coming back." She sighed and pressed her fingers into her hairline.

"Yes. I know. This is important. I'll be more careful," Virginia consoled her.

"Ugh!" Paden grunted and inspected the garment closely. "I don't have time to take this whole thing apart to fix it. We'll go to Mrs. Saul's. She's brilliant with stitching."

"Ow!" Virginia shouted.

"I'm sorry, dear. These fingers of mine should not be handling these teeny, tiny sharp needles because I can hardly see anymore."

Virginia and Paden silently laughed with their eyes. Mrs. Saul looked like she was 150 years old, but no one ever dared to ask. "I haven't seen you in the aid station lately. Has your grief subsided?" Mrs. Saul asked.

Virginia answered with only a breath out of her nose. She knew Mrs. Saul from the aid station where Paden did her work/study program. She was always leaving the treatment room that Virginia was walking into.

"Mrs. Saul?"

She looked up from her stitching.

"How do you live here... in this apartment by yourself?"

"Oh. I don't." She laughed. "My daughter is an old Single who lives here too."

"Lucky." Virginia sighed as Mrs. Saul continued her careful mending on the skirt around her thin frame.

Mrs. Saul finally stood up. She was tall like Virginia. "You should feel lucky too, girl." She touched the Ananta pendant that hung from the chain around Virginia's neck. "It's not a coincidence that a poor girl owns jewelry, and in the shape of the Ananta, for that matter. Nor is it a coincidence that the Ananta has magically appeared in all of the eight cities this season."

Virginia reached to tuck the pendant back under her top, only to find that it was still hiding under her clothes, hidden on the warm skin atop her sternum.

"The two of you hold the key to lifting the curse. The numbers will show you the way," Mrs. Saul whispered.

The curse of the Royals.

They left Mrs. Saul's with a garment that showed no signs of repair. "What happened in there? You look like you saw a ghost," Paden asked.

"I don't know, really. But either Mrs. Saul is as crazy as she is old or she's a Truth Bearer," Virginia replied.

"Why? Did she read your mind?"

"Not exactly. But she said something about my pendant—and she couldn't see it because it was tucked under my top—something about me and someone else breaking the curse."

"Maybe she is a Truth Bearer and you should go back and ask her more questions," Paden said.

"No, I feel a little nauseous. Besides, Mrs. Saul is really old. I don't know if I could believe what she says."

The next morning, Virginia woke up early to make a bean soup for herself and Paden, who would most likely be arriving hours early to ensure Virginia would be at her best for their dates coming from the city of Diony this evening. She wondered what he looked like. But the only thing she felt any excitement for was her future as a plant geneticist, spending her weekends out in space with the Planet Protectors, and going to the movies with Paden.

Her communication button pinged from the living room table. *Who could be calling me this early on a Sunsol morning?* She put the phone clip on her ear to answer.

"Virginia. I hope I didn't wake you."

"Hello, Coach. No, no you didn't."

"I'm really sorry about this, but there's been a change in my schedule, and I can't give you your interplanetary license exam next week. Would you mind taking it this sol?"

"Coach, it's not a good sol for me. I've got an important commitment scheduled tonight."

"Sure. Unity Festival Dinner, right?"

"Mmmm-hhhhmmm."

"Virginia, we'll launch in an hour, and you can be at your dinner table by five p.m., six at the latest," he replied.

She wanted to say no, but the thought of delaying the exam and thinking about it for a few more weeks was painful. "Fine. I'll see you in an hour."

She looked at the clock. 11:09.

She had no doubt that Paden would be furious with her decision and guilt her out of taking the exam this sol—she had to leave the apartment now, before Paden arrived.

Virginia hurried to drop Ridgley off at Ms. West's, the closest thing to family she had left. Ms. West was the only Single in the city who didn't live with family. The city let her stay in a little old student greenhouse in the far northeast corner of Conservatory 1, to keep an eye on the surrounding medicinal crop. She had plants inside and outside that covered the windows of her tiny home and gave her complete privacy, a bed that was also a sofa, a bathtub without running water, a food prep area with one cook coil, a table for one with two chairs, and she used the conservatory's public toilet.

She opened the door to the little glass shack, and her fluffy dog marched his brown little body in first, eager to find Ms. West, who was sitting at her table. "Still watching Amos's gossip, huh? And wow! You're not wearing your robe! Why are you dressed for success?"

"My friend is coming to visit."

Before she could ask more, there was a knock at the door. Virginia's heart nearly jumped out of her chest—she hadn't seen anyone on the path or heard footsteps behind her. Ms. West, however, didn't look away from the entertainment hologram or get up from her seat. It was weird, even creepy. Virginia hesitated before she opened the door to find a familiar jolly face. How could Farro have appeared immediately after she stepped inside Ms. West's place? *It's like he just showed up. Did he teleport?*

The citizens of Alcetra used their magic discreetly, without making a show of it. They certainly wouldn't use it just to get to someone's home quickly.

"Virginia. Hello, I met you briefly last weekend wh—"

"Yes, you did, Mr. Farro," she said and shook his extended hand. He looked so happy, she couldn't help but smile back at him.

Mr. Farro moved a plant off the second chair and sat with Ms. West. "Virginia, I understand you want to create more plants that can grow outside in the Martian atmosphere and have been teaching yourself the science of altering plant DNA."

She took the pot of hot water off the cook coil and poured it into the two teacups on the table, hanging her head a little. "Yes. I've been working on it, watching videos, reading. I just don't really have the proper equipment or all the answers." She watched little Ridgley's curls bounce up and down as he licked the shine off Farro's plump cheeks.

"Virginia," he said, "I'm the Plant Genomics Professor at Nos, and my wife is the Food Sciences Administrator. We would like to offer you a full scholarship to my advanced molecular biology program, which continues the entirety of the Unity Festival."

"Really?"

Mr. Farro and Ms. West looked at each other and laughed.

"What's funny?" Virginia asked.

Mr. Farro looked at her with sincerity. "You can bring along a travel companion of your choice, of course. What do you say?" He beamed as he watched her, waiting for her reply.

There is no way I'm telling Paden about this offer. Am I smiling or squinting? His happiness is contagious. Maybe he's a Joy Giver and I'm caught under the spell of joy. It's not such a bad thing—smiling and nodding my head up and down like this. Wait. Why am I nodding my head up and down?

"Is that a yes?" Mr. Farro asked.

Virginia laughed, then caught herself. "Thank you for your generous offer, but I'm kinda in a predicament and need to stay here and follow through with my commitments."

"Oh, right." He seemed to understand.

"I've gotta go. But thank you so much for the offer," she said. "I'm gonna leave Ridgley with you for a bit," she told Ms. West.

"Virginia," Ms. West said, and she stopped at the door. "Come see me tomorrow. We'll talk about this opportunity in more detail."

"Okay."

As she made her way down Hall 1 toward the old port where the practice ISVs were docked, she opened up the notifications from her communication button on her wrist: one message and one missed call from Paden. Virginia looked at the time. 12:09. *About three more missed calls and Paden will be coming to look for me.*

She paused in front of a pizzeria at the end of the Galleria and stood watching a handful of plump men singing, working without pause in the kitchen. She craved a slice of the warm deliciousness—a treat she only had the luxury of eating on special occasions.

Her transmitter pinged, but it wasn't Paden. "Hello," she answered.

"Virginia. So sorry, but I'll be a little late." Coach Yung was clearly winded. "I'll call you in a half hour." He hung up before she could ask any questions.

With time to spare, she meandered around the Galleria, pausing at the source of the comforting smell of rich, creamy, sweet candy. It was the largest kitchen, where a small army of women toiled tirelessly. Some were laboriously stirring massive pots, others were cutting sticky portions on the counter, and a pair was pulling apart and refolding blue taffy. Not one of them looked up to notice her watching.

Paden called.

She sat on a nearby bench, right outside the port doors. This was the one place Paden wouldn't expect her to be.

As she watched the ladies make candy, the memory of her last visit to a port replayed in her mind: She was running down Hall 6 toward Port 3 to find out why Charles's brother had told her such a mean joke. She stood frozen on the outside of the crowd that circled the ISV, until she felt Paden standing behind her. "This isn't real," she remembered saying.

She'd watched Alcetra's holy man disappear into the crowd. Moments later he returned with two men following behind, carrying a large black bag. That was the moment she'd known it wasn't a mean joke but the truth. How cruel life could be.

Something made her look at the clock: 12:54. *5+4=9. What's with all the nines?*

Sadness dangled above her, but she allowed bravery to convince her to open the doors to a port that was quietly haunted by the life it had once fostered.

She answered a call from Coach Yung. "Virginia. Are you in the port yet?"

"Ye—"

"Perfect. Just wait there. I shouldn't be too much longer," he said with a nervous crack in his voice.

"Yeah. No problem," she replied, sensing he must be troubled.

As she walked around the port, memories flooded her mind of all the after-school meetings when she'd found Charles wrenching on the spacecraft with the head mechanic, Willie. The times when she and Charles would take a plane and fly around the planet or use the flight simulator for hours when Willie was dozing off, or even the few times they'd used Charles's father's fingerprints to take an ISV into space. A lifetime of beautiful memories lived here.

"Hey Virginia, how ya doing, kid?" the scruffy, unshaven, white-haired man greeted her.

"Ugh. I'm surviving, Willie."

"I wouldn't be able to live without my MaeAnne, neither. But you're a young'un. I'm sure hopin' for ya that love'll come again, gal." Willie whacked her on the shoulder as if she were one of the boys. "Coach called. Said you gots to give the ole *Black Centaur* the safety inspection. Get ready ta get up there."

She changed into her flight suit and greeted Coach Yung's ever-coveted matte-black stealth ISV with satin black flames hiding on its streamlines. She began checking the connections on the outside of the vehicle, just as Willie had taught her and Charles how to do during winter break of fourth grade. She sat in the captain's seat and looked at the clock. 2:54. *Again! How weird!*

She stared at the ISV's door, waiting for Coach Yung.

"Welcome aboard!" the boy with green eyes and a large gap between his two front teeth said from inside the open door of his father's personal Mars plane.

Virginia grabbed his outstretched hand and boarded. "Wow. Neat!" She looked around in wonder.

"Buckle up," young Charles commanded from the captain's chair, carefully pressing buttons on the control board. He pushed his wavy brown hair away from his face. "When I turn twelve,

I'll have my planetary license and we'll explore all of Mars together. And when I'm fifteen, I'll get my interplanetary license and we'll sail through space together every sol," he told her.

Her memory dissolved when the warm smile and glossy narrow eyes of Coach Yung filled the open door. "Ready to make the greatest license of all your very own?" he cheered.

"It's getting late, Coach. If we leave now, I won't make it back till like eight."

"Ah. Well, we'll cut it short, then. I'll just test you on the tricky stuff. How about that?"

Anything could happen in space. She thought of the security of remaining in her city, the work in food sciences, movies with her best friend. She needed to go meet her date. Her future depended on the boy she would meet tonight.

"Virginia. Virginia?" Coach Yung was waving his hand in front of her face.

With each pass of his hand, she noticed her anxiety of returning in time for the Unity Dinner dissipating. She waited until the heaviness of going into space without Charles had lightened and the excitement of adventure took its place.

I wonder if that hand-waving trick is a power of the Peace Makers. Their magic is so subtle, it's hard to tell.

After just a few minutes on a heated and bumpy catapulted ride into space, Virginia was reminded of her infatuation with the vast endlessness of it. She applied her safety code into the coordinates and watched Yung input his.

Neither of them moved nor said a word for a while. Virginia stared silently into the star-studded black sea and watched it become a movie of the many adventures she and Charles had had together. Finally, Coach Yung interrupted. "It's not where you're at, but who you're with, eh, Virginia?"

Surprised that he seemed to be reading her mind, she laughed through her nose, comforted that he validated her thoughts and emotions.

"All right, you got us on the catapult perfectly, inserted your birth date as the safety coordinates—that will ensure your safe return home. Now tell me the coordinates to the International Space Station and explain correct docking protocol."

Virginia stated the coordinates to the ISS along with the instructions to give to the computer for docking.

"Now tell me the coordinates to Earth, Jupiter, and the Moon and explain atmosphere hazards and landing protocol for each planet."

She completed his request.

"Good. Now, as one of the planet's greatest pilots, it's important to have the ability to escape anything out here. I have a simulation where you will be required to maneuver the spacecraft manually—without the help of computer-assisted steering—to avoid various meteoroids and space debris. Ready?"

"Yes, sir."

He counted down. "...four, three, two, one." And suddenly there was an influx of meteors flying at the forward window.

She used her manual controls to jolt the spacecraft up and down. She zipped the vehicle horizontally and in circles around the incoming debris almost as fast as it appeared, until the simulations of large and small meteoroids and space debris faded to nothing.

"That was impressive!" Coach Yung said. "Not a single one made contact with the vehicle."

She agreed with a nod and caught her breath.

"Okay, Virginia. The next section of the exam is probably the reason you've been avoiding taking it, but you're going to be okay. I'm here with you," Yung said. "Spacecraft tools," he started.

He knew! He could be a Truth Bearer too—or maybe it's just obvious that I don't want to deal with the equipment that stole Charles's life.

"I will launch images that virtually have the same composition of a meteoroid. And you will use the laser cannon and the X-actionator, at your discretion, to destroy them."

"Just like Spaceball," she mumbled.

"Well, these will be more dense, so prepare for their disintegration to take a bit longer," Coach Yung instructed.

Virginia stared at the buttons to both tools, the two most powerful energy forces at her fingertips.

He didn't interrupt her hesitation.

"There's something wrong with it. I can feel it when it's released. The force at expulsion hesitates," Charles complained to Virginia as they walked home together after his last Spaceball game.

"You'll fix it. Don't worry," she told him before he held her face in his hands and gave her a kiss good night.

Early the next morning, he got under the spacecraft with all his tools and assumed that the power was off, just as he'd left it the night before, and began removing the canister in which the X-actionator power mechanism was housed.

But the power wasn't off. It was active—and the explosion took his life.

When they investigated the accident, they found that the power switch had malfunctioned and the fail-safe connection shorted on account of a defective wire. A complete fluke accident.

The spacecraft started moving from turbulence that quickly turned violent. Nervous, she looked at Coach Yung for an explanation.

"It's part of the exam," he yelled through the noise.

Virginia set a target on the first large virtual meteoroid and destroyed it with the laser cannon. More meteoroids began racing toward them, too fast for her to maneuver around. She took a deep breath. "Danny, turn on maximum shields," she commanded the computer, setting the X-actionator's target on the largest three meteoroids. With a deep breath, she held the activation button until she saw the meteoroids begin to disintegrate.

Time and space became one, and she found herself in a moment of pure bliss, laughing hysterically through the hot, turbulent entrance back into the Martian atmosphere.

"What kind of shoes does a thief wear?" she heard Coach Yung ask. "Sneakers," he responded when she didn't reply. "What did the baby corn say to the momma corn?" He answered for her: "Where's popcorn?"

Am I laughing at him or his jokes? What is going on? This must be the spell of a Joy Giver.

The two sat in front of Port 1, waiting for the gate to open. "We're alive!" Coach Yung said.

Virginia exhaled. "Yeah."

"That means you officially have a license to fly through the universe!"

"I'm glad I finally did it. Thanks, Coach," she said and looked down at her watch. 7:45. "I hope they open those gates soon."

Coach Yung called into the port master's station. "What's the holdup on these gates opening, Willie?"

Willie replied, "We've had a power shortage of a sort. Shoul' be havin' it right here any minute."

It was getting later. *How mad will Paden be?* If she could even make it there in time for the fruit tower and chocolate fountain desert.

But as Coach Yung kept talking, she found herself laughing again. Forgetting all about meeting her date and how disappointed he and Paden would be. By the time Willie had radioed that the port was ready to receive them for docking, nearly another hour had passed.

A knot tied up her intestines with regret and a little shame. She might not even get there in time for the end of the dance.

Virginia raced to change into the almost-new ensemble Paden had prepared for her, then headed straight to the Main Conservatory, where the music was slow, accommodating the dwindling crowd of lovers. She stood still among the thinning crowd, looking for Paden, when a glittery blue pantsuit grabbed her attention. She ran toward her friend, who was walking out of the conservatory toward Hall 6 with two young men she assumed were their dates.

"Paden, I'm sorry, I thought—"

"Ah! Virginia, so nice of you to grace us with your presence," Paden said, giving her a forced smile. "This is Frankie Casmiri. Your date that you missed." She pointed to an angelic-looking young man with olive-colored skin, wavy black hair that rested on his shoulders, and a face that clearly showed his disapproval. "And his brother James," Paden added, smiling at the other insanely handsome boy next to her.

Virginia looked into Frankie's eyes. "I am so very sorry. My space flight instructor insisted I take my exam to become a licensed ISV pilot, and we got held up... for hours, unfortunately. Will you please forgive me... and give me another chance?"

"For sure, Virginia." Frankie spoke gently; his face was kind, his voice serious. "This would be a great Union for both of us, and Supervisor Lox has secured us a sponsorship here next week so that we can stay and get to know you and Paden better. Hopefully a Union will work out for us."

Virgina was soothed by his response. She knew from his reaction that a Union with him would be safe, and quite possibly bearable.

The boys walked toward Port 3 to return to their home in Diony, about an hour away by Mars plane. Paden was quiet, but clearly put off by Virginia's choice.

"What?" Virginia argued with her silent disapproval. "They're coming back. It all worked out. It's all going to work out. It has to. I won't let anything get in the way of this courtship. I promise."she saw the meteoroids begin to disintegrate.

"Bringing food and offering your ear is the best way to help someone who is suffering from loss at any level."

~ Bee Davis

CHAPTER 3

Mars has a high content of iron oxide, which makes its surface appear red.

Virginia looked down to see the Ananta around her neck glowing purple and watched it rise gently from her chest, pulling her forward into flight. She was alone above Alcetra, then soaring above the mountains and craters, flying faster and farther above the barren red land of her beloved planet. The wind began to blow violently around her, and the mysterious force of the Ananta continued to effortlessly pull her forward.

Through the dust and haze she thought she saw two figures. As she got closer, she recognized one of the shadows. "Charles? Is that you?" she asked, knowing that he couldn't hear her through the wind and the distance.

He was waving her toward him. She didn't recognize the other shadow with Charles, but it appeared to be another boy, both walking toward a dust devil that took the shape of the Ananta.

The city below her looked much like Alcetra: shaped like a three-pointed star, with three massive ports at the end of the points. Six giant main conservatories, half the size of the ports, that circled the midsection of the star, and one small conservatory in the dead center of the city's star.

It could be any city, since they were all the same. But which one, and why was she here?

The pendant stopped pulling her as she floated atop one of the conservatories, where the figures of the two boys reappeared. They were playing some sort of game, chasing each other, appearing and disappearing inside the loops of the hovering Ananta.

She called out to Charles, "Wait for me! I'm trying to get—"

"Gin!" He waved her to come. He was saying something, but she couldn't hear anything but her name. And he continued to wave her in.

Virginia turned on her side, feeling the warm companionship of her little dog at her back. She opened her eyes and stared into the darkness of the room.

He was trying to tell me something.

She looked at the clock. 7:09 a.m. *Ugh, I gotta get in and out of the lab before Ms. West wakes up and hounds me about going to Nos.*

She rolled out of bed in the clothes she'd worn the night before and hurried out of her apartment with Ridgley following suit.

There were no sounds or movements under the early-morning darkness in her little lab, nestled beneath the tall banana plants in Conservatory 1. Laborers and students had no work after the winter harvest of the greens and berries that grew in the hydroponic tiers along the sides of the conservatory's domed walls. Supervisor Lox, the planting managers, and the hydroponic tank technicians wouldn't meander in until midmorning, and Ms. West rarely left her glass shack before ten a.m.

Virginia stood undisturbed at her lab table, carefully dropping various enzymes in microfuge tubes. This was the banana forest her grandmother had picked bananas in. The lab her grandmother had cleaned up, where Virginia discovered books and videos on how to alter plant DNA, along with some old tools to begin experimenting. The lab where she'd found her passion. Worried that she might not get United this season and stay to continue her studies, she wasn't as enthusiastic about DNA engineering as she'd once been. But she did have one more project to complete for graduation, and it was the one place she felt close to her grandmother.

The silence was interrupted by birds chirping like an alarm.

Virginia stowed her gloves and lab coat in the closet to investigate. She walked through the dark, weaving between the wet leaf sheaths on the stems of the towering banana plants, until she came to the gravel path just outside of the banana forest that circled the entire conservatory.

No lights were on in Ms. West's glass shack, so she walked along, searching for the disturbance, remembering how Charles always seemed to know everything and would point things out and explain things wherever they would go. She'd enjoyed just listening.

Finding only memories in the darkness, she went back to work in her lab until she was interrupted by a humid draft on her face.

I know I closed the door, she thought and looked at the doorway, where Ms. West, disheveled as normal, with a smile that stretched from ear to ear, was shuffling her slippered feet straight toward her.

Virginia exhaled disappointment before Ms. West was close enough to hear.

"Gin? Where have you been?" She held out a cup of tea for Virginia to take. "You were supposed to come over and talk to me about Professor Farro's offer."

She sipped the warm sweet tea. "I just had a lot of things I wanted to get done." Her nine thirty alarm sounded, and she turned it off. "How did you know I was here early?"

"A little birdie kinda told me," Ms. West replied. "Will you come help me move one of my big hanging plants?"

Virginia huffed and hastily stowed her equipment away. "Sure, I'm done in here anyway."

The awkward silhouette of Supervisor Lox was moving toward them on the gravel path, just before Ms. West's little shack. A harmless woman, really. Just one of those people who acted so nice that it was downright annoying. Virginia assumed she was about to be shamed for missing her date. They stopped in front of Supervisor Lox, who held her position in front of them with one hand on her hip and her head tilted to the opposite side.

"Vir-ginia," she said, with an awkward exaggerated upper lip movement.

"I'm sorry, Supervisor Lox. I won't even think about missing my date when he comes back this Sunsol night," she hurried to explain.

"Good to hear." Supervisor Lox strained her pitch to be cutesy and sweet. "Because that Frankie Casmiri is a fine catch. And assuming you Unite and remain here in your city, you should also continue to take your plant DNA engineering more seriously." She moved her gazed toward Ms. West. "Rather than fraternizing with your friends."

Ms. West shuffled forward, tilted her head to the side, and put her hand on her hip, mirroring Supervisor Lox. "Now, Loxy-Poo," she said, mirroring her squeaky pitch, "I can assure you the girl is doing her best. Now, please excuse us." She shuffled past Supervisor Lox's dropped jaw, Virginia following.

The two spewed laughter as soon as they were far enough from her hearing.

Virginia stood outside the open door of the glass shack as Ms. West removed a large potted fig tree from the second chair.

Ms. West nearly disappeared, rummaging through a box under her sofa/bed. Virginia turned on the cook coil to heat up the pot of water for more tea, watching Ms. West search for something around the tiny room that was cluttered with plants and blankets and various bowls, pots, and containers.

"Oooooh!" Ms. West suddenly exclaimed. She rolled her eyes upward and gave the top of her helmet of hair a pat. Contentment washed over her puzzled face. "You're gonna love it." She moved her fingers to the base of her neck, patting it, squeezing it, narrowed her eyes, then started digging into the mass with her fingers.

She hoped Ms. West wasn't going to let her hair down. She had seen it down once when she was a little girl, and it was frighteningly long. But instead, Ms. West continued digging until she pulled out a Swiss Army knife and held it up in the air, admiring it. "Been looking for that!" She shook her head and laid it on the table.

"Wow!" Virginia said, analyzing the small tool. "This is one of the greatest inventions ever. It's from Earth. Only seen one other. How did you get it?" Then she laughed. "Better question: how do you keep it in your hair?"

She watched in awe while Ms. West dug inside the hair at the top of her head, her brows pressed together, concentrating. She wriggled something out, making an effort to preserve the helmet shape of her hairstyle. Finally, she released the item, put it on the table, and patted the tousled hair back into place.

Virginia was surprised, even embarrassed. "A pudding cup? Ms. West, why did you have a pudding cup in your hair?"

"Multipurposes, girl." She smirked.

She started pulling something else out. "Ow! Ow! Ow!" she cried, until she had removed the item from the clutch of her hair. She laid it on the table in front of Virginia and explained, "It was the rubber band that hurt."

Virginia unraveled a handful of coin storage units. "Ms. West, why do you have so many different coin storage units?"

She laughed while she searched for something on the other side of her head. "Not all mine. Just holding 'em for you."

"For me?" Virginia wondered aloud.

"Yeah. It's your money. Blane had me save it for you." With a satisfied smile, she pulled out a transmitter button and laid it on the table, before wrestling with her pile of hair and pulling out another. "That's it—er, well, it's one of these two," she said, looking at the two transmitters on the table in front of her.

"You could join the rest of society and put one of these in a wristband," Virginia suggested.

Ms. West sat silently, beaming at her.

"Oh. Okay. Right." Ms. West broke the silence. "You're probably wondering why you just sat through my little search party." She picked up a transmitter and pressed the clear dome to turn on the hologram.

It didn't turn on.

She pressed it again and again. Still no hologram. She grabbed the other transmitter and pressed its dome. No hologram.

She tried again. "This is it; this is the one!" Ms. West exclaimed as particles of purple light floated above the button.

The pair watched, expecting an entire hologram to appear, but instead it slowly fizzled away. Ms. West smacked the transmitter into her hand a few times. "Is this stupid thing broken or what!?"

"Let me try," Virginia said, rubbing her hands together to warm them. She held the transmitter between her palms, and within a few seconds, billions of particles of purple light rose from the glass dome of the transmitter and formed a glowing purple Ananta.

Virginia looked at Ms. West for an explanation.

"Just wait," she replied with wide and excited eyes.

The Ananta quickly faded away, and a glowing purple outline of a thin woman with wide-legged overalls, like the laborers in the conservatory farms wore, appeared. As more details materialized, Virginia recognized the small round eyes, set in perfect proportion on the heart-shaped face, that reminded her of her grandmother's face.

The hologram moved her arm, revealing a long white banana hook. Like the one her grandmother used to pick bananas with.

The hologram pushed it out to virtually poke Virginia's shoulder. "You're pale, girl. Seen a ghost?" She raised her chin high in the air with laughter.

"This isn't funny," Virginia said to Ms. West.

"It's fantastic!" said the carefree hologram, grasping her banana hook in both hands, lifting it above her head, and dancing around, as happy as a bird in a puddle.

Virginia looked at Ms. West, shaking her head. "This is a sick joke."

"No, it's really her," she replied.

Childhood memories of her grandmother, who was her everything, rushed in: Grandmother waiting in the dark to scold her after she snuck into the apartment late at night from adventures out with Charles and Paden, Grandmother's embrace that calmed every storm, her laugh that amplified every joy. Grandmother stroking her head as she cried, whispering, "Wish upon a tear, dear. Now is the time to imagine what you want. This is how you Create—through the pain."

"How can this be?" Virginia asked the holographic resemblance of her grandmother. "Dead people don't just show up on holograms."

The glowing purple hologram waved her banana hook around Virginia and teased, "Can't stop love—two only separated."

I wish it were her, but there's no way. I watched them send her body through the embarkment door at her funeral. "If you are my grandmother, tell me where you stowed your banana cane when you were done working."

"In the gutter. You know," Grandmother said.

Virginia remembered her grandmother stowing her banana cane in the long scooped shelf above the door. *It's gotta be her. No one else would know that.* "Okay. But how are you able to come through on the hologram, when a hologram has to be captured from your physical image?"

The image of Grandmother's small face with close-set eyes moved forward, close to Virginia. "Can't explain all Royal magic."

She looked at Ms. West. "I've always known my grandmother was a Royal United. Have you been talking to her this whole time she's been gone?"

Ms. West remained silent, and Grandmother replied, "I was a voice in her head." They laughed together, reminding Virginia of the sols when life was good, when they were all together, sitting in Ms. West's tiny cluttered shack, drinking chamomile tea with kumquat syrup.

Virginia smiled cautiously. Curious, she asked, "Assuming it's you, Grandmother, why are you here?"

"As a guide. To help you see!"

She wanted to know. "To see what?"

Grandmother planted the bottom of her long banana hook on what seemed to be the ground and looked upward. "The leaves. They fall and then?"

"Lay on the ground," Virginia said.

"And?" Grandmother prodded.

"Aaaaand they decompose."

She waited for Virginia to elaborate. When she didn't, she prodded more. "And?"

"Grandmother. You know just as well as I do that the decomposition creates hummus. A perfect environment for new life."

Grandmother clapped her hands. Virginia looked at Ms. West for a reprieve.

"You know, Gin… the circle of life," Ms. West said.

She held her palms up in exasperation. "Yeah. Okay. Life goes on. So what?"

"A new opportunity reveals the secret of the souls' journey to true love," Grandmother said.

"If you're my grandmother, you should know that my one chance for happiness is here. In Alcetra. I've got too much to risk. I'm not gonna risk that just for an advanced molecular biology course in a city that would take a whole entire sol to fly to."

"The accident was fixed. In a new port," Grandmother said.

"Oookaaay, whatever that means." Virginia was annoyed.

Grandmother's hologram form disintegrated into a cloud of purple particles, then took the shape of a large city with a massive windstorm blowing around it.

"That's the way I saw it in my dream this morning. I think I saw Charles there too. Is it Nos? Why is everyone pressuring me to go to Nos? Why don't you all understand!"

"Many are building to aid the important couple. Beware of the one who has much to gain from your defeat," Grandmother's voice whispered from behind the hologram scene.

Frustrated by her lack of understanding, Virginia grasped her head in her hands. "This is just all too weird."

Grandmother's hologram returned. "Don't worry, girl. Soul chooses the right numbers always."

Virginia took a deep breath and got up from the table for one. "I recognize some of what she's saying, but it's like she's speaking in riddles." She wandered around the little glass shack, silently pulling yellow leaves off Ms. West's plants.

Ms. West replied, "She has to guide you. The truth is for discovering. Respect that little voice in your head, that strange knowing you get, girl—your power of sense."

The silence was broken by a cheerful voice outside the clear walls. "Hello! Anybody here?"

It was Paden. Virginia wasn't surprised to see her. Without even thinking about Grandmother's hologram being on, she opened the door.

"Tea?" Ms. West asked as soon as she stepped in.

"Suuuure," Paden said, looking at the glowing hologram of Virginia's grandmother. "What's this?" she asked, pointing.

"Me!" Grandmother said.

"That looks just like your grandmother," Paden said to Virginia, unscathed by Grandmother's repeated pokes and whacks with her holographic banana hook. "If your grandmother was a purple hologram."

"It's her. Just ask Virginia," Ms. West said.

Paden raised her brows and stared at Virginia, waiting for an answer.

Virginia nodded with a side smile. "I get a sense that it's really her."

"I've never known your sense to be off. But how could this be possible?" Paden said. "And why? I've never heard of someone coming back from the dead in the form of a hologram."

"For adventure!" Grandmother blurted out.

Virginia frowned and fervently shook her head, replying in a firm tone, "No adventures, Grandmother."

"Since when don't you want to go on an adventure?" Paden replied. "I wanna go on an adventure! Where we goin'?"

Virginia stared at her grandmother, still shaking her head no.

"She has a sponsorship to an advanced molecular biology program at Nos," Ms. West said.

Virginia hung her head, thinking of how she could make those words go away. Searching for the right lie.

"A sponsorship to Nos?" Paden questioned.

"Don't worry," Ms. West chimed in, flailing her finger toward Paden. "Virginia refused the offer so she could court your friend's brother."

Paden dropped her jaw. "Whoa. Wait. You seriously did get a sponsorship to Nos, didn't you."

Virginia shook her head in denial. "No. I'm not going. And neither are you."

"You were invited to Nos and you didn't tell me?"

Virginia felt a little guilty. Her best friend had always dreamed of going to Nos.

"Yes. Fully sponsored. And the invitation comes with a sponsorship for any companion she wishes to bring," Ms. West said.

"Virginia Dale!" Paden said. "This is a chance in a lifetime! To go to the first city ever established on Mars, the largest city. Where extinct life forms are found every sol! We must go! Opportunities like this never knock on our door."

"I can't, I'm sorry. I gotta stay here, get United. I want to live the rest of my life here—doing the things I love to do."

"Virginia. This isn't like you."

She hung her head. "I have too much to lose, and you don't."

"Please. Just for a week or two!" Paden wrapped her arms around her limp best friend. "The brothers really want Mrs. Lox's job. Frankie's a super-nice dreamboat. He will wait for you," she insisted. "You would take the chance if Charles were here. You don't have to die too."

Virginia rested in her friend's embrace, closed her eyes, and saw her dream. She could see Charles waving her through the Ananta's loop and somehow understood what he was saying. *I fixed it, Gin.*

She looked up, into the faces of the three most important women in her life.

She looked at her grandmother's hologram, who stared into her eyes and didn't say a word. But the words her grandmother always told her whenever she had a question replayed in her mind: *"Trust your power of sense—it's the language of your soul."*

Virginia looked at her best friend and shrugged. "Okay. I'll go. But only for a few weeks—*if* Frankie agrees to wait for me." She sighed. "I don't even know how we'll get there." She looked down and brushed her favorite skirt with her fingertips. "Or if they'll let me in looking like a poor person."

Paden clapped her hands together. "Don't you worry! Charles's father would do anything for you—and probably me. I'll call Mr. Bryant now—he'll take us! Frankie will wait. I'll tell him that you'll talk to him on a hologram call every sol."

Virginia gave her a disapproving glance.

Ms. West waved the handful of coin storage units in the air. "And you'll get some new clothes so you don't stick out like a sore thumb!"

Relief filled her body, and she smiled at Paden. "Yeah. Just a few weeks. It'll be fun."

"To weep is to make less the depth of grief."

~ William Shakespeare

CHAPTER 4

The tallest mountain in the entire solar system is hosted on Mars—Olympus Mons—and it is nearly three times the height of Earth's Mt. Everest.

"Really. I don't need all this," Virginia said to Ms. West, who was hurrying her toward the shuttle with two dozen other shoppers, also boarding to go to the city of Erbos.

Ms. West didn't reply. Instead, she counted through the wad of coin storage drives that she removed from her hair. "...nine, ten. Yes, that's it. Now girl, you'll use these to pay for some new clothes so you don't stick out like a sore thumb at Nos. A new workboard too." She placed the coin storage units in Virginia's hand. "When you get there, you can even eat in the restaurants in the Upper End. It's yours to spend. From your parents and grandmother."

Over the top of Ms. West's helmet of hair, Virginia saw Paden waving for her to hurry to the shuttle.

"Mr. Bryant will be there to take you and Paden to Nos in the morning, so you can be there for the Sunsol Unity Dinner and Dance," Ms. West said. She grabbed

Virginia's hand and put a transmitter button in her palm. "Take your grandmother with you."

"But I don't understand what she's saying."

Ms. West tapped her finger on the center of Virginia's forehead. "Listen with your power of sense, not your brain. And do yourself a favor..."

"What's that?"

"Have some fun! Don't bury your face in your plant work the whole time."

"Wow! The ports look massive." Paden said, looking out the window as the Mars shuttle hovered above the great consumer city, nestled among the mountainous red terrain, waiting for the port master to open the gates. "Is that where they manufacture all the things they sell? In the ports?"

"No. I think they have underground manufacturing facilities. They need large ports for the imports from Earth," Virginia replied. "At least, that's what I've heard."

The two girls exited the port into a bustling Main Hall and stood paralyzed by the mass of people wearing brightly colored hats, their clothes very different from the basic skirts or pantsuits the people in Alcetra wore. There was a collage of perfume and popcorn aromas and a strange glow reflecting off all the new toys, gadgets, and jewelry displayed on the vendors' tables.

"Welcome to Erbos!" a brightly clothed man yelled into the crowd in front of them. He held his hands in the air, and the items in his hands changed every second. "Buy anything you could never imagine! Right here in Erbos."

The girls looked at each other, puzzled. "Looks like they may be using their powers here without discretion or necessity," Virginia said.

~Reserved for emergencies and transport of consumer products only~ the sign on the hyperwalk read.

"Perfect! We'll lollygag up the hall, and I won't miss a thing!" Paden said.

While Paden looked at every trinket the vendors had, Virginia peered through the crowd. A violinist played his own rendition of the planet's top pop songs, while an artist painted a portrait of a young happy couple who sat posing for him, who both then instantly disappeared, assumably after their portrait was complete. *Teleporting?* Virginia had never seen it done in broad sunlight.

A man decked out in a completely purple ensemble walked in front of Virginia. He looked her in the eyes and said, "You have a lot of magic that you haven't yet found," as he pulled a big fat rabbit from the hat he took off his head.

"Oooh," Paden exclaimed, mesmerized.

Virginia pulled her away. "I don't think we should be partaking in how the people here are using their sacred powers."

Virginia found a store with a helpful clerk, informed on the styles the citizens at Nos wore, and purchased a new black coat. Returning to the hall, she found Paden gazing inside a little vendor booth that was decorated with dozens of different styles and sizes of the Truth Bearers' red flag, listening intently to a silver-haired woman, also dressed entirely in red. The old woman stopped talking when Virginia took her place next to Paden.

"One of you will be in a strange battle. Somewhere. Anywhere maybe," the silver-haired woman said and waved them to enter her booth. "The whole truth. Come in."

"Uh... no, thank you," Virginia said.

"But... I... I think she knows something!" Paden dropped her voice to a whisper. "Her booth... all red... She's got to be a Truth Bearer!"

"The future is for discovering, not for sale," Virginia said and hastily walked away.

They stopped to look inside the window of the biggest shop yet, mobbed with people and store clerks, who were easy to find with their bright leaf-green shirts. Paden darted in, Virginia in tow.

"Can I help you?" a young store clerk asked politely.

Paden lifted Virginia's wrist to the clerk's face. "This girl here needs a wristband from this century. And a new workboard," she said.

The clerk laughed. "Yeah, it looks pretty old. What type of workboard are you looking for?"

"One small enough to take anywhere, but big enough to see," Virginia said.

As the clerk carried on about all the new technology, functions, and options on the workboards, transmitters and holograms, Virginia and Paden watched dumbfounded as the devices appeared as magically as they disappeared and some even floating through the air.

The store clerk noticed their amusement. "Haven't you ever seen United magic before?" she asked.

"On rare occasions. The people in our city are definitely discreet about using their powers," Paden said.

"Ah... well, we use our powers here for everything. Maybe more so now, with all the excitement of the Ananta and Royal love returning to Mars. It all has people in a good mood, so maybe they're using more magic than normal." The clerk shrugged.

Virginia smirked and mumbled, "I don't know why that's so exciting when death takes true love anyway."

Paden gave her a disapproving elbow in her ribs.

The clerk plugged Virginia's coin storage into her computer. "Why, it's the end of the Royal curse. It's hope.

Hope that I—and many other Singles—can Unite as a Royal again. It's so exciting, isn't it? I'm excited to see who the couple is who breaks the curse!"

Paden and Virginia looked at each other and together asked the store clerk, "*The couple?*"

"Really? What rock do you two live under?" The clerk sighed, then explained. "It's been told by a Truth Bearer, one right here from our city, that when a certain couple, who have seen many past lives together, Unites this winter, the curse of the lost Royals will end!"

The girls walked on, Paden rambling on and on everything Royal, fantasizing aloud about a planet storming with Royal magic. "We should find our room," Virginia said as the two finished their lunch in the community cafeteria in the Main Conservatory, under the bright glow of its Ananta, just like the one in Alcetra.

As they walked toward the Main Conservatory to inspect the symbol of perpetual love that had magically appeared in Erbos too, Paden coaxed Virginia into a dress shop.

Inside the store filled with special occasion skirts and suits, some similar to the blue sparkly one Paden was wearing, the girls noticed an elegantly dressed store clerk talking to a woman who just suddenly disappeared.

Dumbfounded by another blatant display of their United powers, Virginia noticed that the store clerk was eyeing her from neck to ankle.

"Whay wear such old style?" the clerk asked, in what was assumably an Erboan dialect. "They's a-trending." She pointed to the display of glittery pantsuits.

Virginia shrugged. "I need the pockets. There's always something helpful that I keep in my pockets. Aaand... I don't feel so skinny with the excess fabric at my hip."

The seamstress looked surprised. "Ha! Aye understand this." She grabbed an ensemble from the wall and gave it to Virginia. "Here. Put on, inside out."

The clerk tucked and pulled at the garment atop Virginia's body, then pinned it. "Now, take off. I fix, you wait," she commanded.

Waiting for the clerk to return, Virginia sat patiently, watching Paden try on some of the newest styles fancy enough for the Unity Dinners, until the clerk arrived with a garment in hand and signaled for Virginia to try it on in the dressing room.

"Wow! I love the new V hemline," Paden said. "It's soft. And it almost looks black, but it's... purple? Or burgundy?" She touched the rouching at the hips. "And it fits!" she exclaimed, running her finger along the border of the top that completely covered her torso.

"You don't look like a girl from Extension 220," Paden whispered with a smile.

The next morning the girls carried their bags of new goodies to Port 3, excited to be chauffeured to Nos.

"Coffee," Paden grunted as soon as they arrived in front of the port doors.

"Grab me some," Virginia said. "I'm gonna tell Mr. Bryant we're here."

The port was quiet, with only mechanics wrenching on ISVs. Mr. Bryant stood by his Mars plane, talking to a mechanic. "Virginia. Good morning."

Her shoulders and countenance dropped. "What's wrong? Something's wrong. I can sense it."

He laughed. "You sure did. My plane has had a breach in performance safety. There's a part that needs to be printed. It could take a few sols."

Relief and disappointment wrestled in her head until she finally sighed. "It would be better for me to stay at Alcetra anyway."

"Oh no, Virginia! You would be letting a planet full of people down if you don't pursue this special opportunity."

"I don't think it's that serious." Virginia laughed, shaking her head.

"Class starts tomorrow morning. The Spaceball team will pass over here en route to Nos early tomorrow morning. They have one empty seat and will pick you up before sunrise."

"Oh, that's worse. I can't go with the Spaceball team."

Mr. Bryant hugged her tight and rested his chisled chin on top of her head. "I know, Virginia. Reminders of my son make my soul sad all over again too."

She took a deep breath and allowed Mr. Bryant's embrace to replace the grief that came with the memory of her favorite person. She always felt peace when he was around and assumed he was a Peace Maker.

Paden hid her disappointment with optimism. "Without me there, you can be hyper-focused, learn what you need to learn, come home in two or three weeks, court Frankie, Unite, and we can all live happily ever after!"

"Paden and I will go home on the Dot freight vehicle soon. Before we leave, I'd like to have a minute alone with Virginia," Mr. Bryant said to the two girls, who had spent the last few hours playing hologram games in the port waiting room.

He took Paden's seat across from Virginia, put his satchel on the table, and pulled out a charcoal-colored box. "This is a little congratulations present for earning your interplanetary license," he said. "Every ship captain should have the upper hand whenever she can."

She opened the small hinged box to see a pair of glasses with a gold UV shield, much like the shield on space flight helmets, conservatory domes, and all the city rooftops on Mars.

"UV protection?" She started to put them on.

"Wait," he said, gently pushing her eager hands down. "There is something I don't want you to see right now. Try them out later. When you get settled at Nos."

The next morning came soon enough, and Virginia boarded the big gray plane with the sparkling red cosmos scene and *A-Team* painted on each side and the tops of the wings.

She walked between the seats, fighting to shut down her emotions while greeting Charles's Spaceball team, who, although they had been nothing but kind and gentle to her after his accident, she just couldn't bring herself to spend any time with. His memory shined through their faces. They were all happy to see her, saying her name and furrowing their brows to show her empathy and grabbing her hand as she walked up the aisle. She stopped at a pair of waving arms that were undoubtedly Marita's, the teammate she was closest to. "Why didn't you tell me you were going to Nos?" she asked Virginia.

Before she could reply, she noticed a myriad of flipstones, little pieces of an exploding bomb from a hologram game, crash into her skirt and fizzle into nothing. Marita stood up and turned around, yelling at her twin brother, Marcus. "Annoy someone else with that game, would you!"

Virginia continued to the back of the team shuttle until she noticed one vacant aisle seat—right next to a tall, lanky, overdressed bald guy.

She didn't want to sit next to Amos. She was happy that he'd taken her out of his limelight after Charles died, and she didn't want to go back in it. She didn't want to be his friend. She just wanted to be left alone—and the seat next to him was the hot seat for questioning. She looked back down the aisle, wanting to take the frustration boiling up inside her right off the plane, back to the safety of her best friend and her quiet apartment.

Then suddenly her anxiety evaporated. She looked toward the bow of the plane, where Coach Yung was smiling and waving at her. *Ugh. I can't be angry with a Peace Maker on board!*

"Can I stow your bag for you?" Amos asked Virginia.

She silently shoved her overstuffed bag in the compartment above the seat, hoping he wouldn't say anything else to her.

The plane took flight, the sun not yet risen to reveal the barren red mountains, plains, and canyons that they were flying through, and Virginia soon became confident in a silent ride, as Amos began playing Flipping Mars with Marcus.

"Sorry there wasn't another seat. I know I'm not your favorite person. But I don't have my recorder on, so we can talk in complete confidence if you'd like," Amos said while he continued playing his game.

Just my luck—he can do two things at once, Virginia thought, getting comfortable in the seat next to him.

Suddenly, he closed his game. "I just lost my ninth life." He opened the bag on his lap, pulled out a box of juice, and offered it to her. When she declined, he put the straw in the box and sipped it. He pulled out a pack of crackers and offered it as well. She could smell that they were sweet peanut butter crackers, but there was no way she was taking anything from him, even if they were her favorite.

She shook her head, again declining his offer.

"Your new coat looks nice. Did you get it from Erbos?" Amos asked in between bites of cracker.

"Yeah."

He ignored her aloof reply and continued to talk as if she was the friendliest passenger on the plane. "I know you're mad at me for turning your adventures with Charles into my news. But I had to. You two were exciting. I had to share you both with the city. And your adventures."

She made eye contact with him. "The only reason you got away with all the hidden cameras was because you were so close to Charles and Grandmother... and because you didn't post anything private."

"You inspired others to find a best friend and not be so fearful. To live. Now, that's not really a reason to hate me, is it?"

Virginia stared at him.

"You know, I had a lot of recordings that I didn't show."

"I knew you were creepy."

Amos ignored her snarky remark. "Like your first kiss under the banana trees. That's why I posted the one where the camera was all screwy in the spacecraft, when you and Charles were on an unauthorized adventure. I made people believe that was where your first kiss was... so that your privacy was respected but the viewers still got a juicy detail to talk about."

Virginia was shocked, then suddenly relieved. "Like I said, you're lucky it wasn't that bad, and Charles and Paden and Grandmother and the rest of the city love you.

You probably wouldn't have a job if it weren't for me and Charles subjecting ourselves to your 'news' show."

"Cocoa Ball?" He offered her a round candy, its wrapper made to resemble an exploding Spaceball.

She slowly unwrapped it, preserving the decorated wrapper, hesitantly put it in her mouth, and the jelly-filled center oozed strawberry between the pressure of her teeth.

Virginia relaxed, finally noticing Amos's genuine character, and he seemed happy to see her softening. With mouths full of candy, the two laughed at each other—together for the first time since they were kids.

"Gin, wherever he is, I'm sure he misses you too."

"I just hope he waits for me to cross, so we can come back together as Royals, with wild magical powers. And we spend our every sol sailing through the cosmos."

"I loved the heck out of your grandmother too. Remember how, when we were kids, she would make a fancy meal and set the table every Unity Festival Dinner so we would feel included? Like we were part of the festival. And how she would stand up and make a toast to each one of us, mentioning something specific that we did that she was proud of?"

"How could I forget? I wished you weren't there at every single one."

They both laughed, and she sensed the heaviness of disdain she had for Amos and his news sloughing off her shoulders.

"How did you get all these candies?" Virginia asked after a bite into a soft candy apple slice covered with hard caramel.

"My mother makes them. She and my two sisters and my aunties make all of the candies for the city."

She remembered all of the candies, wrapped in dainty packages, that Charles had brought her throughout school, remembered seeing the women making candy in the old shop in Alcetra's Galleria in Hall 1. "Oh wow! I'm surprised you're not rich, with the Upper Enders being the only people who can afford to buy them."

"The Upper Enders think that just because we're poor Mother shouldn't charge a lot for her candies. So the candy business will never make my mother rich. And my dad is a musician whose paycheck is also determined by how much money the Upper Enders can save by paying him and my brothers fractions of coins for live music at their parties. It's fine—we're just happy to have work."

"Wow. I didn't know they were that stingy. How 'bout you? Tell me how you got interested in news and video."

Amos fidgeted with a small recording device in his hand. "I'm the oldest, ya see. I was five when my first sister was born. While they doted over her, I figured out how to record her with my dad's transmitter. They thought it was cute. When I continued to record my sister's first year, they bought me a pole recorder for my next birthsol. And on and on that went, through three other siblings. Now my father's pressuring me to start making more money for the family—or Unite and get out of the apartment. That's why I'm traveling to new cities with the Spaceball team. So I can grow my audience and get advertising sponsors."

He turned to her. "I know what'll happen if you don't Unite this season. I'll help you get hitched. You know… be your wingman, your confidant, your good-guy detector, your—"

"Okay, Amos. Thanks." Virginia blushed.

"I don't think I can wait another season to get out of my parents' house! My brothers and sisters are so noisy!"

"Yeah, is this like your third Unity Festival since you came of age?"

He laughed. "Yeah, but I believe there's someone very special for me. I've only told your grandmother this, and it's why I hate that my parents are pressuring me to Unite, but I feel like there's a match that will make my soul jump for joy." Amos lowered his voice to a whisper. "You know… a love I've had before in another life." Then he leaned in, to ensure no one would hear him, and finished, "A Royal match."

Virginia watched him pin his recording device onto his jacket pocket and then a wilting leaf next to it. "I guess I can count on you recording me while you're here at Nos?"

"Are you giving me permission?" he asked eagerly.

She rolled her eyes. "Only if you have to, and nothing that could mess up my courtship with Frankie."

The plane hovered above the city of Nos, waiting to come into port. "It's magnificent!" Amos said with his face against the window.

"Like a dream come true," Virginia said under her breath, dreading the pressure that came with meeting new people.

"It's okay, Gin. I'll be here for you."

"Loss, trauma, sadness, and grief are crippling. It's only because of our own determination and the people who are there for us that we survive."

~ Bee Davis

CHAPTER 5

In 2004, NASA discovered evidence that water once flowed on Mars—a potential sign of life as we know it.

"What are these things?" Virginia whispered to Amos.

"Oddly magnificent," he gasped.

Paying no attention to the Spaceball team in front of them or the woman dictating orders, the pair stood silent, mesmerized by the outlandish little creatures with glowing red wings that fluttered like fins, their wheat-colored bodies glistening like water as they weaved fluidly through the trunks of the finely pruned mature walnut trees that outlined Nos's Main Hall.

"Are they birds or fish?" Amos whispered.

Higher into the branches, Virginia noticed the same sort of creature, but smaller, with bright orange faces that faded into muted yellow tails. She nudged Amos with her elbow, silently signaling him to look up.

The pair moved their gazes to the tops of the trees, where more of the creatures glistened, with walnut-sized white bodies and miniature silver wings, moving as faintly as a gentle breeze between the leaves.

CLAP, CLAP.

The awestruck friends realized Alcetra's Spaceball team was no longer in front of them. Only a mysterious, dark, yet somehow captivatingly beautiful woman—with a head full of slithering and hissing creatures. Black sunglasses covered her eyes.

"Snap out of it, tourists!" she yelled.

Was it a woman? Or one of the beings that the scientists at Nos were rumored to have found among the Martian rocks? No such strange creatures existed in Alcetra.

Amos and Virginia stood frozen, staring impolitely at the serpents atop the quite possibly evil woman's head as they slowly wriggled against the hood of her burgundy knee-length velvet poncho.

"Hey! You two! This ain't no freak show," she yelled at them again.

Virginia and Amos quickly changed their view to their toes.

Did this creature make Yung and the whole team disappear? Has it teleported them somewhere? What sort of strange magic is going on at Nos? Are we being held captive? She stepped closer to Amos for comfort.

"You only have to be scared if I take off my glasses." The woman laughed.

The pair watched her lift her sunglasses on and off the bridge of her nose, never revealing her eyes.

"That's why I'm the guardian of this hall, the five other halls, and every extension and nook and cranny in this city. One look into my eyes and you two will be sorry you loused up. So don't. Don't you dare louse up in my city!"

Amos and Virginia nodded in compliance.

"My name is Sofia. These guys here," she said, pointing to the knee-high reddish-brown rocks that were double the width of her narrow body, "are my assistants. They will be watching you, reporting any and all of your behavior to me."

The rocks rolled themselves around in place, confirming Sofia's delegation.

"Now. Who exactly are you kids? And why are you just standing here with your jaws on the floor? Are you here with Alcetra's Spaceball team?"

"I am. I'm the news reporter for the team," Amos said and then pointed his thumb in Virginia's direction. "This here is Virginia Dale. She's—"

Sofia stomped her foot, interrupting Amos, then stepped forward in front of Virginia and planted her hands on her hips. "She was supposed to be here last night! Missing functions and poor time management is unacceptable for a girl who is being sponsored by the administrator of the planet's food sciences program."

"Yes, ma'am," Virginia humbly replied.

"Fine then," Sofia agreed, and she marched swiftly toward the top of the hall. The Rock Friends rocked back and forth, picking up momentum as they followed behind her. "Come on, tourists!" she yelled, and without looking back, she waved for them to follow.

The Rock Friends began rolling faster. Virginia and Amos were nearly running behind them, up the hall that was quiet with serious-faced pedestrians and tall walnut trees that blocked the sun and made the hall dark with shadows. They stopped when Sofia did at Extension 670, the first residential extension, right outside the Main Conservatory.

"There are no empty beds with your team, so you two will share a guest suite," she said, pointing down the brightly lit extension. "The Rock Friends will show you to your suite and answer your questions." The snakelike creatures protruded in front of her and stared Amos and Virginia down with hundreds of glassy eyes. She wiggled her sunglasses on the bridge of her nose again. "You two better walk a straight line while you're here." Her face revealed a devious smile. "Or I may just have you join the Rock Friend community." She laughed, then she and her head full of exposed creatures whipped around toward the north side of the Main Hall, her velvet burgundy poncho following in an elegant circle around her as she walked away.

A crackling noise came from the Rock Friends on the floor, and without haste they began to roll down the extension. Amos and Virginia followed them.

"I can forget about ever fitting in here. This place is weird. I gotta get the information I need and get outta here," Virginia whispered to Amos, following behind the rolling rocks.

"Maybe you should try wearing your brains on the outside of your head," he snickered.

The Rock Friends stopped at Door 67211. With loud crackling noises, they began getting bigger. Nearly as tall as a short human.

Virginia and Amos stared, dumbfounded, watching little rock arms come out of their giant rock bodies and little rock legs come next. Before they knew it, the rocks had sort of distorted faces, complete with eyes, noses, and mouths.

"Mostly scary, Sofia is," said a rock with a raspy masculine voice and a blotch of reddish brown over the indent where an eye would be.

"Welcome here. We good," a rock with a raspy feminine voice said, and muted cheers came from the other rocks.

Fascinated by the rock creatures, Amos and Virginia walked through the door they opened to inspect the lush guest suite. Each put down their travel bags on the smooth dark carpet, which was unlike Alcetra's rough natural floors. Virginia inspected the oddly-colored plants and strange fruits in the food garden in the kitchen, fully stocked with fruit and fresh breads in the cabinet, while Amos turned on the entertainment hologram in the living room.

"It's really cold here," Virginia said, rubbing her arms.

"I'm cold too. Could use a warmer coat."

"Hurry, hurry," a rock whose every edge was jagged yelled into the suite. "Girl rush. Class now."

Virginia looked at Amos with worried eyes.

"I'll go with you. This place is too sketchy to explore alone," he said to her.

They returned to the extension to find the Rock Friends in their roundish form, rolling toward the exit. They hurried, following the Rock Friends through the Main Conservatory, where a large Ananta also hung from the dome's center and which was decorated for the Unity Festival just as brilliantly as their Main Conservatory in Alcetra. They continued into Conservatory 5, where winter crops grew in hydroponic trays along the sides of the glass dome, and stopped in front of a bamboo tent in the center.

"Welcome here! Farro program. Veeery special," the Rock Friend with the reddish-brown blotch over his eye said.

"Only best! Martian scientists!" the jagged-edged Rock Friend said.

"Hurry now. Black laboratory. Behind red. Don't blunder!" the Rock Friend with the reddish-brown blotch said and then collapsed back into its rock form and rolled away with the others.

Baffled, Virginia and Amos looked at each other, and then at the tentlike structure that stood under a shortened stack of hydroponic growing trays. "Behind red?" Virginia said, looking at the white fabric walls of the tent, held together by tall bamboo.

Amos grasped the door handle, then paused and looked at her.

"Might as well." She shrugged.

They walked through the flimsy door into a nearly vacant large room. At the end of it, two girls were taking photometric measurements of liquids from a tray of microcentrifuge tubes on a high table with a red circular top. As the exploratory pair looked around, they noticed all the tables and chairs in the laboratory tent were red. They smiled at each other, silently confirming they'd found the red laboratory.

Only a few steps behind the table of girls was a wide door, just as temporary as the four walls of the structure. They walked toward it, and Amos put his ear against it, then opened the door just enough to peer into the next room. After a long look, he closed the crack he'd made with the door and whispered to Virginia, "Looks black to me. Are you ready?"

She brushed her new long black coat smooth and straightened her skirt. She glanced at Amos, silently asking him for a vote of confidence.

"I think you'll probably fit in just fine with all the other DNA-altering nerds," he replied.

She moved to peer into the room without being noticed, just as Amos had, but before he could move out of the way, Virginia stepped on his foot. He lost his balance and grabbed the door handle for stability—at the same time she was opening it.

Amos couldn't stop his fall, taking the door down with him and leaving Virginia fully exposed to her new classmates.

She saw nothing but bright lights broken up with various shades of gray and could hear only a room full of laughter. Of course it was funny to see a silly accident. But she wasn't one of them watching.

She *was* the accident.

Virginia looked at Amos, now attempting to reattach the door. "Forget about fitting in for now." He laughed under his breath.

She pulled her shoulders back, forced a laugh, and focused on the familiar jolly face with plump, shiny cheeks walking toward her.

"Uh. Hello. What are you doing here?" a voice to the side of her yelled. "This is an advanced genetic engineering program. Not a training program for Neanderthals."

She looked to find the source of the verbal onslaught: a gruff voice attached to girl with mystical blue eyes, creamy skin, and smooth black hair cut in a straight line across the top of her neck.

"Now, Iris," Farro said as he made his way toward her from the top of the room, "this isn't just any unevolved human. This is Virginia Dale, genetic engineering prodigy from Alcetra." He greeted her with the same joyful presence that he'd met her with in Alcetra.

"Well, Virginia," Iris said, "I would say let's be friends, but my mother told me that being poor and stupid is contagious, and I certainly don't want to catch any of that." She looked around to accumulate the snickers of her peers.

"Welcome to class, Virginia. Who is your friend?" Farro asked, looking at Amos, who stood confidently, with a blazing smile, behind her.

A voice from the front of the room yelled excitedly, "That's Amos! He's got the juiciest news stories on Mars!"

"Amos, you're welcome to stay if you think genetic engineering could be 'juicy' enough for your news," Mr. Farro said.

"Thank you, sir. I think our unscripted entry was just that! I'll come back another sol for more," Amos said. He smiled at Virginia and left.

"Come to the front of the class, Virginia. I believe I have the perfect class partner for you." Farro stopped at a table where a tall, thin boy was playing a game on his workboard, paying no attention to the ruckus or his instructor. "Virginia," Mr. Farro said, "you might catch flak from Iris, but Korbin Xander here is one stand-up guy."

The boy turned to look at her, then froze with a troubled expression.

He had a long face with short dark hair and olive skin, and he wasn't cute at all, but for some reason, Virginia was a little confused about him too. She couldn't find a word to greet him either.

She pulled away from his puzzled gaze as Farro continued with his instruction. Finally she spoke. "Should we have the instrument Farro's using on our table?"

She looked at him, waiting for his reply, but all he gave her was a shrug.

Virginia caught the eye of a heavyset boy with gold-rimmed glasses and curly hair at the table next to her who had the instrument Farro was instructing with. The stranger pointed to the symbol on the side of his machine and then to the side of the room, where a few of the same instruments sat sparse on a shelf.

"Here's the machine we need for this assignment," Virginia whispered after she retrieved it.

"Okay," Korbin mumbled without looking up from the game he was playing.

A wave of emotions swashed around inside her body. *I definitely don't fit in here. Even the ugly guy doesn't like me. I don't want to stay here for another sol—forget staying a few weeks. I need to go home now!*

Class broke for lunch, and Virginia followed the crowd through the connector, into the Main Conservatory. As she walked around the lavish Upper End cafeterias, she thought about all the coin storage Ms. West had given her and contemplated sushi or pizza. The giant pizzas with five toppings, basking in the lights under the glass case, were calling her name, and a salad came with a choice of twenty different dressings.

But she gasped when she looked at the price. *I only need one topping and one dressing*, she thought and walked to the community cafeteria at the Lower End, where the food was simple and didn't cost anything.

"What'd I miss?" She looked to see the smiling face of Amos, walking with pep in his step next to her.

She laughed through her nose. "No one in my class likes me, my class partner is weird—the whole city is weird—and I'm ready to go home."

Out of the corner of her eye, Virginia noticed the gold-rimmed glasses of the boy who'd helped her in class. He was sitting next to a girl who was half his size. She walked up to them with her tray of food in her hands. “Hi. I’m Virginia, by the way, and this is Amos.”

The boy continued to chew his food, silently offering Virginia and Amos a seat across the table with his open hand. “I’m Jeremiah. This is my girlfriend, Ellis. She’s the quiet type,” he said after he finished chewing. “That was funny when you two fell into class this morning… and like what… two hours late?” he said in disbelief. “I think I should let you know that it’s socially unacceptable to be late for anything in this city.”

Virginia hung her head. “Yeah. Pretty embarrassing. Not exactly what I wanted for my first sol. My class partner is even embarrassed to work with me.”

Jeremiah laughed. “It’s not you, it’s him.”

“What’s wrong with him?” Amos asked.

Jeremiah pushed the gold wire rim up his nose with his pinky finger. “He’s a know-it-all. Thinks he’s hot stuff just because he’s smart and his father is the administrator of Living Rock Sciences.”

“What’s Living Rock Science?” Virginia asked.

“It’s the program that’s discovered all the weird creatures you see around here—from out there.”

She wondered if that was where Sofia and the Rock Friends came from, but Jeremiah continued before she could ask. “Korbin is a real genius. He can find cells and bacteria that no one else can. Some of his findings have even been developed." He paused for a drink.

"Which is probably why he's so arrogant," Ellis said. "No one likes him. You should stay away from him too."

"Anyway, all that changed though... after his accident," Jeremiah continued.

"He's not arrogant anymore?" Virginia asked.

He laughed. "Yeah, he probably is. But he's not interested in science anymore."

"Still just as miserable as he was before his accident, too," Ellis chimed in.

Jeremiah seemed to notice Virginia's and Amos's curious faces, and he continued. "One night Korbin stayed late in the lab, and he mixed a bad batch of chemicals. The janitor found him on the floor and called emergency aid. When Aid Carrie arrived at the scene, his heart had stopped and he wasn't breathing. Within a few minutes she brought him back to life."

"Oh, what a lucky schmuck!" Amos commented.

Ellis added, "He doesn't talk to his best friends anymore. My oldest brother included. He's got some new fascination with space and flying—I heard he spends all his time in Port 1 with the mechanic, wrenching on Mars planes and old interplanetary spacecraft."

"When did the accident happen?" Virginia asked.

"Not long after the close of last year's Unity Festival, I think," Jeremiah said. "Maybe he's gotten better—I'm not sure. I only know as much as I do because I'm fascinated with politics and pay attention to what's going on with the city's administrators and professors."

Virginia returned to class and stood next to Korbin, who only seemed to acknowledge her with a brief dumbfounded gaze.

He could have suffered brain damage when his heart stopped. He could be suffering from PTSD. I should have compassion for him, not take his aloofness to heart, she thought as Farro resumed teaching and her class partner shamelessly played a Spaceball game on his workboard. *Although the rest of the class hates me, they don't ALL have a death-and-revival story for an excuse. I don't see how I can survive here for a few more weeks.*

She typed Paden a message through her workboard: *This place is not for me. I'm ready to come home.*

That's too bad. But me and Frankie will be happy to see you sooner than later. Call Mr. Bryant. He'll come scoop you up in a heartbeat, Paden messaged back.

I will, as soon as I get out of class.

"Virginia Dale has been practicing genetic engineering on her own for quite a while."

She looked up, shocked that Farro had just called her out in front of the whole class, sensing dozens of eyeballs staring at her.

"I think the class would like to see what you have accomplished with your bean invention. Would you like to give us an informal presentation on the work you've done so far?" Farro asked.

The proposition was as uncomfortable as the boulder that had just landed in her stomach, but she couldn't tell Farro no in front of the whole class. They would think her a fraud in addition to being a joke.

Virginia forced her pressed lips into a smile and nodded in agreement to Farro's proposition.

"Ugh! I don't know how to read this DNA sequencer," she complained under her breath. "I'm gonna look like an idiot. I'd be better at presenting use of the X-actionator."

"You've never used an X-actionator," Korbin replied in a whisper without looking up. "It's the most powerful and precise tool ever created, and it can only be used in space. Additionally, you must have your interplanetary license to use it."

Virginia peered laser cannons into the side of his face.

When he looked back at her, she noticed how much his ears stuck out, the unsettling vertical wrinkle between his brows. And there was something in his eye. In both his chocolate-colored eyes. A light? A reflection?

She narrowed her eyes to get a closer look at what exactly the reflection was, unapologetically stepping closer and moving her head from side to side.

And, unexpectedly, he smiled a little at her.

Ugh. Now I'm the weirdo. She took a step back. "I think I saw something... I think I saw my reflection in your eyes. Do you see your reflection in my eyes?" She shook her head. "No. No, never mind." She looked down and mumbled, "That couldn't happen more than once in a—"

He laughed under his breath as he packed up his workboard. He finally said, "It's okay, there's a lot of weird people in this city."

She didn't know why she wanted him to make her feel warm and welcome; she only knew it bugged her that he didn't. "By the way, I *do* have my interplanetary license."

Before he could reply, little alarms from dozens of transmitters sounded at four o'clock, and the students hurried out as fast as they could.

"Korbin and Virginia," Professor Farro called, waving them to the front of the class.

They walked up together.

"Korbin, you need to start helping Virginia get caught up on using our tools—and please take her to Mister and Missus's office on Hallway 2. They want to meet her."

"Ugh." Korbin quietly sighed.

"Who are they?" Virginia asked.

"They're the Unity Administrators."

She was puzzled. The Unity Administrators were very important people. They were in charge of the whole Unity Festival, the registering and unregistering of courtships; they oversaw the program, matching any interested Singles. They were also responsible for any quarrel that a United pair had.

Why would they possibly have any interest in meeting me?

Korbin walked out. Was he waiting outside for her, or had he just left without her? She finished packing her bag and walked through the red lab to the exit, stopping when she heard voices.

"No way," a boy's voice said. "Definitely would never consider courting her. She's clearly poor, looks weird—not someone who would have anything to offer as a future."

She opened the door to see Korbin talking to Iris. He'd been talking about her, she knew it—and to the most evil girl she had ever seen.

Virginia hurried away toward Hall 2 to find Mister and Missus for herself.

There is no way I'm going to stay here and be that guy's class partner. I'll call Mr. Bryant as soon as I get back to the suite.

How am I supposed to tell this foreign girl that I was only telling Iris what she wanted to hear so she wouldn't bully me? She won't believe me, Korbin thought as he ran to catch up with her. *I'll just be extra nice.*

He caught up with her in Conservatory 3. "Rice," he said, pointing to the hydroponic trays that filled the entire center of the conservatory. "It's our biggest food export."

He walked with her through Conservatory 2 in a weird silence, then onto the southbound hyperwalk of Hall 2. The hall was shaded with almond trees, overdue for pruning, and the Galleria that separated Hall 1 and 2 was barely in use. He couldn't help but admire Virginia's cream-colored face, prettier than the most visible Martian sunset. He didn't know why, but he wanted to be close to her and bask in whatever mysterious warmth she possessed. He couldn't do that, couldn't tell her that she reminded him of a sweet and happy song that he'd heard a million times. She would think he was as awkward as everyone else in this city did, as strange as everything else that had been going on since his accident.

He noticed Virginia looking up at the pictures hanging from the hallway's clear domed roof. The men in the portraits were plain with long hair pulled tight against their heads and wore white shirts with stiff high collars. The women also looked plain and old, their long hair pulled tight and with no fancy collars.

Maybe he could tell her enough Martian history that she would forget what she'd heard and believe his attempt to be friendly was genuine. "Those are portraits of the founding mothers and fathers of Mars, the original settlers. The people who risked their lives in the great unknown, the people who built this city. The people who are responsible for life as we know it." He spoke with confidence as he pointed to a beautiful woman's portrait. "This woman here is Eleanor Greene. She was the first girl born on Mars. Also my great-grandmother, who four generations ago founded the Unity Festival.

"You see those people over there?" he said, pointing to a flamboyantly dressed couple in front of Extension 220 wearing orange, green, and yellow ensembles with large feathered hats, talking to a small group—likely Singles, because they were flaunting flags and various Unity paraphernalia in red and purple. "That's Mister and Missus, the Unity Administrators. The next opening is on Hall 4, you can exit the hyperwalk there. I'm riding this thing to the end."

"Where are you going?" she asked.

"To Port 1. I work there."

"I used to love being in our ports with Charles."

"Who's..." he began to ask, but stopped when he noticed the sadness in her eyes, right before she tucked her chin. He didn't want to make her cry. This could be a great opportunity to redeem himself and maybe get her to like him a little. "Why don't you come with me and see our port? You can tell me about Charles, if you want, and catch the Unity Administrators on your way back up the hall."

Virginia didn't respond, so he kept talking about Martian history, until they were suddenly standing in front of the port doors together.

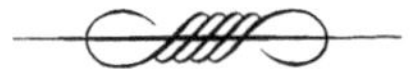

Korbin opened the door to Port 1, and she walked in. It looked the same as Port 1 in her city, where they kept all the older planes and ISVs, as well as the newer ones that had major mechanical problems. As she followed him up and down the rows of ships, Korbin told her their stories, which the old port master, Jerry, had told him. Entertained by all the history, she forgot about what he had just said about her to Iris—until the gruff voice of the meanest girl on the planet rumbled into the back of her head.

"Miss Dale, shouldn't you be practicing for the presentation so you can prove that you have no business in our advanced class?"

Virginia turned around and looked into Iris's ice-blue eyes. "What exactly is your problem with me? Are you angry that I'll end up proving *you* have no business in this class?"

Iris shoved herself between Korbin and Virginia. "Whatever, Neanderthal," she said as she walked away, toward the break area just under the port master's tower.

Virginia stared into Korbin's eyes, rage running through her blood. "Did you bring me here so she could insult me? What did I ever do to you to deserve this?"

"Look, Virginia. Iris is a bully, and I only said those things about you so she wouldn't make up some strange story to get me in trouble with my father."

"I don't believe you," she said, pointing her finger at him.

"I don't know why she's down here. I see her and some of the others who wear the black coats with their hoods up all the time hanging around in the break room a lot."

They both looked toward the break room, where Iris was getting a drink from the vending machine. Korbin continued, "She doesn't work here. Her family doesn't have any ISVs here. She has no business here. Unless the rumors are true."

"What rumors?" she asked gravely.

"Rumors that there is a secret passage to Hall 1 from this port. Maybe even from the parts closet." Korbin pointed toward the break room.

"Why would there be a secret passage to Hall 1?" Her uncertainty in his truthfulness rang through in her tone.

"I don't know." He shrugged. "The hall is closed, prohibited to all residents. It's like a forest over there. Just storage mainly on those extensions. No one has lived there since... well, for a long time."

Virginia sensed there was a bigger story behind the one Korbin told, but the hurtfulness of Iris's words and her doubt of what his intentions were made her unsettled. She took a deep breath in, let it out, and looked at the time on her transmitter. 4:09. "I'm going to go talk to the Unity Administrators," she said and began to walk to the port doors.

"Exit on 4. Extension 220, Door 2211," Korbin said loudly as she walked away.

She rode the hyperwalk up the hall, trying to put together the pieces of Iris and Korbin. Was he telling the truth? *If these two are up to something, I have to figure it out.*

Exiting the hyperwalk near Extension 440, she walked up to Extension 220, only to find that no one was in Office 2211. Virginia leaned against the wall next to the Unity Administrators' door and let out a deep breath, exhausted from the sol and questioning everything since she'd met Farro in Ms. West's shack.

Searching for a stable thought, an answer to settle the waves inside her body, she decided that tonight was the perfect night to have a call with Frankie, whom she would soon be spending forever with. Frankie had no connection to her; he was a distant vibe. A place to go where no worries or concerns existed.

"The risk of love is loss, and the price of loss is grief. But the pain of grief is only a shadow when compared with the pain of never risking love."

~ Hilary Stanton Zunin

CHAPTER 6

Mars has extreme temperature changes, ranging from 20°C (70°F) to –153°C (–225°F). Because of the thin atmosphere, the planet doesn't retain the sun's heat for long.

Korbin sighed and slung his bag on the ground next to Virginia's seat. His shoulders were slumped in defeat, and she felt a heaviness of compassion for him—that was, until he didn't ask her a single question to connect, but started playing his game on his workboard. "There are other things I'd rather be doing after class too," she replied to his display of discontent.

"Ah, don't worry about it. We gotta help each other, right? Besides, I owe Farro big-time for getting me the mechanic's job. He's a highly connected professor, you know. It would be disrespectful if I didn't do whatever he asked."

"Then I have Farro to thank," she said under her breath. She remained silent, hoping that he would express more eagerness to help her, address her concerns about his dealings with Iris and her dealings in Port 1.

He didn't.

For some reason, she wanted him to care. "Well, thanks. I don't know how I could learn to read this DNA sequencer without your help." She could feel his eyes peering into her skull. She looked at him, and he quickly looked away.

"Ah, you'll give a great presentation, and no one will have anything to say about your talent."

There was no one else in the lab. The only noise was Korbin's quiet voice explaining the machine and the steps she needed to use it, until a familiar gruff female voice broke the calm of the room. "What is this?"

It was Iris, standing in front of the door of the red laboratory, followed by a miniature version of her, wearing the same floor-length black-hooded coat, mirroring her with her right hand on her hip. "Korbin, I'm here to save you from this inferior excuse of a human." Iris cackled loudly while she marched toward them.

"Again? Really? What is up with this girl?" Virginia said under her breath.

"Korbin. Really, friend? Spending time with this Lower Ender from a fruit-producing city won't help you break into a career in space flight."

Virginia waited two seconds for Korbin to insert some sort of defense. He didn't.

"The only thing lowly about our fruit-producing city is that we allow monsters like you to consume our precious fruits," she snapped back.

Iris snarled through her scowl and stuck her neck out toward Virginia. "Your only friends will be Rock Friends once Sofia sees what a mischievous, lying, good-for-nothing intruder we have in our city."

Korbin had closed the scientific tool and put his workboard back in his duffel. "Let's all just go home. Virginia, we'll get together tomorrow," he said, attempting to break the death stare between the two girls.

"You can do way better, Korbin. Way better than this one." Iris whipped around, her coat smacking the back of her ankles, and marched out of the laboratory with her little duplicate following behind.

There was pain in Virginia's eyes. "Why is she always showing up to attack me when I'm with you? Do you two have a plan to make me hate it here and leave? Because it's working."

"No. Not at all, Virginia, I've got nothing to do with her. Promise." His voice was sincere. "She's probably harassing you because you haven't shown any fear like the rest of us have. Don't take it personally. I think she has family problems."

"Whatever," she huffed. "I've got to go back to Hall 2 next. The Unity Administrators weren't there when I left the port tour with you the other sol."

She'd hoped that Korbin would offer to walk her down, but he didn't.

"Okay," he replied and threw his bag behind his back.

I wish I knew why I just want to go with him right now and figure all this out, she thought, noticing the cells in her body anxiously whiz as she watched him walk out the red laboratory's door. *I should figure out what Iris is doing in that parts closet—maybe that will lead me to some answers.*

The door to the Unity Administration office was wide open when Virginia arrived. The walls of the waiting room were plastered with pictures of kissing Uniteds and quotes about love and Unity powers. The space didn't make her happy—the happiness of Union had become a memory of a dream she'd had long ago.

There was another door, closed, with words painted in cursive letters on it: *Knock and the door will open for you. Seek and you will find.*

KNOCK—

The door slid open before Virginia could knock a second time. The room that it opened to was dark with a calming melody playing from speakers in the ceiling. A little weirded out, she went in, walking around a round table toward a dimly lit hologram panel on the wall.

"Hello," she called out loudly. When she heard nothing, she waved her hand in front of the panel. The number nine lit up brightly. Virginia took a step back, toward the door.

"Coming!" a woman's voice yelled from somewhere far away.

The floor began moving clockwise, stopping after a half circle.

A brightly dressed pair suddenly appeared at the door. The man, wearing a dark green suit with bright green trim and a small green brimmed hat with a feather sticking out of the side, approached. "Miss Virginia," he said, pulling her into his arms as if he had known her his whole entire life.

"Welcome," said the woman, whose asymmetrical skirt and top with extra-puffy sleeves and wide-brimmed hat were the same colors as the man's. "We are Missus..."

"...and Mister," the man continued. "Unity Administrators for the city of Nos. Say, Virginia, do you plan on courting one of our fine young men while you're here?"

Normally, when a couple wanted to court each other, they registered at the Unity Administration table during a Unity Festival event. Too shy to ask why they were singling her out to have a personal meeting with her, she fervently shook her head back and forth. "Oh no. I have someone back home. Waiting for me. I think I will likely go home early and Unite with him."

Missus started laughing. "You must be brave, daughter, and follow your power of sense when it comes to courting this season."

What is this wild-looking woman talking about. Uninterested in what seemed like gibberish, Virginia began to look around the room. A picture on a shelf caught her attention. She narrowed her eyes to look closely at it. "Is that..."

"Your father? Yes," Mister replied. "He was my best friend in interplanetary flight school. You know, you have the same power of sense he had when he was young... before he and your mother were United."

"You knew my father?" she mumbled in disbelief.

"Many know each other," Missus said. "And *many* will be with you to help you on your important journey."

"*Many*? Important journey?"

"Yes, dear," Missus began. "All the souls whose energy lives on, who have powers that are greater than what the eyes can see."

"Maybe we should slow down," Mister said. "We brought you here so you would know that we are here for you. Friends of your family that you can count on while you are here in Nos."

Still confused, Virginia stared blankly at Missus.

Mister laughed to lighten the mood. "Yeah. It's deep. Just know you're not alone. Any question, we have the answer. We're here for you."

"And we understand how important Union is for you this season. Don't underestimate our understanding for your situation."

Mister clapped his hands and lit his face up with a smile, attempting to ease the uneasiness she held in the lines of her face. "And United and well educated you will be this Unity season."

"Uh, yeah. Sure," Virginia replied.

Missus walked to the hologram board, waved her hand in front of it, and watched it become a beautiful glowing purple Ananta. "There's a bigger story than what your eyes can see. And whatever you may learn or understand, count on us. For anything." She looked at Virginia with a warm smile and soft gaze.

The meeting was odd. Mister and Missus were odd, and at the same time, oddly comforting. She decided trust them, for no other reason than their connection with her father, and hold their mysterious concern safe. *But what did they mean by "it's deep"?*

Virginia lay on the sofa in silence, staring through the roof in the living room, watching the sky grow slightly darker with each passing minute, and talking to Paden about the strange conversation she'd had with the Unity Administrators. Amos walked into the suite, rattling around, not even noticing her.

"Oh geez!" He jumped and threw up his hands. "Didn't even see you sitting there," he said with his hand on his chest, catching his breath.

As soon as she ended her call with Paden, she asked him, "Did you have to meet the Unity Administrators too?"

"No. Why? Are they interesting characters that deserve a spot in my news?"

"Absolutely. And guess what? They knew my parents."

"Oh. Wow. Interesting."

"Yeah. Small world. But they seem to really like me. At least someone here does, because that heinous flower in my class sure has the strangest disdain for me. And my class partner, I can't tell if he's hot or cold. Or why I sense that there's some reason I need to see him, some reason that I should be interested in him."

"Heinous flower?"

"Yeah. Iris."

"Funny. Maybe you have a subconscious crush on him and so does she?" Amos said.

"Me? A crush on Korbin? I doubt it. Her? I doubt that too. But I think I'm sensing something important about him. Maybe her too."

"Like what?"

"I don't know, but I'm thinking it's complicated."

"Superhuman senses on the fritz?" he teased.

"Possibly. Or maybe I'm confusing my senses with plain ole curiosity. I keep going back to the question of *why*. Why would my generally aloof lab partner show me, on my first sol of class, the suspicious activity of the girl who hates me? I'm getting a sense that there are some puzzle pieces I need to put together."

"Is it a setup maybe?"

"It could be. But why would two strangers have it out for me that bad? This is exactly why I need to have the upper hand. Maybe I need to figure out just what exactly Iris and the other kid dressed in black were doing disappearing into the port parts closet."

"Maybe you should figure out if they were snooping around because of that secret passage you told me about. That would give you the upper hand if they decided to start some trouble with you," Amos said. "I wish your grandmother were here. She would know. She always had the answer for everything."

Virginia whipped her head around, narrowing her eyes his way.

He turned the palms of his hand up. "What?" He laughed. "You know your grandmother and I were friends."

"It's not that." She disappeared into her room. "It's this," she said after she returned, placing a transmitter button into his hand.

Amos looked at it, then at the transmitter in her wristband. "What's this?"

"It's Grandmother." Her curls bounced as she shook her head. "But she speaks in riddles. I'm not sure what she's saying exactly."

He opened his hand and laughed. "Gin, this thing looks older than your grandmother."

"Just turn it on."

Amos gave it a squeeze and almost dropped it when a wild purple windstorm appeared from the little glass dome in his hand. "What on Mars!" he exclaimed as the little windstorm turned into an image of Grandmother Blane.

He set the transmitter button on the coffee table. "This is crazy! It looks just like your grandmother."

The hologram lifted her head to the sky and laughed. "The girl doesn't even recognize him! Hahahaha!"

Amos laughed as well. "It even sounds like her!"

Grandmother pulled her banana cane from behind her narrow body and poked Amos with it. He watched the light of it pass through his body. "That's certainly something Grandmother Blane would do. She was constantly poking people with that thing." He chuckled.

"It has found you too." Grandmother giggled, waving her banana cane in front of Amos's face.

He furrowed his brows and pressed his lips.

"Yes, you remember what we spoke of, young friend," she confirmed.

Amos got up and stepped toward Grandmother's hologram. He tilted his head, staring into the small, closely set hologram eyes that resembled Grandmother's, and said, "Grandmother Blane?"

"At last! I live forever!" She giggled.

"It is her, Gin," he said to Virginia, who sat cross-armed on the sofa. "I sense it. It's really her!"

Amos looked back at Grandmother, who nodded her head and drew her shoulders up with each little laugh. "And what you fear is only that, young man."

He took a deep inhale. "I hope so, Grandmother."

"You're replying like you know what she's talking about," Virginia said.

He shrugged. "Repeats from our previous talks... We talked a lot. Many a heart-to-heart conversation—she helped me figure some things out."

The two looked at Grandmother, who was now dancing to music that only she could hear. "Can you tell me why she's so giddy?" Virginia asked.

"I celebrate the important couple!" Grandmother sang.

They looked at each other, puzzled. "She said something about this important couple the first time, when Ms. West showed me her hologram," Virginia complained. "But she doesn't say who. Could you and I be the important couple she's talking about?"

Amos spit out his laugh. "No! She's your grandmother," he replied. "There's no other reason she would be here except for you. And she knows... well... she knows me well. And you and I never, ever have a shot at being a couple."

Grandmother bent over and smacked her knee, laughing. "It's his new shell! It hinders her sense!"

Virginia stared at her, trying to make sense of what she was saying.

"Gin, remember when you were just talking about Korbin, and how you were either curious or sensing something about him?"

She remembered the last time she saw him walking away, how the cells in her body had gone wild, disrupting her innards. "Yeah, but she would never want to see me with someone who gives me anxiety."

"Only the two hold the key!" Grandmother sang, clapping.

Virginia nudged Amos with her elbow. "I think she's talking about how we can get into the forbidden extension that Korbin was talking about."

"Forward Union after defeating the white light," Grandmother continued.

"Maybe she's trying to give me a clue that Iris and Korbin are plotting against me," Virginia whispered.

Amos shook his head. "No. Your awful classmates aren't exactly a clapping matter. She's giving you clues about the future."

Virginia tilted her head. "How do you know that?"

With a smirk, he shrugged. "I don't know. Forward means ahead, so I'm just guessing it's in the future. Maybe it's *my* superhuman senses?"

Grandmother poked Amos with the light of her banana stick. "You help pink and blue along the dangerous mile. Two must not be separated again. Many are building to aid the important couple." She twirled in a circle until she disappeared, leaving a hologram scene of Amos and Virginia flying in an ISV together, shooting off laser cannons, ray guns, and the X-actionator.

"Whoa! Look at us!" he exclaimed, and soon the purple glow of Grandmother's hologram dispersed into innumerable particles and faded away. "I miss your grandmother. I always kinda thought she was a Royal. Did you know?"

"Of course I knew. She tried to hide her magic, but the fun little child in her made it a little too obvious. I'm kinda glad I knew though, her powers made me feel safe. If I were a Royal, I would use my powers to make my children feel safe too. And for fun, of course—I'd fly around Mars without a plane! If I had Royal powers right now, I could get into that forbidden extension and figure out what Iris and the hood-wearing character—maybe even Korbin—are up to."

"If you had Royal powers, you wouldn't need to get into that extension—you would already know," Amos said, then he put his arm around Virginia and gave her a squeeze. "We'll go put some cameras down there on Satsol, when most of the city is in the conservatory watching the Spaceball game. We'll figure out, together, what that heinous flower is up to."

She laughed, delighting in the ease that flushed through her body from Amos's concern for her.

"And about understanding what your grandmother is saying... She's having fun. We should too, and not take her too seriously."

Virginia watched Amos cram a handful of tiny little black cameras, no bigger than the tip of her pinky, into his bag. "Port 1 parts locker, here we come," he said.

They passed through the Main Conservatory, gracefully dodging the rambunctious Singles who had gathered to watch the Spaceball game, and scurried through the connector, hastily passing through Conservatories 5, 4, and 3, exiting into the main hall of Conservatory 2. On the hyperwalk toward the port, they passed white hairs slowly strolling along, parents and their little children watching the Spaceball game on the hall holograms, and some older kids going in and out of the eatery with popcorn and fruit ices in hand.

"Gin, you can relax. We're not doing anything wrong. We're just going to Port 1 to look around. I'm a reporter. That's what I do," Amos said, noticing the look of concern on her face. "In addition to being suave, of course." He smirked when he got her to smile.

"Let's go to the observation tower first. So we can see who's there and get a read on the port before we go planting cameras."

Standing in the observation tower high above the ground floor, hidden behind mirrored glass, they watched as the port revealed no movement at all. On the opposite side, in the port master's tower, they could see the shadow of a person, presumably the port master. They waited for him to get up or even move his head.

"Looks like it's nap time for the port master," Amos mocked.

"The stillness is kinda creepy," Virginia added.

"And look!" He pointed to the tall, thin young man who had just rolled himself out from under a spacecraft almost directly below the observation tower. "There's the source of this drama right there."

Virginia leaned forward to see Korbin in the port below. "I don't want him to see us, just in case he and Iris are better pals than he's led me to believe," she whispered. "The parts closet where he said he saw her is under the port master's tower, behind the break room." She peered at it with narrowed eyes.

"Perfect," Amos said. "We'll lollygag around in the break room, sit at the picnic table, buy a drink from the machine. You can check out their flight simulator while I plant the cameras. If anyone asks us anything, I'm a reporter looking for a story. That's all."

She agreed with a nod.

"But first..." He strolled along the long observation window and stopped at the corner, pulling out a small camera from his bag. "We should get a view from this angle too," he said and carefully stuck a little camera on the window, directing it toward the break room where the suspicious parties would be seen.

Virginia watched Korbin slide back under the spacecraft. "C'mon, let's get to the ground now so Korbin doesn't see us."

She walked to the soda machine. "What do you want?" she asked Amos, but he was gone. She got herself a drink and sat, waiting for him at the picnic table.

"Virginia. What are you doing here?" Korbin asked, his face dirty and his expression confused.

Startled, she fumbled for her words as Amos strolled confidently out of the parts locker. "Hey, man! I'm Amos.

I'm a reporter. Virginia said I could come and get a good story from… What's your name?"

"Korbin."

"Yeah. Exactly. Korbin, she said I could get a great story from you."

"In the parts locker?"

Virginia immediately decided the best approach was the truth. "Korbin, Amos is just here helping me. I'm trying to get the upper hand on Iris, in case her disdain for me goes any further. I thought that if I knew what she's doing back here…"

"You'd have some leverage. I get it," Korbin replied gently, his brows drawn in concern. "I know she's been really rude to you." He sat down next to her, his gestures peaceful. "I know how difficult it is to be a stranger. I sometimes look at myself and think I'm a stranger in my own body."

Amos put another camera high in a corner that gave a perfect view of the entire break room area.

"I sure hope Sofia doesn't find those," Korbin said.

"They just look like spots on the wall. Amos is a reporter—he can get away with a lot," Virginia replied.

"I'm not gonna say a thing about this. I hope you find some answers. But please stay out of Hall 1. Sofia means business about people staying out of there," Korbin said.

They left Korbin in Port 1 with their secret, hoping he truly wasn't in cahoots with Iris, or a snitch. "Now what?" Amos asked as he stared, puzzled, at the Galleria that separated Halls 1 and 2.

"I'm hungry." Virginia looked at him with a devious smile.

"You want to find a door."

"Maybe."

"Even if the Galleria was home to some mysterious open door, it's forbidden, so if we get caught by the snake-head lady, we're, uh, probably gonna be turned into some sort of rock freak show or something."

"But you're a reporter. You're not even from this city," Virginia said, leading the way to the lower end of the Galleria, past the aid station, and standing in front of a narrow door. She gave it a push with the tips of her fingers. It opened, and her eyes widened. "No way! Maybe they aren't serious about keeping people out."

"Or this is a setup," Amos said. He looked around, making sure no one was nearby, and slid the door open wider. "We're visitors. We don't know any better." He confidently hurried through the door.

"Wow. I can see why they don't want anyone in here now," Virginia said, looking at their surroundings, exposed by a dim glow from the moon. It highlighted sparse leaves on tall trees and the hyperwalk that was on a forever halt, covered with vines and withered fruit. The safety lights above flickered randomly, the air was stagnant—it smelled like nothing was alive or dead—and the creatures in the walnut treetops barely moved, trapped in a fog.

She led the way on what looked like a path toward the lower end of the hall, each step gentle so as to not disturb the dead leaves underfoot. They had passed two extensions when Virginia froze. The two friends stood still and silent, waiting to hear something, waiting for a reason to turn around and run.

"Down there," Amos whispered and pointed toward an extension where the *x* on the exit sign was the only illuminated letter that pulsed steadily. Holding on to her shoulders, he tapped his fingers to the rhythm of the flashing *x*. "*Don't. Go. Any. Further,*" he whispered in her ear.

"Goofball," she whispered back.

"Look at that." He pointed to Extension 190, the extension closest to Port 1, where the entrance was clear of all vines and overgrown flora.

The two had started down the extension when Amos whispered for her to stop, just in front of a door that didn't close all the way. Door 1903 was partially open, a bright white light seeping through the crack.

Virginia turned her head toward him and whispered, "Look above the door. Do you see that?"

"I do." The two of them watched the shadow of a large body with short bent legs creep along the wall. It turned its long, narrow head as if it had just noticed them too.

"We gotta go—that thing could be on top of us at any moment," she replied from the breath in the back of her throat.

The shadow creature moved its tail to the side, revealing a shadow of spikes along its back.

Amos scurried to the wall opposite the door and added a camera that could record anything happening around it. "Let's get out of here, fast!" He grabbed Virginia's hand, and they hastily made their way back to the Galleria.

They stopped between the suspiciously open door and the aid station to catch their breath and dust the fear and suspicion off their clothes.

"What was that?" Virginia said to Amos, noticing the horror that lingered in her veins.

As the two lifted their faces to discuss it, they were met by the bearded scowl of a tall, thin man and innumerable hissing snake tongues.

Amos and Virginia remained silent as they followed Sofia and the dark-bearded man, who used a walking stick taller than he was, across Hall 2, to Extension 250, Door 22511.

"Wait outside my office," Sofia commanded.

She could feel doom weighing heavily in her stomach. "I can't stop thinking about that thing on the wall, Amos. What on Mars was that? It was huge and had like a dark energy," Virginia whispered.

He leaned against the wall. "Everything here in Nos is weird. And it was something we weren't supposed to see or ever talk about again. Now, let's get our story straight," he whispered directly into Virginia's ear, so as not to be heard by the surrounding Rock Friends.

Before they could confirm a story that would paint them innocent, the door opened and the dark-bearded man slammed the narrow tip of his walking stick into the ground, looking at the fright in their faces as he exited Sofia's office.

"Dad," a voice from the top of the extension called.

It was Korbin. He walked forward and stopped in front of his father.

"Administrator Xander," Virginia gasped.

Korbin noticed the scene with Virginia and Amos, heads hung low, and Sofia standing at her office door with the serpents on her head all riled up. "Virginia! I've been looking everywhere for you," he blurted out, moving hastily toward her, past the rigid body of his father. "What are you doing here? I was worried when you didn't show up."

“I found them in Hall 1, coming in from a door that said no trespassing,” Sofia said before Virginia had a moment to explain the worry on her face.

“But I told you to meet me in Port 1, not Hall 1,” Korbin said.

Virginia stared into his long face. *What is this guy up to?*

Amos nudged her with his elbow.

“Oh. That’s why I didn’t find you in that creepy place, huh?” she replied.

“See that, Sofia, she thought I told her to meet me in Hall 1. She’s not from our city—she doesn’t know any better.”

“What is your dealing with this outsider, young Xander?” Sofia questioned.

“I… I was gonna… talk to her about something.”

“Like what, boy?” she demanded.

Korbin shrugged and sighed. “To court me,” he replied to the scowl on Sofia’s face. “Officially. Starting this Sunsol, the Unity Festival Dinner and Dance.” Then he turned to Virginia. “This isn’t how I wanted to ask you, but will you?”

She was so shocked she could have thrown up. She forced a gleaming smile and agreed with a nod.

“Hall 1 is forbidden,” Sofia said, leaning into Virginia’s face. Then she leaned into Amos’s face. “You didn’t know that, so I won’t destroy you *this sol*,” she said, pressing one last drop of fear into them.

Amos, Virginia, and Korbin walked away from Sofia's office together.

"Wow. Thanks for saving our tails back there," Amos said.

Virginia couldn't figure out what to say. She knew she should be grateful, but Korbin didn't even like her. Why would he care? Why would he choose courting as a solution to save their hides?

"Yeah, thanks," she finally said. "Does Sofia really turn people who break the rules into rocks?"

"That's what all the Rock Friends are, apparently. I don't really know what type of infractions call for the stone sentence, but I didn't want to find out. Not if I could help it," Korbin said.

"This is not the life you pictured but here you are. You can still make something beautiful. Grieve. Breathe. Begin again."

~ Thema Bryant-Davis

CHAPTER 7

Mars was first seen through a telescope by Galileo Galilei in 1610.

Within a few short hours, United volunteers had magically transformed the conservatory from daily life to a space rolling with a glow of enthusiasm and hope, just like they did in Alcetra. The Ananta, magically suspended above, illuminated Nos's entire conservatory dome in purple.

Virginia was puzzled, anxious even, about her courtship with Korbin. *He's nice, and then he's weird. Hot and cold. Frankie's my guy. Just get the courtship over with so Sofia doesn't turn you and Amos into rocks,* she told herself as she walked to the table where she would sit with her new friends for her first Unity Festival Dinner at Nos and wait for her date.

Jeremiah and Ellis were cool, easy to talk to; they didn't take sides or hold any judgment.

"Do you think he likes you?" Jeremiah asked Virginia.

She shrugged. "Enough to keep me and Amos out of trouble."

"Do you like him?" Ellis asked.

Virginia's face became flushed.

"It's okay if you do," Ellis replied. "We told you what we knew about him. But people speak different languages with their heart."

"I think my one true love hasn't even been gone for a year and it would be hard for me to like anyone right now. But maybe I can at least decide if he's a friend or a foe," Virginia replied, content with her answer.

The seats at the tables around them began filling up, and the quartet onstage picked up the tempo.

"Who's Amos talking to over there?" Virginia asked. "He looks kinda like a peanut."

Jeremiah laughed. "Yeah, that's our city's news reporter. He's up-and-coming, but only because he's an Upper Ender who schmoozes for views."

Ellis leaned in to whisper, "No one really watches him. He wouldn't even have a news channel if the mayor wasn't funding him to produce the news that he and other administrators want him to."

Amos strolled toward their table, took his seat, and leaned across Virginia to stare at the empty seat next to her.

She swallowed the lump in her throat. "Yeah, well, he's not here. What's important is he got us out of a bind."

Mister and Missus, decked out in a rainbow of colors and cheerful large hats, stepped on the center stage, and the music faded away, replaced by the cheers of everyone under the dome. Just like in Alcetra, they too spoke the Unity Creed to open the evening festivities.

Inside the room with the door that wouldn't close all the way sat a small group whose shadowy appearance was as unknown as the darkness around them. They sat upright atop storage containers surrounding the empty center of the room, dispersing the heavy silence with their whispers.

Without warning, a strange cloud of light appeared in the circle, revealing the faces of four teenagers, outlined by the shadow of the black hoods pulled over their heads. The door shrieked on its tracks as it opened, revealing two more people. As they walked closer to the center of the room, the cloud illuminated the hooded faces of Iris and her smaller sidekick as they took their seats.

The group solemnly stared at the dim cloud of light as it became brighter and formed a cyclone, soon revealing a holographic pair of mighty wings. As the wings expanded, the cyclone took the form of a man's heavy chest and finely chiseled torso. His long hair blew back from a wind that wasn't in the room to show his eyes, so deeply set they looked like black holes.

His voice was suave and enthusiastic. "Whew! It feels good to be here! And with your help I will soon be out of Anywhere so that I can break the Royal curse, living in this body, right here on beautiful Mars with you! Or maybe I'll try—"

"And we will have the infinite powers of the Royals!" a girl's voice from the group cheered.

"Ah. Enthusiasm. You're my kind of girl. A new recruit to our team?" the Dutch said as he moved his hologram around to acknowledge each person in the group. "It's a fine group of highly intelligent and deserving people you have joined."

"Yeah, um... that... I've been wondering: how exactly will you give us our Royal powers? Do you have access to a Unity Element or something?" the extra-tall boy in the circle asked.

The Dutch swung around and addressed him. "Tell me, young man, do you know how important it is to keep these two from Uniting?"

"Uh, no," the boy said lackadaisically.

"To find each other twice in the same lifetime would give two humans more than Royal power—some would call it Legendary." The Dutch spoke poetically. "From where I am, I have seen the future of this boy and girl. If they Unite, their powers will be dangerous. Dangerous enough to destroy the planet."

He raised his head, swayed his long hair across his back, and exhaled his words. "And when you keep them apart, the master of the world where I am will reward us all by releasing me. I will return to Mars, break the Royal curse, and give you fine young people the great magic you have so rightly earned! We must keep them apart! And if that boy makes it to the Unity Administration booth tonight, we will need to end their courtship!"

Iris spoke up. "I've known Korbin since grade school. He trusts me. I've been dropping hints about Uniting into opportunity, reminding him of exactly what he wants."

"Yes. This is a brilliant young lady. Keep him distracted and on mission to make his life better. And maybe you should introduce him to someone—or bring him into the Love Counseling Booth—and I will help him," the Dutch replied.

He moved in front of the tall boy. "How will you earn your Royal powers?"

"My uncle, he owns the fleet of freight transportation vehicles. He has a daughter—I'll introduce them."

"Perfect. Everyone gets a pretty face in front of this boy. Only thirteen more weeks to save the future of the Royal Uniteds."

"Uh, Dutch?" One of the boys spoke up quietly.

He spun around to face him. "Yes?"

"If this is so important, why don't you do it? Why us?"

The Dutch sighed, drew his wings into his body, and assured the timid boy, "I cannot take form until these two are separated forever, or I would have ended things the sol the girl arrived." He opened his wings again and asked, "Any more questions? Or are you ready to earn your Royal powers?"

The group was silent, and without a farewell greeting, the bright white hologram of the Dutch turned into a cyclone, spinning faster and faster until it disappeared.

Embarrassed about his tardiness, Korbin arrived at the table in the middle of dinner. "I'm sorry," he said quietly into Virginia's ear.

She looked at him, seeming to spot every detail. He was freshly cleaned yet disheveled, and he noticed that she noticed. Flustered, he slicked back his hair and exhaled a giant breath that he might have been holding for the past hour.

Virginia responded to his late arrival with a smirk and rolled her eyes. Her friends were staring, dumbfounded, at Korbin. "I'm really sorry," he said to Amos and Jeremiah and Ellis, whose faces showed their disapproval.

"I was hoping you didn't make it because Sofia turned you into a rock," Virginia said to him loudly, eyeing her friends, like she didn't want them to think she was a pushover.

He knew he was wrong for being late, but he couldn't tell her it was because he was nervous, that his stomach was in such knots that he'd buried his head in his work for hours, trying to avoid this moment as long as he could. "We better register with Unity Administration or Sofia may still add us to her collection," he replied.

They walked toward the Unity Administration booth, silent, until Korbin finally told her, "I was nervous. I'm not really sure why I made this choice—I don't even know you. This is not at all how I thought I would end up courting someone. But I like you. I really do. And I hope we can become good friends."

Virginia looked at him, puzzled. "Okay. Thanks, Korbin. I hope we can be friends too. And this is really awkward for me too. In more ways than one."

He sighed a sigh of relief.

They arrived at the Unity Administration booth to register their courtship. Korbin typed in his name, and Virginia followed.

How do you wish to register?

☐ *Courtship*

☐ *Union*

"We should probably take it slow, eh?" Virginia said playfully.

Relieved, he checked the *courtship* box, and she did the same.

"Do you want to court anyone this season?" she asked him.

The question troubled him. He sighed again and ran his hands through his hair, speaking into the air above him. "Yeah, actually. And I'm under a lot of pressure to make a Union this season without my father choosing my mate. I would like to find a Union that will connect me to some sort of opportunity in space flight. If I don't, I could be stuck working in Living Rock Sciences forever."

"It's funny—we both need to get United this season, and now we're courting each other, but neither of us is a good fit for the other," she replied with a nervous laugh.

We both need to, but we're not a good fit?

"Hey, would you like to maybe ditch the dance and go to the observatory where it's quiet and we can talk?" Korbin asked.

Virginia's face lit up. "You have an observatory?"

"Yeah! It's the connector at the end of the Upper End hallway."

They walked up Hall 6 through the Upper End, and Korbin wasted no time in explaining. "The seats in the observatory came from Kepler, which of course was the very first passenger shuttle to Mars. And Messier..."

Virginia contentedly listened to the history lesson he gave her, which reminded her of Charles's knowledge and passion for history, forgetting his awkwardness and noticing there was a bit of happiness racing around her as they walked together. They arrived at a set of shiny silver doors. Above read *Galilei Observatory.*

"We don't have an observatory at Alcetra, but I've read about them," she said.

It was a dimly lit room with no windows and only a few pale blue lights under the circle of seating in the center of the observatory. Around the wall there were six telescopes, two of which were occupied.

How could he know that I would love it here? Virginia thought as she followed Korbin to an open seat. "Do you know of any constellations we can see tonight?"

"We can probably see Orion's Belt if it's not too windy. Let's try."

She scooted to the side of the seat so Korbin could use the telescope, but not far enough. *He's sitting too close. We're touching. Why am I not moving? All I have to do is move over just a little more and we won't be touching. Does he know we're touching right now? I've got to move away.*

"Virginia. Virginia. Ginny!"

Korbin was saying her name. He grabbed her hand from her lap. "Hey, are you okay?"

His hand was warm, so warm she could feel her whole body getting warmer. *Just pull your hand away. If there was light in here and you could see his odd face, you would have no problem moving away. What's wrong with you? Get it together now!* she told herself.

"Uh yes. Yes, I'm fine." She pulled her hand away.

She put her face in the viewer and listened as Korbin began his information ramble. "...Orion's Belt. As seen from Earth—but who can honestly make out an archer with a bow from a couple of distant stars?" he said. "Start with the brightest star you see in the top left corner of the nebula. That's the tip of Orion, the hunter's bow."

As she gazed at the stars, she no longer heard his voice, only the gentle and caring voice of her beloved Charles, showing her the magic of the universe, telling her the countless stories of the gods from Earth.

"Gaia sent a giant scorpion to challenge the hunter Orion and her daughter, Artemis. They fought the great scorpion together, but one of Artemis's arrows hit Orion, and he was killed. Artemis was so sad that she killed her best friend and lover that—"

Virginia playfully put her hand over his mouth. "That she placed him in the sky as a tribute to his memory," she said, finishing the story.

He caught her hand with both of his before she could return it to her lap. She could feel his breath on her fingertips and the heat of his hesitation. She felt a buzzing of warmth through her body that she wished would go away.

Through the dark, they stared into each other's souls.

Virginia had a knowing, in that moment, that Korbin was safe. That he was a friend. That there was a connection that she hadn't had since... Charles.

Korbin's transmitter button lit up bright yellow on his wrist. He took a minute to read the message. "That's Jerry in Port 1, gotta go. I'll see you around," he said, as if it was no big deal to just leave her without even offering to walk her back to the conservatory, without setting up a time to talk again.

She sat in the darkness of the room, staring at the stars billions of miles away, noticing relief and disappointment that Korbin had left so soon.

I don't know why I care; I don't even really like him! she told herself as she walked down the hall alone.

The band was slowing down the tempo and the lovers on the dance floor were holding each other close when Virginia arrived back at the table.

"I got into a conversation with a group of administrators." Jeremiah could not restrain his excitement. "Met the Food Science Administrator, who turns out to be Farro's wife, and the Air Quality Administrator, Jung, who is friends with Farro and the Spaceball team coach, and Administrator Xander, of all people. This night confirmed my calling for an administration position." He was grinning, giddy. "What about you? Where have you been? Where's Korbin?"

Virginia smiled, hiding her disappointment. "Port 1. He had a work call. Strange guy, but not terrible." She slumped into her chair, relaxing into her loneliness.

Amos came strutting over, asking every question with merely his eyes. "Spent the last hour and a half with Korbin, eh? I want the scoop! I'm not recording this for my news—tell me, are you into him?" He smirked.

She looked down at the floor. "I'm embarrassed. I mean, I never wanted to have a real moment with anyone else, but we kinda had a... a moment. Right before he ran out the door to answer a message from Port 1."

"Not that you asked my opinion, but he's always been a bit odd." Ellis cut into their conversation from across the table. "You can do so much better, Virginia."

"Don't worry. It was just a foolish moment. I had a love once, and I would be a fool to even think that it would ever come again. And if it were to, like you said, it certainly wouldn't be with Korbin Xander. Besides, we both agreed that we should be courting other people, not each other. For our careers' sake," Virginia said, embarrassed that she'd even let any moment transpire with Korbin.

"It's odd that he left during a hot moment to go to the same port that your buddy Iris has been up to some questionable activity in. Don't you think we need to get to the port and do a little spying?" Amos suggested.

"Only got about an hour left before curfew is up," Jeremiah warned.

Virginia raised her eyebrows. "Nah. I think he's a friend," she replied, shaking her head in tiny movements.

Amos shrugged. "Just sayin' we should use my news reporter status to go check out the subjects in question—just to make sure."

"Do a live recording so we can watch from our rooms," Jeremiah said, smiling suspiciously.

"Yeah, we've been watching your news channel. It's actually pretty good," Ellis added.

Virginia was nervous, but said, "You're right. An innocent visit could show us a lot. Let's go check it out and, at the very least, get you some news."

They hadn't expected to be interviewing an old potbellied man, who was sleeping sitting up in the port master's chair.

"We startled you, sorry. I... I'm Amos, a news reporter from Alcetra, and this is my friend Virginia. She is a licensed ISV pilot, in fact. I was hoping to interview you for my news channel." Amos pointed at the camera stationed right under the flower on his coat pocket. "And to learn about this port and what goes on here."

The old man scratched his little round belly. He looked down at his feet and shuffled something around with his toes, then nodded and said, "Sure" with a little enthusiasm, as if he was relieved that his old port had not been forgotten. He cleared his throat. "Well, I'm Jerry, the port master. Started working here as a mechanic, been here fifty-two years now." He stood and walked to the window and looked down at the floor, filled with old and new planes and ISVs, docked in no apparent order. "There's a boy down there who's my apprentice. Fixin' mostly older ISVs and Martian planes, personal and transport ones." The port master pointed to a large ISV that wasn't new, but not too old either, where Korbin was working on one of its wheels. "He really knows his stuff, that kid," he continued. "Like he's been fixin' these vehicles longer than me."

"What about the two girls walking toward him with the black hoods—do they work here too?" Virginia asked, pointing to the girls she assumed to be Iris and her smaller sidekick.

"Hmmm. No. I've been seein' 'er around a bunch. But she don't work here though. I think maybe she's workin' for Sofia. 'Cause she came up here a lil bit ago, told me that Sofia needed that ISV fixed immediately. So I put an emergency call to Korbin just a little while ago."

"Why didn't you fix it yourself if it was such an emergency?" she asked.

The port master shook his head. "I'm kinda slow. Be seventy-three in a few weeks. Don't see as well, don't move as fast. Better the boy do it. Wish I could talk him into taking my place."

"You want him to take the job as port master?"

He confirmed with one nod. "But he wants ta fly too badly. Ain't gonna take the job here."

"It looks like your protégé and that girl are arguing," Amos said, looking out the window. "Oh. And here comes Sofia. Looks like she's here to get after someone," he added as Sofia and her head of monsters marched toward the argument, in hot pursuit.

"Ah, Sofia. She's probably here for me," the port master said. "I called her to ask what the problem was with her ISV." He shrugged. "Not really sure what's goin' on. Talked to her, and she said there weren't nothin' wrong with 'er ISV." The port master nodded his head toward the window. "The boy checked it out anyway. About to find out what's goin' on now."

Virginia and Amos stared at each other, dumbfounded, as he walked slowly toward the stairs.

"Did he just tell us that Iris set this up?" Virginia exhaled.

With their eyes glued to the little event below, they watched Sofia step inches closer, pointing her finger at Iris, who stood unaffected even as the slithering creatures creeped closer to her face each second. Korbin and Iris's sidekick watched, horrified.

Amos shook his head. "Sofia is fuming."

"Why would Iris go to such extremes to get Korbin working on a vehicle near the middle of the night?"

"She's in love with him, and she wanted to keep Korbin away from you?" Amos suggested.

"Keep Korbin away from me," Virginia pondered aloud. "Why is that so important?"

"*Important couple*," he sang in a tune similar to Grandmother's, staring into her eyes.

She made a face. "Noooo... it couldn't be. What could be so important about me? Or Korbin?"

"Maybe it's the two of you together," Amos said casually.

"It's not just about missing someone when they're gone, it's missing the part of you that shined in their presence."

~ Bee Davis

CHAPTER 8

There are windstorms on Mars that blow up to sixty mph. Because of the prevalent red dust, these storms can add a layer of dust to the entire planet.

Virginia was relieved when her presentation, which took maybe five minutes, was done and over with, and that she'd now proven to the class that she belonged. But Korbin hadn't been there to see it. She hadn't seen him in sols and was getting increasingly anxious about their courting status.

She hurried back to her suite to call Paden and tell her all about the success of her presentation, reminding herself not to tell her about the courtship with Korbin. Besides, she would need to end it soon. Maybe after just one more Unity Festival date, just to make sure there was nothing there with Korbin.

"It's been a few weeks," Paden said. "Are you going to make a plan to come home and court Frankie?"

She wanted to but couldn't let Paden down by telling her that she still needed time to figure out the connection she had with Korbin. "Yeah, but I'm kinda starting to get some new information, that I, uh... just may need a few more weeks to learn a bit more about, so that I can come home and be valuable to the city," Virginia said. "And I just had a hologram call with Frankie the other sol. Told him a few more weeks. He was perfectly fine with that."

Hidden camera activity in Hall 1, Amos's message said on her transmitter.

She and Amos had been waiting for weeks to see what was going on in the Port 1 break room. Now she had an excuse to end the conversation about Frankie and going home.

"Amos just messaged me. I gotta run and meet him. Talk to ya tomorrow!"

Her face lit up when she saw Amos waiting for her in the connector between Halls 6 and 5. Excited to discover what suspicious parties might be doing exiting Port 1 or even lingering around the door in the Galleria between Halls 1 and 2, the two friends hurried through the connector into Conservatory 4, noticing all the people who were also heading in the same direction.

"Look. The Rock Friends"—Virginia pointed to the sides of the traffic path—"are lined up like little guards."

"Maybe they're taking names," Amos teased.

"I guess we're on their list now."

They arrived at Conservatory 2, where a mass of people crowded on the paths among the winter vegetables that grew in a hydroponic system. Amos held one of his mini cameras up over the crowd of heads. "The entrance to Hall 2 is completely blocked by bodies," he said, looking at the recording on the transmitter on his wrist.

He pushed through the bodies and asked, "What's going on here?"

Finally, an elderly woman explained. "There's been a breach in security on an extension in Hall 1. I'm just tryin' to get back to my apartment."

Virginia's heart raced. "What if they found your cameras?" she whispered.

"If I'm going down, I'm taking you down with me," Amos teased.

"It's not funny. That shadow creature could have escaped, and Sofia and Xander already know we were down there, so let's get out of here."

They made it back to Conservatory 5, where Jeremiah was talking to Professor Farro outside the red laboratory door. "You two look like you saw a ghost," Jeremiah said when they stopped to talk.

"Just a shadow of a massive monster," Virginia said with a smile and a tilt of her head so no one would take her seriously.

"She's joking," Amos said. "There's some security issue going on in Hall 1, holding up the residents in Hall 2."

Professor Farro silently disappeared into the lab.

"My cousin Heath will probably know what's going on," Jeremiah replied. "Let's go down to Port 3 and talk to him. He's probably down there now, getting ready for tonight's Spaceball game."

The group halted at the eerie, rhythmic *click click* they heard moving toward them on the gravel path. Administrator Xander had locked onto them.

"You two," he said into the frightened eyes of Amos and Virginia. "You like being in places you aren't supposed to be, eh?" Xander lifted his cane just a few inches and slammed it back down into the gravel. "Something terrible has happened because *someone* has been in the part of the city that is forbidden." He stopped and silently stared, waiting for a reply.

Virginia's heart was racing. *Something terrible? Did we accidentally release a monster in Hall 1? If those cameras don't show that someone else was there—like Iris or one of the other kids wearing a black hood—Sofia will surely turn me into a rock.* She noticed she wasn't breathing. She looked at Amos, who also might not have been breathing.

"Okay, then. You two silent mates, you're coming with me to Sofia's office for formal questioning."

The door of the red laboratory flew open, without anyone behind it. They all watched, nervous, waiting for what would happen next.

"They will stay right here." It was the voice of Mr. Farro, who somehow mysteriously appeared on the opposite side of the open door.

With one look at Professor Farro's smile and jolly cheeks, all her troubles melted away.

"You can question them another time. They are working, with my permission, on something important," Farro said, building a silent hostility with Xander.

Xander forced a smile and stepped toward Amos and Virginia, spiking his cane into the ground. "I'll be watching you," he said, turned on his heel, and walked away.

"Pompous beanpole," Farro said in a cheerful whisper. "Virginia." He waved her closer, away from Amos and Jeremiah, and handed her a little bag.

She took it, speechless when she looked inside. "We didn't—" she began to explain.

"No need to explain." Farro stopped her. "You are an important part, girl. I couldn't let anything get in the way of your doing something great!"

"No," she said, shaking her head, sensing that he was trying to tell her the same thing Grandmother was. "There is nothing important about me or anyone else I know, and there is nothing but ordinary on my to-do list." She held up the bag. "But thank you, Professor Farro."

She crammed the bag in her coat pocket and returned to Amos and Jeremiah, who were waiting.

"What was that all about?" Amos inquired.

She pulled the bag out of her coat pocket for him to peer inside. His eyes grew large.

"What is it?" Jeremiah asked.

Virginia held the bag open for him to look. He laughed. "What is it?" he asked again.

"Cameras!" Virginia and Amos replied simultaneously.

"Amos was helping me get some dirt on Iris, who might be trespassing in the extensions off Hall 1. We were trying to catch her on video. I guess Farro found our spy operation," Virginia said.

"You two are lucky," Jeremiah said, shaking his head.

The red light was on in Port 3. "Incoming!" Jeremiah announced. He led the way to the observation tower stairs, where they would wait until the incoming spacecraft had completely docked and the green light came on, signaling atmosphere stabilization and that the port was safe to walk about again.

The observation tower was packed full of the boisterous bodies of the Nos Spaceball team. One strikingly handsome tall boy pushed through the crowd and greeted Jeremiah. "Cuz!" The beautiful young man hugged Jeremiah like he was his favorite person on the planet.

Jeremiah and Heath discussed the security breach. "No official news on it, so it's probably some strange experiment of Xander's that escaped," Heath said.

Virginia's heart started racing. She immediately thought about the shadow creature, imagining it lurking in the halls and extensions until it found her. She looked at Amos, who seemed unconcerned and completely devoted to the conversation with Heath.

Heath looked like the physical incarnation of Zeus: a smile as bright as the sun, tall and strong, with glowing skin and strawberry-blond hair that waved down to his shoulders.

Her daydreams came to a halt when she noticed he was talking to her. "Do you really have your interplanetary license?" he asked.

The green port light flashed on, and everyone in the observation tower began to exit. "Let's talk laaater!" Heath said before he was swept through the doors with the others.

Virginia sat on the bench in front of the window with Jeremiah, watching the Nos Spaceball team prepare for the game, watching Amos follow Heath around, likely asking a million questions and recording him for the night's news that he'd send to Alcetra.

"There's your boy. I wonder why he hasn't been to class all week," Jeremiah said.

She watched Korbin below, following an extra-tall boy and a girl, both with black hoods pulled up over their heads, raising her suspicions that he and Iris and those hooded goons had some sort of plan going on.

She gave Jeremiah the evil eye. "He's not mine. Soon I'll be wrapping things up here and going home to court someone whose intentions are clear."

Korbin and the tall black-hooded team unloaded gray mesh containers of fruit and vegetables and dry goods onto the city rover's cart. "But maybe with one more date I can figure out what his dealings are with that hooded crew," she whispered under her breath.

She watched others start loading a second cart, and the tall boy pulled Korbin away, likely introducing him to the captain. The hooded boy, Korbin, and the captain walked around the large freight plane, disappearing.

"You should go down there and talk to Heath about your piloting experience. I think he's in need of a fill-in pilot or something," Jeremiah said.

Virginia released her clenched hands from the seat. "That makes sense—why he was talking to me about my interplanetary space license." She stood up. "Are you coming?"

"Can't. Ellis wants to grab tacos. I'll see you tonight, at the game."

"Oh good, Virginia! So glad you're here!" Heath said when she approached his and Amos's conversation. "Tell me about your piloting experience."

"My deceased boyfriend's father is the Planet Protectors Administrator, and we, uh... got away with a lot of extracurricular events, like space flight. In addition to all-time access to the Planet Protectors' official flight simulators," she said with a side smile, rolling her eyes.

Heath laughed. "And you have your license and you're a legit pilot."

She nodded.

"Would you be confident in piloting for our team? We need a fill-in pilot for a few games."

Virginia hadn't gotten her license so she could play Spaceball. *And I can't play against Alcetra. If I screw up, no one will like me.*

Amos elbowed her hard. "What she means is yes! Yes. She would love to!" He looked at her, nodding his head up and down.

She stared at him, wide-eyed, rubbing the pain in her arm from his elbow. She wasn't really in love with the idea, quite nervous about it actually, but Amos was into it, so she went with it. "Yes. Sure. It will be fun… but I won't play against our home team," she said to Heath firmly.

The ten-minute buzzer sounded, and the team scattered toward their ISVs for the Spaceball game. "Great. Be here tomorrow afternoon for practice," Heath said before he darted off to prepare for launch.

"Why did you make me say yes? I'm supposed to be here cultivating plants to grow outside that will produce food for our planet. Not playing Spaceball in my free time."

"Don't you like Heath? Don't you think you should do something cool and not so nerdy? Become good news again?" Amos stopped when they passed Korbin closing the freight vehicle, the vertical wrinkle between his brows deeper than a lava tube as he looked at Virginia. "Don't you think it's weird that Korbin is hanging around with those hooded goons?"

"Yeah. They look like a special group of misfits or something," she agreed.

Korbin followed Virginia and Amos up to the observation tower as the light turned red again. Sitting next to Virginia, he greeted her cheerfully, as if he'd never left her in the middle of their date, as if he hadn't been missing from class, hadn't missed her presentation. His only concern was why she'd been talking to the most-loved guy in the city. "So, uh... I saw you talking to Heath." He paused. "What were you two talking about?"

Virginia looked at him with her arms crossed. "I'll tell you—if you tell me what you're doing palled up with those goons wearing black hoods," she demanded.

Korbin thought about what she'd said, about how he wasn't even friends with them, but how over the last few weeks Iris and the rest of them had infiltrated his life in Port 1. "I dunno, really. They showed up when I was working. That tall kid just asked me to come and help him here after Sofia shut down Port 1."

Some kind of pain flickered on her face. What was she was upset about? Maybe if he showed her he was concerned, she would look happy again. "I heard Sofia's on the march for answers about the breach in security on Hall 1. I don't know what you two were up to down there, but you may, uh... you probably want to stay low tonight. If you know anything about anything happening down there, that is," he added.

Virginia pointedly turned to Amos.

Korbin interrupted their silence as they stared at each other. "Sofia's Rock Friends have already been here questioning people. You should stay here as long as you can tonight. Wait for things to cool down."

"Great idea!" Amos blurted out.

Korbin watched Virginia scorn Amos with her eyes.

"Gin," Amos whispered, "in a few hours, probably, Sofia will have all this figured out. You don't want to be in her path right now."

The green port light came back on. "Just an idea. Don't want to see you hassled by Sofia again so soon," Korbin said as he got up from his seat to return to the port.

Virginia rolled her eyes and huffed, "Fine."

He turned around, surprised by her answer.

"I'm gonna lie low here with you for a bit," she announced.

Noticing the scowl she was trying not to show, he smiled at her gently, hoping to relieve her discontent. "Can I buy you a soda?"

She didn't say no and followed him to the machine.

Amos abruptly arrived on the scene. "So, kids, I won't be hanging with you two any longer tonight, as I have news to catch." He gave Korbin a pat on the chest. "But Virginia is going to stay here with you—and you'll keep her from Sofia's scrutiny, right?" Amos said, rubbing his heavy hand on Korbin's chest.

Korbin looked at him, puzzled, wondering what called for all the extra affection.

"Good man," Amos finally said, retracting his hand. "I'll be here to walk her back to the suite after the game."

And he left Korbin and Virginia awkwardly staring at each other.

"You know, you never even apologized for acting like a baboon and walking out of our date. It was rude, you know. To up and leave me in the observatory the night of the dance."

"Sorry, Gin. I didn't know you were interested in courting for real."

She shrugged. "It would have been worth a try, since we had to register with the Unity Administration and all."

They sat next to each other in the break area and watched the game on the port's hologram, Korbin narrating the game, telling her about each one of the ISVs, their pilots, and the game statistics. Virginia seemed to enjoy listening to it all, forgetting her disappointment with him.

The visiting team, the Tartarians, were the first to shoot laser cannons at the Spaceball that slowly formed the shape of a sphere connected by curved, bright and glowing lines. Both teams made their shots, failing to disintegrate it by hitting it dead in the center, where the four lines crossed, until at last, Nos's team captain, Heath, was the first to destroy it.

Korbin was still determined to get a gauge on what she and Heath had going on. "Check out your boy Heath." He nudged her with his elbow.

He stared at her, waiting for a reaction. She didn't give him one. Only remained silent, watching the game. Heath's spacecraft was blocked by a Tartarian ISV with a green fire-breathing snake with legs painted on it.

"Heath asked me if I would fill-in pilot for someone on the team," she told him.

Another Spaceball was shot.

He was relieved that Heath wasn't asking her for anything else. "That's probably who he needs a replacement pilot for," Korbin said, gesturing to the ISV with a red, yellow, and orange mandala painted on it, which had just taken the winning shot. "Her name's Bora. She's good. I heard she's leaving to court someone in the city of Aguan."

Virginia focused in on Bora, who was being blocked by a Tartarian moving back and forth in front of her, cutting off any shot at the Spaceball.

"Can you do it?" Korbin asked.

She looked at him with contempt. "Of course I can! But it—"

Buzz, buzzz.

There was a long pause.

Buzz, buzzz.

The loudest and most annoying alarm in the city was the alarm for an atmosphere breach. Even a pin-sized hole in the glass conservatory dome or the roofs covering the halls, extensions, or ports could set it off. They could always find it fast, but sometimes the repair could take hours. The safest places were the apartments, where there were breathing apparatuses in case of an excess infiltration of carbon dioxide.

"We can go up to the observation tower and wait it out, or we can wait it out in this old team plane," Korbin suggested. "It's airtight with an oxygen converter on a backup battery, and we can watch the rest of the game. We could run the battery for sols if we wanted to. There's snacks and drinks onboard too." He pointed to the plane, only steps from the break room area. "I've been helping Jerry with it for months now. We just moved it over here from Port 1."

With wide eyes and a giant smile, Virginia walked toward the plane. "You had me at snacks."

She stepped slowly down the aisle, exploring the plane. It was just like Alcetra's team plane, with two large captain's chairs on each side. She slumped down in the window seat on the fifth row, looking out as if there was a dusty red terrain to watch. She was almost disappointed she hadn't chosen an aisle seat when he crashed into the seat next to her. She crossed her arms and closed her eyes. Korbin leaned his seat back and settled in to watch the

Spaceball game on the little hologram on the seat back in front of him.

Her grandmother's words appeared in her head like a giant flashing sign. *"We've fixed the accident in a new port."* Her eyes popped open, and she straightened, trying to figure out why she'd remember those words right now. She dug in her pockets, searching for Grandmother's hologram.

"Are you alright?" Korbin asked.

"Yeah."

He leaned forward to look through the window at the empty port that was now nearly dark. "I'll turn the heat on in a bit. You're probably getting cold."

"For someone who spends his time finding life inside of rocks, you sure know a lot about these vehicles," Virginia said.

He chuckled. "It's weird—everything after my accident has been. Especially in the beginning. I found myself so uninterested in my normal sol-to-sol life. I was searching for something, or maybe even someone, and well, I just stumbled into the port one sol. Jerry asked me to hand him a tool, and I accidentally handed him the right one. I started working with him, and I keep getting these hunches about mechanical issues—that are usually right. I was never really happy before the accident, and now I'm finally starting to be."

Korbin tucked his chin and picked at his fingers. "It's funny too: when Farro was talking me into taking his program, he had some Amos News reruns playing in his office." He paused to look at her. "I saw you and your boyfriend, and you both looked so familiar. Like I had met you before. And in one clip, when he was telling you how to change gears on the laser cannons, I knew what he was going to tell you."

"Maybe you have a natural superhuman sense. And you know a good soul when you see one," Virginia said in an attempt to disperse the heavy energy.

He let out a nervous laugh. "Yeah, maybe."

She watched his gaze into her eyes become trapped. Nothing but silence exited his frozen, slightly open mouth. The space around them became a blur, and any thought dissipated into a heated sensation.

When did he grab my hand? Am I okay with this?

She moved her fingers in between his, noticing the warmth of his breath, sweet like caramel pears, close to her face. She drifted her hands up his long arms, which felt stronger than they looked. She couldn't see his long, strange face anymore, only his lips, right in front of her.

Korbin wrapped his finger around the curl in front of her ear, and her head gave no resistance, moving forward until her lips melted into his. Her mouth watered as he kissed her more.

An uncomfortable heat and a dizziness came over her, and she gently pulled away, his lips slowly separating from hers. A warm sensation lingered in her body as she relaxed into the chair. "Ummmmm... How did that happen." She sighed, unsure about her unconscious decision.

Korbin's voice was scratchy. "I think it was meant to happen. I'm comfortable around you, Virginia."

"I have someone back home that I should be courting. But even though you've been somewhat hot and cold with me, and I've been annoyed with you, there's still something that makes me think you and I should just give it one more week of courting—and I think it's for reasons more than just that kiss. What do you think?"

He was silent, laying his large head on the seat's headrest. "Yeah, sure. Just one more date will be plenty," he finally agreed.

She was worried. She couldn't sense anything in his voice expressing that he wanted anything else to ever happen between them. For some reason she was disappointed that he'd agreed to only one more date. That he wasn't interested in more time with her. She attempted to dissolve the tension rising in her head with conversation and still bring connection between them. "Do you think Iris and that black-hooded crew have a reason that they don't want to see us together?"

"I don't know, Virginia. I don't pay much attention to her. I don't see why she would care who I court or don't court. Unless she were to benefit from it. Don't know how she would benefit from me courting or not courting."

Her transmitter pinged. "It's a message from my Aunt Norma, from Earth." She sighed. "I really don't want to have to go live with her."

"Don't worry, Virginia. You will Unite, and it will all work out for you this season," Korbin said, pulling her under his arm.

He smelled nice and he was warm, but she couldn't relax. What was she doing with him right now? It could mess up her whole life if that kiss meant nothing—and Frankie found out.

Still, as she rested against Korbin, she let her imagination run wild, picturing her and Korbin using their Royal powers to repair broken planes and ISVs, watching the faces of people they passed turn bright with their powers of joy, until she fell asleep and was woken with banging on the plane door the next morning.

"Never. We never lose our loved ones. They accompany us; they don't disappear from our lives. We are merely in different rooms."

~ Paulo Coelho

CHAPTER 9

The first photograph of Mars taken from its surface was taken by Viking 1 on July 20, 1976.

Tonight was the second, and likely last, Unity Dinner she had with Korbin, and all she could think about was why she enjoyed spending time with him—and that kiss. She couldn't tell Paden about it, definitely not Frankie, and probably not Amos. *Why did I kiss him? Why did I want to kiss him? Could it have meant anything more than just a kiss? If maybe, just maybe, we are the important couple, then maybe Grandmother is showing up for me magically because she knew I could have another special person. I need to talk to him tonight about the kiss. See what he thinks it means.*

Her thoughts were interrupted by an unexpected knock at the door. Nobody ever knocked. If you wanted to see someone, you sent messages to make plans to meet up. Virginia came out of her room to see if Amos had already opened the door. He looked at her from the desk, puzzled. They waited for another knock.

"I would think if someone was waiting, they would have knocked again."

"I'm not in the mood for any trouble," Virginia replied, worried that it could be Iris—or Sofia or Xander with a pack-your-bags notice.

"I'll open it, and if someone asks, you're not here," Amos said, getting up and moving toward the door.

She ducked down low in the sofa, under the blanket, listening to the door slide open.

"Just a package delivery!" he yelled. He placed a bundle that was wrapped in decorated dried banana leaves on top of her blanketed body. "We both got a package," he said, smiling, looking at the beautiful wrapping on his.

Virginia tore into the package to inspect the garment that was inside.

"From my sisters," Amos announced, reading the card that was hidden in his package. "They said, 'We love you so much and made this so that you would be warmer. Congratulations, your show is now being viewed in all the cities!'" He put on the long, straight coat that was a deep violet, almost black, with a hemline right below his knees.

He looked at Virginia next to him, who was admiring herself in her new coat in the mirror. "Same color—we almost look alike. But yours kinda reminds me of..."

"...Sofia's?" she replied.

"What does your note say?"

"'Believe in miracles. Love comes again. We believe and made this for you so you would stay warm and look as special as you are.'" She turned to Amos. "I thought you said you wouldn't post me in any of your news stories without my permission."

"Oh Gin, no! I've only shown a few past clips of you from Alcetra and a few still photos of you here, along with special commentary, just so people remember you, just to keep your story alive. But nothing that you wouldn't like. Nothing that would make Frankie think you're interested in Korbin. And nothing that would link us to Hall 1, that's for sure. But apparently good enough to pick up new viewers!"

Virginia looked at him out of the tops of her eyes. "Well, that's not bad. Congratulations." She discovered the deep pockets and smiled brightly, spinning around and watching the bottom of the coat spin with her. "Just make sure nothing gets out about me courting Korbin. I can't mess up the sure thing I have with Frankie."

"I'll meet you back at the table when I'm done," Amos said when they arrived at the bustling Main Conservatory. "I have stellar news to create."

"You mean gossip?"

He shot her his most evil eye, then smiled before hurrying off.

Nervous to talk to Korbin about their kiss, Virginia wandered around the conservatory, through the building crowds, and stopped at the cluster of bodies standing in front of the Love Counseling Booth. Peering through the heads, she noticed the peanut-like Nos news reporter interviewing a very tall girl with a black hood shadowing her face. Wasn't that the girl she'd seen hovering around Korbin in Port 1?

"...now that the mayor of Nos has given his official approval on the Love Counseling Booth, do you think it will change the long lines that we've already been waiting in to talk to the Love Counselor?"

Her voice was quiet and monotone, but the pitch was just right for Virginia to hear. "We will be taking referrals and appointments first."

The little reporter went on, but Virginia's eyes caught Korbin Xander in front of the Love Counseling Booth with no one else but the dreadful Iris.

Before she knew it, she was moving toward them. After all, she and Korbin were in an official courtship—and it was customary to be by your courting mate's side during all Unity events. As soon as she stepped under the rope, she sensed something bad. Every neuron went crazy, and the sensations in her body were entirely uncomfortable.

She stepped away from the booth, back to the viewing side of the rope, and her nervous system returned to normal. *What was that?*

She watched him receive a few words from Iris and nod. Iris was awful. And seeking answers outside of your soul was not the natural Martian way to Unite and gain your powers. How could Korbin partake in such a sham? To Virginia and many others, the Love Counseling Booth was a disgrace, a blasphemy to sacred Unions. She couldn't wait to confront him.

As soon as he exited the roped-off area of the Love Counseling Booth, she hurried toward him. "Korbin!" she said loud enough to get his attention, but not as loud as her growing rage.

He turned around, revealing a sullen face, which he forced into half a smile.

Her brows drew in, and her lips quivered. "What are you doing over there? Please tell me you had nothing to do with the mayor's approval of that stupid Love Counseling Booth!"

Korbin looked down at the ground and shook his head, but he wouldn't tell her what he was up to either.

"We are in an official courtship, Korbin. I know it's not because we're madly in love, but we are still in an official courtship, honored by the Unity Administration of Nos! I was starting to like you, and I am betraying someone who certainly wants to Unite with me back home by agreeing to court you one more week! Not to mention that you are participating in a mockery of everything that our world was founded on." There was a sadness in her voice. "And with Iris? Really? How could you?"

Korbin pressed the corner of his lips down. "It's not like that. Not with Iris. I told you, we've been in school together since we were little." He shook his head. "Listen. I like you. There is something strangely magnetic and... uh, almost familiar about you? But I want to fly in space. And only a Union into a family of space flight will give me that opportunity. If I don't Unite this season, my father will announce me as the junior administrator in Living Rock Sciences."

"And you went into the stupid booth and some dumb hologram told you there was someone out there who was going to Unite you into space flight?"

Korbin shook his head. "No, that wasn't what happened at all," he said, looking in the direction of the Unity Administrators' Booth.

His face had sadness and disappointment written on it. She waited for him to tell her what was going on, but he kept his lips pressed tight and looked at the floor.

"Something's up. Something with Iris convincing you to court someone else for some reason." A rage began to boil through her bloodstream, and she pictured the Love Counseling Booth burning from the ground up.

He started moving in the direction of the Unity Administrators' Booth. She stayed with him in their cold and awkwardly silent walk, finally realizing where they were going, "Unregister. Perfect," she spat. "I'm very happy that I no longer have to court you anymore!"

With no line to have to wait in to be further tortured by the silence, Virginia signed the Courtship Cancellation agreement.

"Unconditional love isn't something I can risk in this lifetime," Korbin said after he signed the document. "Really, Virginia, I'm sorry. I want what's best for you too, and I want to remain friends. I care about you."

She threw up her hands. "I don't even know why I'm bothered by this at all. I didn't even like you all that much anyway."

Virginia's emotions were like an electrical explosion in her body. She needed to calm down and figure out why she was so upset about Korbin Xander, who was really nobody at all. *"We're here for you..."* She remembered the words of Mister and Missus. And who else would be better to talk to about love and Uniting than the Unity Administrators?

Hall 2 was too quiet. Most of the city was either at the Unity Festival or watching it from inside their apartments. There was a Rock Friend on guard in front of Extension 220.

She hoped that Mister and Missus would be there, but didn't expect it. Sure enough, the extension looked almost entirely dark. She stood there in dismay, about to turn away, when a purple flash of light called her to proceed down the hallway. She passed the door to Mister and Missus's office, which was slightly open, and continued down the dark extension to where a sliver of light creeped from under Door 2215. Its sign read *Administrator Xander - Living Rock Sciences.*

Virginia gasped when she heard the recognizable and dreadful gruff voice coming from the other side. "I'm leaving, and if you have any more problems, take it up with someone else," Iris said.

She was shocked. What would Iris possibly have to do with Korbin's father? *Could Administrator Xander be the one directing her to steer Korbin away from me?* She hurried along the shadow of the wall, back to the safety of Mister and Missus's office, past the waiting area, and straight into their office, where they were both sitting at the round table, not even surprised she was there.

"I was looking for someone to talk to," she blurted. "I think I'm sad. I didn't think I liked Korbin—but as unrealistic as the idea was, I wanted to court him."

"Separate, thus sad," Mister said.

"Together is the key," Missus said in a warm and comforting tone. "We saw the withdrawal for your courtship with Korbin."

"His soul has yet to convince his brain that he has found you again," Mister said.

His soul? Why would his soul know something his brain doesn't, unless he's spent a lifetime with me before?

Mister and Missus looked at each other and laughed at the secret they shared.

"Found me *again*? But Korbin and I have never met," Virginia said, puzzled.

"The truth can only be discovered with your power of sense—and yours has been made stronger since the kiss," Mister said.

"How do you know about our kiss?"

Missus stood up and walked toward her, put her arm around her, and lifted the chain from under Virginia's top. She rubbed the Ananta between her fingers until it began to glow purple—and orange. "It's the law of true love. Like the Royals, but a bit different for you two. More powers come with the orange glow."

"Are you saying Korbin and I are Royals?"

"Stronger than Royals—legends!" Missus lifted her hand toward the center of the table, then displayed her palm. An image rose up, of Korbin being revived from death on the floor of a lab, the same way Ellis had described it. He got up and walked toward a glowing purple Ananta. And there was another boy on the other side walking toward it too. Just like the vision she'd had before she left Alcetra.

"I've seen this image before. Who is that other boy?"

Missus closed her hand, and the image faded to nothing. She whispered, "The souls of true love always find each other again."

"Is the other boy Charles? Do Charles and Korbin have something to do with each other?"

"True love is a life itself, and it never dies," Missus said.

Mister spoke up. "You have to be careful, girl." He aimed his fist at the table and opened it, revealing an image of Grandmother holding Virginia's head in her lap as she cried.

"Wish upon a tear. Now is the time *you Create* through pain." Virginia whispered the words Grandmother had always told her when she was sad.

"As a Royal, you can Create without the pain. Your powers are not yet Royal, yet much stronger than your natural human sense, and the images that you imagine can take shape immediately. Make sure your imagination is clear and pure during your creation moments," Mister said.

Virginia bunched up her face. "If Charles and Korbin have something to do with each other, and I have some sort of Royal powers that are also on the fritz, that means there's something bigger going on here—and more to Grandmother's clues."

She looked at Mister and Missus, who stared at her with wide eyes, their brows lifted, smiling from ear to ear and nodding their heads.

"This is scary," she said.

Missus relaxed her brows and smile and spoke softly. "The truth of our souls does not hold the power of fear..."

"...but of power and love and clarity of mind," Mister finished.

Virginia shook her head and cleared the angst on her face with her hands. "If you say so," she huffed.

"It will all become very clear at the right time," Missus said.

"Just believe and know we are right here for you. Many that you don't see are here to help you along this important journey," Mister finished.

"Ah! You're here! I didn't see you all night," Amos said. "I thought you would be with Korbin tonight... Maybe something... mmm, special going on with you two?" he asked excitedly.

Virginia narrowed her eyes, looking at him suspiciously. "Ummm... special?"

His smile was devious. "Yeah, like maybe another kiss?"

"Amos! How do you know about that?" she snapped.

He held up a clear square sticker. "It's a new invisible micro camera. I just put it on Korbin again so I could get some ground footage of the Spaceball team docking after the game. I never anticipated you two would kiss!"

Virginia blushed and buried her head in her hands.

"Don't worry, don't worry, Ginny," he consoled. "It's not the kiss that was the showstopper—it's the magic that came with the kiss."

"What magic?"

Amos sat at his desk, fiddling around on a few workboards until the living room entertainment hologram turned on with an image of Virginia boarding the plane that she'd been trapped inside with Korbin. She watched until the camera found her sitting cross-armed and slouched in the seat.

"I don't want to see... I don't want to see..." But she watched, knowing every movement that would happen next.

As Korbin and Virginia drew closer and closer, Amos paused the video. "Gin, don't worry. No one has seen this, nor will they."

"I really don't want to see this. He just dumped me tonight. He's a jerkface," Virginia pleaded.

"Fine. But it's not about this kiss," Amos said with wide eyes and raised brows. "It's about your necklace. Just watch your necklace."

She pulled out the dangling silver Ananta and rubbed it between her fingers.

"Okay. Watch closely," he whispered and then paused it a few moments later, as Virginia's blue top approached the camera.

"Is it… is my necklace glowing—orange and purple? That's weird. Why would it do that? Is there something wrong with your camera?"

"I think it started glowing the moment you kissed."

"How do you even know we kissed?"

Amos looked at her through the tops of his eyes. "Oh please, I wasn't born yestersol." He unpaused it, and they began pulling apart. "Now watch. See?"

"Yeah, it stopped glowing."

"Gin, what is your necklace made of?"

She held up the dull silver chain and pendant for him to see. And under her breath said, "It glowed purple and orange when Missus touched it too. But orange doesn't represent a color of any United."

Amos reached for the pendant and rubbed it between his fingers. "It's the same color as the Unity Stone. At least, from what I've seen in images of it." He gasped. "Aaaand oddly enough, it's an Ananta. Look at it, it's dangling from the chain, just like eight of them are dangling from the center of every city on Mars."

"The Ananta is a sacred symbol. There's probably hundreds of them dangling around people's necks in every city. And it couldn't be part of the Unity Stone.

That's hidden and locked up when not in use. How could my grandmother ever get a piece of the Unity Stone and make it into this pendant?"

"Long, long ago maybe," Amos said. "Before it was locked up."

"Like from my grandmother's grandmother?"

"Exactly! Gin, you didn't come from a family wealthy enough to spend on frivolities such as jewelry. That has to be where it's from."

"If in fact it is a piece of the Unity Stone," Virginia argued, "that would mean that kissing while one person is touching it activates it."

"Maybe that's why it also glowed orange—partial activation." Amos grabbed the Unity Festival event workboard from the side table, turned it on, and began reading: "'It is understood that souls of a Royal pair hold the purest of love, Unconditional Love, which cannot be destroyed by death; they can only be separated until they are United in their next life. Because of the many lifetimes they have spent together, their powers are mysterious and immeasurable. The Unity Stone will produce a purple glow when the pair whose souls cannot be separated by death touches it.'"

Virginia collapsed her face into her hands and mumbled, "No, no," shaking her head back and forth. "Not Korbin Xander. He doesn't even have enough sense to Unite for the love of the soul. That fool ended our courtship because he needs to Unite for his future career. How could I ever have loved such a fool in a different life?"

"'They must not be separated again,'" Amos whispered under his breath. "That's what your grandmother said to me. Your grandmother knows. That's why she's here!"

She threw her head back. "Ugh! Why is she telling me? Why can't we just get United and find out our powers when it happens? Why do I have to know now? And what does Charles have to do with all this?"

"What do you mean about Charles?"

"I don't know, but some images Grandmother and Mister and Missus have shown me look like Charles and Korbin walking toward the Ananta."

"Hey! Let's find out. Get Grandmother's hologram—let's talk to her and get some more clues."

Virginia dragged her feet as she retrieved her backpack from her room. She didn't want to talk to Grandmother. Her clues were frustrating because she couldn't figure them out. And she didn't want to think about her powers and how she would use them. She flopped her duffel atop the round dining table, reached into the inside pocket, and pulled out Grandmother's transmitter button. She pressed the domed glass and put it on the table, waiting for Grandmother's hologram to arrive.

The small frame of a woman with a tall banana hook and farming suit appeared. She was laughing. "So close!" she said.

"We are? To what, Grandmother Blane?" Amos asked.

"Can you give us a clue about the pendant on my necklace, Grandmother? And what Charles has to do with all this."

She did a pirouette and laughed. "You have been shown, daughter."

Virginia and Amos looked at each other. "I've been shown so many things lately," she said.

Grandmother stopped laughing and changed her tone to a serious one, pointing her banana stick at Virginia. "Incomplete powers—you must control your images." She tapped her head with her index finger. "Magic is here. Keep your imagination pure, daughter."

"I think she's scolding you. What did you do?" Amos asked.

"I don't know."

"Happiness arrives again when the boy remembers. Peace for all when he defeats the one who benefits from keeping them separate. Evil wants them separate." Grandmother waved goodbye as her image dissolved and was replaced with a new one. An image of the explosion in the port that had taken Charles's life. It quickly transitioned to Charles walking toward the Ananta. The image panned out, and there was another boy, coming from the other side, walking toward the Ananta.

"This is the third time I've seen this image. 'We fixed the accident in a new port,'" Virginia whispered. "Amos, read the message about the Royals from the Unity Festival catalog again, please."

"'It is understood that souls of a Royal pair hold the purest of love, Unconditional Love, that cannot be destroyed by death; they can only be separated until they are United in their next life…'"

"Amos, when a person dies, the soul leaves the body, right?"

"Yeah. All life leaves the body."

"So if a soul can come back, generally it would return in a new baby's body. But it could come back into a body that was maybe void of a soul for a few seconds. Like in a body that died and was revived?"

Amos scrunched his face, pondering the idea silently for a moment. "Like I die for a minute, and you're already dead, then your soul takes life inside my body when my original soul leaves during death?"

"Yes. But why would my soul need to return inside your body?"

With a devilish grin he replied, "To spend a sol being me would be more than enough reason!"

"Very funny. But really, what purpose do we know a soul has to return?"

"The purest love of all, of course—Unconditional Love!" Amos said and then began to ponder out loud. "And let's see... Charles died. There was unconditional love between you, aaaand... and there's some sort of magic between you and Korbin." He paused. "Korbin died and was revived." He stopped talking, his mouth hanging open, until he finally spoke. "Really, Gin? Nooo... Do you think Korbin got Charles's soul when he died?"

Virginia tilted her head, pressed her lips together, and lifted both palms up. "Remember when Grandmother said something about not recognizing his new shell?"

Amos drew his chin into his neck and pulled his eyebrows down. "Woah! That's what she meant when she said, 'You have yet to put the two together.' This is wild!"

Virginia sat silently with a weight in her core, her thoughts so heavy she couldn't feel herself breathing. She didn't know whether to believe it or not. *What would it be like, being with Charles's soul inside Korbin's body? Could this be real?* "That's probably the reason Grandmother is here, why they convinced me to come here to Nos and gave me these clues. But it still seems too bizarre of a concept to believe." She became silent, her head spinning.

Finally, she said, "Maybe I can get some clarity if I tell Korbin and show him the video. See what he says."

"No. No way." Amos fervently shook his head. "You can't just tell a person something like that! That's something someone has to have a natural sense about. Certainly can't tell him that his body is being operated by your deceased boyfriend's soul right after he dumped you! He'll think you're not taking the dump like a lady."

"Yeah. I see your point, but I can't expect him to look at me one sol within the next eight weeks and say, 'Hey, I believe our souls belong together. I don't care if I ever fly in space, I just want to be with you.'" Virginia exhaled and leaned her head on the back of the sofa. "It's science. He's a scientist. And it's a clue I believe he should see, just like I'm seeing. I've gotta believe that if he sees the evidence it will put a crack in his current Unity strategy. Amos, this is nuts, but if it's real, neither of us will be happy for the rest of our lives if we Unite with other people." He nodded in agreement. "And I still need evidence that this is real. Maybe if I spend some time with him, I'll see some sort of proof that he really is... Or maybe he'll remember me. Or himself, like Grandmother just said."

"Without risking your whole entire future."

"Right. I will just keep up my calls with Frankie, set a timeline to go home no later than a week before the closing ceremony. And in between Spaceball practice and class, spend all my extra time with Korbin. Hopefully he'll realize how happy he is around me and that I'm the one." She shrugged and took a deep breath. "This is crazy, but it could be possible, and I have to at least try. I was happy with Charles, and I would do anything to be that happy again." She felt wrung out. "Whew! I'm going to my room to process this alone in the quiet," Virginia said and walked to her room.

She sat in the chair next to her bed, stretching her neck, trying to de-stress.

"Holy cow!" she heard Amos yell.

She went back out into the living room to see what he was yelling about.

"Look at this." He swung around in his desk chair to turn on the entertainment hologram.

Virginia lay on the sofa and pulled the weighted blanket with the yellow-and-blue Nos symbol on it over herself, watching the hologram of Nos city news.

"We still don't know how the fire started, but take a look." The peanut-looking guy walked over to the corner of the Love Counseling Booth and focused his camera on the bottom corner. "See, it started here." He moved his camera up to the top. "And it smoldered out by the time it got here. Nothing else around the Love Counseling Booth was damaged. It almost looks like it was targeted."

"That's funny," Virginia said. "I imagined that thing burning to the ground tonight when I saw stupid Korbin talking to Iris outside its door."

"Grandmother said something about your imagination—just tonight."

She gasped and sat up on the sofa. "So did Mister and Missus. Amos, do you think if my necklace is made of the Unity Element that maybe..."

"...yes, you're probably radioactive."

She laughed. "Thanks, but I was thinking that... maybe I got some United powers? I mean, if this Charles-slash-Korbin thing actually is real. Like Grandmother said, 'Incomplete powers—you must control your images.'"

Amos was silent as his cheeks filled up with the air he was holding in. He finally exhaled. "Are you saying you started this fire with Unity powers of your imagination?"

"I was boiling angry when I saw Korbin exiting the stupid Love Counseling Booth. And when I was a child, Grandmother would always stroke my head when I cried and tell me to Create through pain, with images in my mind. And I just automatically pictured that." She nodded at the hologram.

He scrunched his face up. "Like that? Did you picture it burning down like that?"

"I don't remember how, I just remember creating an image of it on fire in my mind." Virginia shrugged.

"Have you done anything like this before?"

"Sure. I've been doing it ever since I was a kid. My grandmother taught me to 'wish upon a tear.' Every time I cry, to picture something I want. Like me and Charles flying through the cosmos and feeling how peaceful and safe it was out there with him. Sniffing a lavender plant in bloom and feeling the relaxation of the scent. Winning an award for my plants growing outside and the elation of success that came with it."

"But did you ever imagine anything that actually happened? Anything that came true?"

Virginia dropped her head, twisting her mouth to the side, and shook her head. "No. But it makes me feel better inside." She shrugged. "She said that's why I'm rarely sad, because I keep replacing the painful moments with beautiful images in my imagination."

"Got it. But this time is different because of that Ananta pendant you wear and that kiss... If it is made of the Unity Element, it may just possibly be actually *creating* your wishes. And unfortunately, you pictured a not-so-beautiful image this time. Gin, let's put your 'undeveloped Royal powers' to the test. See if it's real. You cry right now and picture me with an extra thirty pounds of muscle."

Virginia smiled and rolled her eyes.

"What? You don't think I would look good beefed up?"

"I like you how you are."

"Fine. But if you did get some sort of United powers, you need to heed Grandmother's warning."

"And Mister and Missus? They warned me about it tonight too."

"Don't think too much. Just practice crying me some muscles," Amos said.

Virginia blindly stared at the little Nos news guy, rambling on and interviewing Uniteds who were breaking down the festival setup, thinking about how odd it would be to look at Korbin again and wonder if the soul of her beloved Charles was now in this new strange body. If it was, could they really be as happy as they once were? How would she get him to recognize her? If only he would just do or say something so that she could know it was Charles's soul and not some weird idea she'd put together from a bunch of Grandmother's funny clues.

Every cell in her body was in a tizzy. *Take a deep breath. This can't really be real. I just want to be happy again. It's just my mind playing tricks on me*, she told herself in an exhale.

"...what if it's all real," she heard the Nos news reporter say as she stared up through the clear ceiling into the blackness of night, trying her best to convince herself that there was no way it could be real. Still wishing it was.

I have nothing to lose if I believe—at least until it's time to make a Union with Frankie, she said to herself while the news carried on in the background and Amos commented on the funny-looking reporter. *Happiness is worth giving it all I've got, at least for as long as I can.* She rested on the thought.

"No one feels another's grief, no one understands another's joy. People imagine that they can reach one another. In reality, they only pass each other by."

~ Franz Schubert

CHAPTER 10

Mars has two moons, Phobos and Deimos, which are small and irregularly shaped.

Virginia was hoping to see Korbin at lunch, to smooth things over with him after they ended their courtship—and before she showed him the video—but he was still missing from class. Nervous about what his reaction might be, she stalled, opting out of looking for him in Port 1 and visiting Farro's office instead, where she could check on her plants that had been put outside only sols ago.

Inside Farro's office, she dodged the water droplets that dripped from the freshly watered hanging plants. She didn't see him, but assumed he was there. "Hey, Professor Farro?" she called out. "Do you know when my lab partner is coming back to class?"

As she waited for his reply, the sound of running water became louder. She followed the sound to the old carved rock sink, painted white with a hose attached to its spigot. She turned the water off, and in the mirror above the sink, she noticed a curl that refused to gather with the others atop her head, hanging down in front of her ear. As she reached for it, she was startled by Korbin's reflection, looking at the curl and reaching for it, one finger aiming to inspect. She reached to touch him, but it was only the mirror. She looked behind her, and he wasn't there either. When she looked back into the mirror, Korbin was waving for her to follow him. She watched as his image got smaller, and then suddenly they were together, in a Nos ISV, looking at a gigantic red cyclone of light in front of them.

Out of the windows she could see Grandmother and her mother and father and Professor Farro and Mister and Missus and thousands of other unrecognizable faces standing behind them, all outlined in a bright purple glow, smiling and waving for her to follow.

"Did you find the many?" she heard Farro say from far away.

She looked away from the mirror to find his voice but couldn't see him, and when she looked back, the reflection was an image of Korbin and Charles, walking toward each other.

Farro's voice moved closer, sounding more like a whisper. "Why are you looking for Korbin?"

Fixed on what was happening inside the mirror, she watched Korbin and Charles walk into each other, transforming into a glowing orange Ananta. "I have to see who he is. See if he knows who he is," she replied in a whisper as the image of the Ananta faded away and her own reflection returned.

Farro moved next to her. "He's probably in Port 1. He will know who he is when he remembers you."

"What do you mean?" she whispered back, still staring into the mirror.

"I mean he doesn't remember you. His mind is louder than his brain right now."

When she finally looked away from the mirror, everything around her was far away, as if she was surrounded by a great distance. Out of the corner of her eye she noticed a drawer creep open at the other end of Farro's endlessly long desk. Farro walked to it and began searching through its mysterious depths.

"This will help." He dangled a long, narrow white bottle from an attached string in front of Virginia. She reached for it as if her arms were stretching for miles, until she at last grasped the little bottle, which fit inside the palm of her hand.

"It's a mighty water. With grand powers. It will quench your thirst."

She opened the cap and tilted the bottle into her mouth until a drop came out. "That's it? Only a drop? Good thing I'm not thirsty."

"Was it enough?" Farro asked.

She looked around—the distance between her and everything else had normalized too. "Yes. That was really weird. Like all these clues about Korbin having the soul of Charles are getting stronger."

"It'll get weirder," he said with a chuckle.

"You know about this? You're in on it too?" Virginia said and extended the white bottle to return it to Farro.

"Keep it. You will need it on your journey, for there is a tax to pay for such a grand Union."

"A tax?" She walked toward the observation window and silently watched her little bean plant standing strong in the cold Martian wind.

"Sure. Nothing is free, not even the greatest love of all. Don't worry about any of it, girl. Many are around, helping the important couple who hold the key."

"Many helping? The key...?" she mumbled.

"Many are we. I only tell you so you never feel alone, no matter what you're going through. Just have fun and trust your power of sense, girl. That's all you need. And the numbers. They guide you."

Virginia looked at the time. 3:45. "The numbers. There's always a nine around."

"It's the number right before completion."

"Completion?"

"When you two Unite."

"Can you tell me what me and Korbin have to do with the Royal curse? Unless it's me and Charles..."

"The two boys are one now. And only a Union as strong as yours has the power to end the one who is evil, who wants to keep you separate at the soul's crossing point."

"The one who is evil?" She grasped her forehead with her hand. "Ugh. This is a lot! Why does everyone want me to know all this? It seems like I'm responsible for the happiness of everyone on the planet."

"We tell you so that when the time comes, the information we share overrides your mind's resistance."

Farro noticed her shaking her head. "Breathe, girl. Go have fun in Spaceball practice. Your little plants are growing fine for now. Come back and check on them tomorrow."

Virginia liked Spaceball practice. She liked her copilot, Nicolette, she liked knowing that she could spend two hours inside a flight simulator and not think about anything that had to do with Korbin or Charles or the

Royal curse.

In her suite the next morning, Virginia mentally prepared to show Korbin the video and discuss the pendant around her neck, wondering what she would say and how she

would say it. She put on her best suit, the one that Paden had refurbished, and wore her curls down and tame. She made herself a cup of tea and a cup for Amos, who was already sitting in front of his workboard at the desk.

"I'm going to show Korbin the video clip this sol after class."

He lifted an eyebrow and looked at her sidelong.

"Yeah, I know your thoughts on it, but I don't have much time left to Unite. I think if I'm getting clues, he should too."

He didn't argue. "Tonight is your first Spaceball game."

Virginia rummaged through her travel bag for something, then ended up dumping the contents on the table. Intrigued, Amos got up to look at the exposed belongings. He picked up a small rectangular case from the table. "What's in here?" he asked, shaking it next to his ear.

"Solar shades. Mr. Bryant gave them to me before I came."

He opened them. "Niiiice!" he exclaimed and put them on his face. "How cool do I look?"

"Not very." She laughed.

"C'mon now. Tell the truth."

She took the glasses off him and put them on her own face. "This is what cool looks like." And she strutted to the other side of the room.

"So cool that no one would recognize you!" Amos teased.

"Hey!" Virginia stopped and leaned in toward him, pushing the solar shades on and off her nose. "You're lucky I'm not Sofia or I'd—"

Amos jumped back, fear covering his face. "What the... Sofia? What are..."

"What's wrong with you?" she asked.

"Y-y-you... Sofia... The glasses!"

She took the glasses off and looked at them in her hand. "Amos, are you okay?"

"Gin! You turned into Sofia with those glasses on!"

"That's crazy," she said and put the glasses on, looking in the mirror. "It looks just like me, Amos..." Virginia stared at her image—that suddenly morphed into Amos—and then tore the glasses off her face. "Did you see that? I said your name and I looked like you."

Dumbfounded, the friends stared at the glasses in her hands.

"Is this real?" Amos said.

"Maybe, but I definitely don't want to be Sofia again." She waved him to come closer and held out her hand for him to hold. "I wonder if it will change both of us if we are together."

"Try Professor Farro," he said, grabbing her hand.

Virginia put on the glasses and looked in the mirror. "Only one Professor Farro—where are you?" She lifted her fingers to feel her new jolly cheeks.

Amos's eyes were wide with wonder. "It's like I disappeared. And you still look like Virginia to me."

She took the glasses off, and they both returned to normal. "I wonder if Mr. Bryant knew what these things do? If he gave them to me for a reason. Like if there's something I'm supposed to do with them."

"I know one thing: you can probably get all the answers you're looking for with those things on."

"Amos. These glasses have just topped everything that has been progressively getting weirder for the past nine weeks," she said as she stowed the glasses in the depths of her pocket.

"If Grandmother Blane figured out a way to be here for you, it's all going to be okay," Amos said kindly.

Hall 2 was bustling with administrators and professors gathered in circles to talk, grandparents eating lunch with their little grandkids at the few public eateries that remained open, and some teenagers riding airboards on the hyperwalk railing or teasing the Rock Friends stationed around the old Galleria. As Virginia watched everyone move about, she wondered what she would say to Korbin. In her head, she practiced a few different ways to start a conversation, points that would convince him to have an open mind about the glowing necklace and their connection, about the idea that they could very well be a special couple.

When she arrived at the doors to Port 1, the extra-tall boy and his two hooded companions stood facing a wall that had been graffitied quite artistically in a bright orange, yellow, and green floral pattern.

"What happened! I mean, it's beautiful, but it's, ummm—vandalism. Really, why would someone do this?" she said.

The three boys, their black hoods disguising their faces, turned around to look at her. The extra-tall one replied, "I agree. Maybe you can help." He handed her a black bag, and they walked away, back into Port 1.

She looked in the bag but couldn't make out what was in it. She reached in, and her heart sank when she saw what was in her hand.

"Virginia?" said Sofia, who had somehow appeared in the same instant that she held up the can of yellow spray paint.

Virginia looked futilely over Sofia's shoulder for the boys who had just pinned this crime on her. They both stared at the bottle of bright yellow paint.

"I didn't—"

Sofia grabbed the bag and looked inside, going silent with surprise. She and her head of little monsters only looked puzzled.

"Sofia, I promise, this wasn't me. I just came here to talk to Korbin, and these three boys... the ones who wear their hoods up all the time... the really tall kid gave me this bag. I didn't... I would never..."

"I'd like to believe you. I find you to be a curious girl, not disrespectful." Sofia was calm, yet disapproving. "But you're standing here with the same paints in your hand that are on this wall of vandalism."

Virginia looked down at the incriminating bag.

"Someone has to take the blame for this. Clean it up now and there won't be any other consequences," Sofia said.

"But this will take hours, if not sols, and I'm a pilot in a Spaceball game tonight."

"You may be important, but you are not exempt from following the rules." Sofia spun around with her two Rock Friends rolling behind.

She called me important too... and didn't threaten to end my life, Virginia thought, baffled by her comment.

She stared at the painted wall, overwhelmed by how to remove the paint, with hopeless thoughts about getting to her game tonight. And most importantly, how she would show Korbin the video he needed to see and get some solid sense of who he might just be.

Anger crept in as she remembered the tall boy and Iris and all the rest of the hooded crew hovering over Korbin in the port, seemingly to keep him away from her. How she'd accidentally caught the booth on fire.

What if I was intentional with my imagination, gave these undeveloped powers a whirl on making this paint disappear?

She thought about the trip she and Korbin had taken to unregister for courtship, how terribly sad and angry she was that he hadn't even given their courtship a chance. She allowed the sadness to heat up her body.

"Control undeveloped powers." She remembered her grandmother's words.

She allowed the pain of being wrongly accused of this evil deed and the embarrassment of missing piloting the game tonight to rise inside. As the pain was at its highest, she released it all through her tears, at the same time picturing the wall being clean, free from vandalism and restored to its original state.

She opened her eyes and dried her tears, suddenly confident that the graffiti would soon disappear. For now, she needed to carry on with her plan before she'd been falsely accused: show Korbin what she knew he needed to see.

The footsteps of a new person had arrived on Korbin's scene. His long head and skinny body were crammed inside a mechanical panel on the side of some old plane. He waited for the assistant next to him, who wore a black hooded sweatshirt, to address the visitor.

There was silence.

He pulled his head out to look for himself. "Well, hi there!" Korbin said, happy that she was there. "You're the last person I expected to see in here."

His decision to end the courtship with Virginia still filled him with disappointment, but maybe this was his chance to be nice enough that she would forget how he'd let her down. He handed his tools to the spiritless helper and dusted off his arms. "I'm due for a break. Let's go to the break room and grab a soda."

The hooded helper followed closely behind them. Korbin turned around and said, "I don't need any help here."

The small girl, who could very well have been Iris's sidekick, shrugged and stopped midstride.

They sat down in the break room together. "I've been trying to talk to you in private," Virginia whispered, "because, umm... well... Amos put a recording sticker on your shirt the night we, uh, got stuck in the plane together."

Korbin scrunched up his face. "What? You mean he recorded us?"

"Well, not intentionally. He only hoped to capture the Spaceball team returning to port. That's why he put an invisible sticker cam on your coat," she said, tapping his chest with her finger.

"Hmmm... I did find something on that coat, but I just sent it to the laundry. I didn't know what it was. That's a little disturbing that someone saw us kiss. That was a special kiss, Virginia." Korbin whispered a sincere reply. "You are special in ways I can't even describe. I'm really sorry that I just couldn't... umm... see a future with you."

Virginia looked worried. "Anyway, he caught something strange on the recording. Look." She turned on the hologram from her wrist. "Now watch. Right here, look at my necklace. It glows. It lights up purple and a little orange." She let it play until their bodies drew apart again. "And look. As soon as the kiss ends, it stops glowing."

"I don't understand."

She pulled a necklace out from under her blouse. "My grandmother gave it to me after Charles... left. Well, the Unity Stone lights up a certain color when a pair touches it. I think that it may be made of the same elements the Unity Stone is made of."

Korbin scratched his head. "But how on Mars could you possibly have a piece of the Unity Stone?"

She continued, "All I know is that when we kissed, it glowed like the Unity Stone does when two people become United."

Korbin paused in silence, confused. "But it glowed orange. That's not a color of the Uniteds," he whispered.

"Right. At least, not one we know of... and also... some weird things have happened with me since that kiss. Have you noticed anything weird for you? Like having powers kinda weird?"

"My whole life seems weird lately, Virginia." He quietly laughed. "I don't really know what to think about this. It's strange. I can definitely put some thought into it."

Their conversation ended as an all-too-familiar silhouette of a girl dressed in all black marched toward them. She stood confidently in front of Korbin and Virginia, her silky black line of hair falling forward on her face, around crystal-blue eyes that gleamed with rage. "You know that Virginia has someone waiting to Unite with her in Alcetra, right? And if he were to get an image of you two together, her future could be grim."

Korbin felt something like a boulder drop from his head to his stomach. "Yeah, I was kinda aware of that."

Virginia stood up. "What exactly is your problem with me? And me and Korbin? Are you trying to keep us apart?"

"Korbin and I have been friends since grade school, and I think he deserves better than a farm girl who has no business here. Why don't you go home?"

He stood up as well. "That's enough, Iris. Virginia did nothing to deserve this. You don't need to harass her."

Virginia gave Iris the evil eye she walked away.

Seeing the sadness on Virginia's face, Korbin wondered why he was so disturbed that she had someone to Unite with, when he didn't even want her for himself.

Walking toward the port exit doors, Virginia only hoped the graffiti wall would be back to normal, while also anticipating the embarrassment of having to call Heath and tell him she wouldn't be able to pilot for the team tonight.

She peered out, noticing a handful of Rock Friends had gathered in front of the wall, staring at it and mumbling among themselves. Curious, she stepped into the hall and looked.

I did get my powers. It's all really real.

With a surge of confidence, she called the port master as she walked away from the wall she miraculously hadn't gotten stuck cleaning. "Yeah, hiya, Jerry. This is Coach Matz over here in Port 3, and we could use some extra help. Would you mind sharing your port mechanic so we can get more of our team ISVs tuned up?"

Virginia stood in front of her ISV, waiting for her copilot to arrive. Amos peeled the protector off a clear sticker camera and with a devious smile waved it in front of her face, giving her the option to decline the camera's placement.

"Yeah, sure," she said and watched his hands smooth the sticker onto the front of her father's old flight jacket. "I guess everyone will see any mistake I make out there."

"Oh, please. You're a great pilot. The mission will be flawless," he said. "But please try to mess up at least once. For the audience—they love mistakes. And then my ratings go through the roof."

"That's exactly what I want to do, be the star louser-upper of your nightly news show!"

"It's the screwups and romances-slash-failed romances that have given me an additional twenty-two percent news exposure in all the cities. And I've got a big paid product sponsor from Erbos!" Amos flaunted.

"Oh, Amos! That's so great! Your father must be—"

"Yeah yeah yeah, so proud. He'd be astounded if I United and moved out when I got home!"

Virginia drove the burgundy-colored spacecraft with the inconspicuous snake mouth painted on the front nose out of the port, along with the five other ISVs, onto the Space Ascent Ramp. One by one, each little vehicle in front of her disappeared out of orbit and into space with a few loud bangs and a quick flash of light.

"Our turn!" her copilot, Nicolette, said.

Anxiety whirled around in her stomach. She still couldn't believe she was doing this—without Charles.

Their ISV latched onto the ascent tracks and catapulted them out of the Martian atmosphere. Within a few heated, rocky minutes they were in orbit with the rest of Team Nos and Team Morphus, the visiting team. Virginia immediately set her safety coordinates, and before she moved the spacecraft toward the others, she asked Nicolette, "Safety coordinates?"

"Check." Her voice was as mellow yet confident as her stature.

There were 15 minutes in each of the five time segments, and whichever team destroyed the Spaceball the most in each was the winner for that segment. The team who won the most fifths was the winner of that game. The Spaceball was launched, and both teams began to fire, except Virginia and Nicolette and two other teammates on defense, hovering in front of the other team, blocking their shots.

"Grapes? Is that the only thing this kid could think of to paint on his ISV?" Virginia mocked. "Let's squeeze his stupid grapes. Nicolette, I want you to turn on the port, starboard, masthead, and stern lights, along with all the interior lights, then flash them on and off as fast as you can. I'm going to spin us in circles in front of him until he alters course, and then I'll have a chance to take a shot at the Spaceball."

"Good thing I don't vomit easily..." Nicolette said as the ISV began spinning.

The grape vehicle was paralyzed by the madness in front of him and maneuvered his vehicle below Virginia, and she used those few seconds to fire her laser cannons at the Spaceball, just as planned in practice.

"Spaceball 4. Team Nos," the announcer said through the radio.

"I'm a little sick, but that was worth it," Nicolette said.

A dizzying influx came through the group radio: "Good job!" "Genius move!" "Way to go!" "Virginia killed it!"

The Spaceball was launched in the final fifth. Both teams had won two fifths. This was the winning or losing segment for Team Nos.

"Virginia and Nicolette. Wanna use some of those fancy moves to help me out?" Heath asked on the radio. To their starboard side, the defense held a tight in-your-face, one-on-one follow on Heath.

"Yeah. Sure. We'll move our opponent closer first. When you see us close, tuck and roll off his port side, and we'll come over from the top and pick your defense off."

"Brilliant! I'll take a shot from below," Heath said.

"Twenty-five seconds on the clock," Nicolette said as the move was in play.

"Gonna use the X-actionator," Heath said, his voice rolling with his spacecraft.

And as soon as Virginia and Nicolette were in front of Heath's defense, they saw the bright glow of the residue of the X-actionator's impact.

"Spaceball 5, Team Nos," the announcer said through the radio.

"Oh my goodness. I can't believe we actually pulled that off," Virginia whispered.

Virginia made friends with her much shorter and stronger copilot as she and Nicolette rode the hyperwalk together back to the conservatory for the end of the Unity Dinner. There were celebrating Singles cheering as they passed by. "Go, Team Nos!"

"Good game, Virginia," a voice said into her ear, from behind her on the hyperwalk.

"Korbin?" She was shocked, but the smile on her face revealed how happy she was to see him.

He looked down at his body. "Yeah, look at me, hanging out with all the cool kids. I got assigned to work on the team ISVs tonight! Maybe one step closer to getting out there in space with you, huh?"

She shook her head and said, "Yeah, I hope you get out there in space with us soon too."

Korbin walked ahead, and as she continued along with her new friend Nicolette, the skin-tingling sensation of hope and joy raced through her body, producing a smile that lit up her eyes. *Things are going to work out just fine—somehow.*

"If there ever comes a day where we can't be together, keep me in your heart. I'll stay there forever."

~ A.A. Milne, Winnie the Pooh

CHAPTER 11

NASA has calculated a 2.5-year round trip to Mars from Earth, including the time it takes for Mars and Earth to realign for the return trip.

A faint glow just beyond the door that wouldn't close revealed the shadows of those who waited for the brilliant hologram who promised them the greatest gift on Mars. They sat in dark silence until at last the void space filled with a holographic cloud of moving white light, which morphed into a cyclone that unraveled the wings, chiseled torso, and long flowing hair of the Dutch.

His lips were pressed upward, and his face had an easy glow. "Young men and women who wish to possess the greatest powers on Mars, when will you get serious about doing the work to obtain your reward of special un-United Royal powers?" the Dutch said smoothly to the unconcerned faces revealed by the light of his hologram.

"We're trying," one girl said.

"Trying? Then will you kindly explain how Mr. Korbin Xander got placed in Port 3, as the team's official mechanic, while also moving one massive step closer to that girl—the one trying to force herself on him and keep him from someone who will give you all an incredible reward?"

"Things are happening." A boy spoke up. "I told my uncle about him. My Uncle Dot owns the galactic freight transport company. He's going to come here with his daughter to meet Korbin."

The Dutch spun around and looked in the face of the extra-tall boy. "At last! We have one solid plan to keep those two apart and bring him one step closer to the life-changing Union we need. Now tell me why you think this plan will stick?"

The boy replied, "Because my uncle has nearly fifty ISVs of all sizes, he's always going to need captains for the flights. The Union with his daughter would give Korbin what he wants—the promise of a career in space flight. And his daughter is a little older and eager for Union."

The Dutch moved his hologram wings and body around the circle, looking at each face through his black holes. "In the meantime, which one of you has a plan to get Korbin Xander out of Port 3, where that evil girl has daily access to him?"

"I will." A girl's gruff voice spoke matter-of-factly from the darkness. "I'm friends with the mayor's daughter. We'll come up with a plan for Korbin until the Dots arrive."

The Dutch rubbed his hands together and smiled. "Yes. Yes. A power play. Do it quick. We must keep the outsider from corrupting him."

While Virginia and the rest of the Spaceball team were in a heated match against Erbos, Korbin found himself answering Amos's questions. "Is this an interview for your news channel, Amos?"

"That's a great idea, Korbin—do you mind if it is?"

Amused, he agreed with a chuckle and a head shake.

"You've been in this port nearly all week. Could it be true that you're an official team mechanic now?" Amos asked.

Korbin looked around at the port, void now of movement. "Maybe." He shrugged. "I think they needed an extra hand, ya know—our team is on a bit of a winning streak." He wiped a wrench off with a dirty rag.

"What about space flight? Do you ever get the sense that you've already spent a lifetime flying?"

Korbin looked at him as if he were speaking a different language.

"How about this..." Amos continued. "Do you think you want to fly one of these things soon?"

Korbin smiled, admiring the ISV in front of him. "I would love to—if an administrator would sponsor my license. Then I'd fly to the moon, through my birth constellation, and take my love and fly her through hers too."

"What is your constellation, Korbin?"

"The archer."

"December?"

"Yup. The first."

"And how about this love? We want to know who she is."

His first thought was Virginia. But why would she be the first thought in his mind? There was no way she was the one—they were just becoming good friends, there was no real potential for his future or anything as significant as sharing United power together. Besides, she was courting someone. Korbin smirked wryly and looked down at the floor, shaking his head. "You know, Amos, sometimes it's not just as easy as falling in love."

"Sounds to me like you're having a battle between your brain and your power of sense. Don't you believe that the Unity Stone will gift you the greatest powers and your soul's desires when you choose with your power of sense?"

"If the Unity Stone grants us powers at all."

"But you only have to worry about that if you choose someone who isn't suitable for your soul."

Korbin was aware of the risk: the practical girl might not be the best for his soul, and the Unity Stone could very well deny him Union, and he would be stuck on his father's path. Luckily, the conversation ended when the yellow port light started flashing and the alarm sounded, signaling the port doors would open soon.

"Thanks for the interview, Korbin."

"Yeah, no problem. I'll see ya 'round, Amos."

Virginia stepped out of her ISV to Korbin's awkwardly long face, his mouth flashing an equal amount of gums as teeth. "What are you smiling for?"

"It was a good game. Ya can't win 'em all, Virginia," he said. "I'm gonna check out your ISV tonight. Particularly the motor of your X-actionator. I just always get a bad sense about those things for some reason."

She stared at him, dumbfounded, remembering Farro's words. *"The boy must remember who he is."*

Is he remembering?

"Virginia?" Korbin said, waving his hand in front of her blank stare.

No. He can't risk it. What if it happens again? She shook her head fervently. "No. There's nothing wrong with it. Please don't. Not tonight or ever."

His brows turned in and questions strewn across his face, he replied, "Okay, Gin. I won't."

Speechless, she forced a smile through tight lips before she started to walk away.

"Also..." he said, firmly enough for her to turn back toward him. "I want you to know that I've been thinking about, you know, your necklace... when we kissed. I have some ideas. Let's talk here, tomorrow, before practice."

Relief released the clench it'd had on her chest. She wanted to talk about it now, but after all, it was nearly midnight. Instead, she replied, "Oh. Great! I can't wait," and wished him a good night before she headed out of the port with the rest of the team and back to her suite.

The next sol, Korbin finished his morning's work in Port 1 and headed to Port 3, looking forward to talking to Virginia about the necklace, contemplating scientific ideas about its glow. He paused to listen to a message on his transmitter.

"Korbin, I'm Karen, secretary for the mayor's office. We have a request that you work on the mayor's daughter's ISV this week. Go directly to Port 2—we have already notified Coach Matz about your reassignment from Port 3."

Surprised and confused, but also intrigued to be invited to work on a project for the mayor, he headed for the highly esteemed port, which was off-limits to everyone except a Planet Protector or a city official.

When he arrived, Port 2 screamed in silent rigidity. Korbin hauled the heavy weight of his insecurities up the stairs to the port master's tower. The port master stood tall and straight, undisturbed, analyzing a flight plan on the large workboard in the center of the tower. Korbin took a few steps closer, until the port master finally looked away to eye up his skinny body, covered by his wrinkled and soiled mechanic's suit. "I suppose you're the mayor's special request."

"I suppose, sir."

The port master moved next to Korbin at the window. Together they silently observed every meticulous row of Planet Protector ISVs, grouped together in the center of the port and docked at perfectly equal distances like asymmetrical art. The various carrier planes and high-performance ISVs were laid out in order, from largest to smallest, and a half dozen mechanics were at work, filling in their pressed and unsoiled suits like covered rocks.

Korbin knew he was the smallest of workers among the greatest of experts in Port 2. "I don't belong here," he mumbled.

"No. You don't," the port master said, eyeing his disheveled appearance. "But at least try to look the part and keep a professional pace with the rest of my mechanics when you're in my port. No visitors, and absolutely zero shenanigans. The mayor's vehicle is below us. His daughter will be there to talk to you about what she wants done." He returned to his workboard.

Korbin sensed the port master's graciousness and thanked him before he left.

Below the tower, an oddly misplaced girl in a bright red suit spoke up. "You must be Korbin, the one who is going to make all my dreams come true." She reached to shake his hand and added her other hand on top of his.

She wouldn't release his hand and stepped closer into his personal space. "I'm Manda," she said in a low tone, batting her heavy eyelashes like she had a problem in her eye.

Korbin thought her extreme and off-putting, and he gently pulled his hand away. "Yes. Manda. Thank you for choosing me for this project. What is it you want done?"

She laughed at nothing and walked slowly around the bright green personal plane. "It's too slow. You see, I have some friends who like to go out and race sometimes. And, well, I need to win."

"You want me to make it faster?"

She laughed hysterically. "Yes! Exactly."

"I can do that," he said soberly.

"Wonderful. I'll be back to check on it tomorrow!" Manda replied and turned to leave.

Korbin inspected the spectacular paint job, which faded from a deep green into a lime green with silver sparkle at the bottom. As he made his way to the tool box, out of the corner of his eye he noticed someone who appeared to be Iris in her long black cape. She and two very tall figures, their faces hidden by their black hoods, were talking with Manda behind the glass in the observation tower.

"What the heck are they up to?" He sighed aloud and began assessing the plane for its update.

"Why didn't you show up yestersol?" Virginia asked Korbin, who was standing next to the mechanical panel of Heath's ISV, carefully inspecting something. "You make plans and then don't follow through. You didn't even send me a message."

"Sorry about that, Virginia," he said unconvincingly, without looking up from the part he was cleaning. "I got called to work on the mayor's daughter's personal plane, which I think was, uh… um, really weird."

Her feelings were hurt, but she didn't know how to tell him, so instead she sighed and crossed her arms and rolled her eyes in one movement.

"About your necklace glowing… I think we should go to my father's lab, test it there. It could be an element that we've seen before, or it could be a metal that we haven't seen, one that reacts to temperature and body chemicals. Some form of living rock maybe. But at least we'll know with some testing."

He was completely denying the voice of his soul. She stuffed the frustration down her throat. With a deep breath, she asked, "Korbin, do you ever sense something important about me? Something familiar?"

He narrowed his eyes, looked into hers, and nodded his head slightly. "Yeah, but it's... it's strange. I sense that—"

"Korbin! Here you are!" His reply was cut off when a flamboyantly clothed girl walked in between them. She moved her body in direct contact with Korbin's, tapping her pointer finger on his cheek and whispering into his mouth, "Why are you here? I want a faster plane. Don't you want to give me what I want?"

Her stomach upset with disgust, Virginia watched the unknown girl and Korbin share some sort of private quarrel. *Is this the reason he ended our courtship? There's no way he has Charles's soul. Charles would never do this to me*, she thought as she felt pain grow heavy behind her eyes.

The pain lessened and curiosity grew when Korbin pulled away from the overanimated girl. "I finished it. Worked all night. Take it for a ride and see for yourself."

"What are you talking about?" she said in the fakest high-pitched voice, while moving closer to Korbin.

"There's no way you're done so fast. Come show me what you did," she begged, still moving toward him as he backed away.

"Look," he said, putting his hand up in front of her, "I'm not gonna be part of whatever you and Iris are cookin' up. Go tell the mayor I'm done with your vehicle, and let me work on the team ISVs in peace, please."

The girl stomped her foot and huffed before glancing at Virginia as she turned around and left.

Confused about what she'd just witnessed, Virginia asked Korbin, "What was that?"

"That was the reason I missed you yestersol."

Humbled, she replied, "Oh. Okay."

The team entered the simulators along the wall for practice, and Korbin walked to the break room to grab a juice from the machine, where he found Coach Matz and Professor Farro talking and his father walking away, giving him a disapproving glance. "Oh. Excuse me," Korbin said, nervous as to why they were all talking to each other and wondering what his father could be so angry about. He turned and began to leave.

"Korbin, you don't have to go. We want to talk to you," Professor Farro said, waving him closer. "You've been doing a lot of volunteer work in Port 1, helping Port Master Jerry."

"And also here recently on the team ISVs—you're doing a great job," Coach Matz added.

He nodded. "Thanks."

"We thought maybe we could do something for you, a repayment for your work here," Coach Matz said.

Korbin was uncomfortable. "For me? Nah," he said from the side of his mouth. "I don't want anything. I'm just happy to be here."

Coach Matz pressed her lips together until they disappeared. "Mmmm... what if we told you we want to get you out there?" She glanced at the glass dome above, then looked back at him to check his response. "You know, some lessons and a license, maybe, if you can pass the exams in the next seven weeks."

"What? Are you serious?" He looked around the room for someone playing a trick on him. "I don't know any administrators who would sponsor me for that." Surely it was a trick—his father had just been talking to these two jokesters. He laughed and shook his head. "Additionally, there is no way my father would approve."

Coach Matz glanced at Farro, then returned a convincing head nod toward Korbin. "He just did."

He glanced at Professor Farro, then at Coach Matz, staring at her thin, pressed lips and processing what she'd just said. He tilted his head to the side. "You mean he sponsored me?"

"The Nos Planet Protectors Administrator did," Farro said with a smile brighter than normal.

Coach Matz moved her finger around on the transmitter button on her wrist. "I just pinged you the official study guide. Meet me here in the morning for your first lesson."

He watched them walk away, his thoughts still clouded in disbelief. He looked at the time on his transmitter, counting the minutes until Spaceball practice was over and he could tell Virginia the good news.

Virginia was brighter than ever with the hope of Korbin remembering who he was during his space flight lessons and his idea to test the composition of her pendant in the coming week.

"You look fantastic tonight!" Paden cried. "Did you wear your new ensemble to show off to Frankie on a hologram call tonight?"

With things looking so up with Korbin, she'd nearly forgotten that she had a designated call with Frankie on Sunsols before every Unity Dinner. "Of course!" she replied, too optimistic to have any thoughts of dread.

She wasn't paying attention as Paden went on about her courtship with James and her plans for the four of them. What would Korbin say when he realized that her pendant was the same element as the Unity Stone? What would it be like, being with Charles in someone else's body?

The girls ended their call, and she again kept her promise to Frankie.

"You look beautiful tonight," he said.

Virginia blushed. She didn't want him to like her as much as he did. They exchanged pleasantries, as usual, never really talking about anything connected to any type of emotion, which was likely why she was exhausted by the end of each call.

"C'mon, Gin! Time ta go!" Amos called from the living room. She was happy to end the call of superficiality with Frankie, as dear and good-natured as he was.

Inside the beautifully festive Main Conservatory 6, on the way to their table, she and Amos walked past the Unity Festival vendors, including the Love Counseling Booth. He pointed at five figures dressed in black, their faces shadowed by their hoods, who were huddled together outside the booth.

"Looks serious," Virginia said.

"You should go over there and listen to what they're saying."

She looked at him as if he had two heads. "I think things are going to go fine with Korbin. I don't really care what those weirdos are up to."

"I dunno, Ginny Gin Gin," Amos said, pointing to the scene.

Korbin walked toward the group and stood outside the roped-off area. The extra-tall boy approached him, speaking with animated hands and Korbin hesitantly agreeing with him.

"You have those weird glasses in your pocket still, right?" Amos asked.

She reached in her pocket and looked at him with surprise. "Yeah."

"Well... don't you want to know what they're saying?"

"Yeah." She laughed nervously. "Who should I be?"

"What about the really tall girl? I don't think she's with them right now."

"I don't know her name." Virginia thought for a few seconds. "Ellis. Ellis will know. She knows everyone in this city." She hurried to find Ellis, who was sitting soberly with Jeremiah at their designated Unity table, tonight decorated in the Unity color of red.

"Oh yeah. A recognizable gal," Ellis began explaining. "She's an only child of the Aid Administrators. I heard she's uber smart and keeps to herself usually. Beth Taylor. Why? What do you want with her?"

"Thanks! Tell ya when we get back!" Virginia hurried away with Amos in tow. She walked them into a thick crowd of Singles who were bouncing up and down on the dance floor to the most danceworthy song on the planet. She held up her glasses to show Amos that she was ready to make the change, put them on, tucked herself into her giant coat, said the name *Beth Taylor*, and came up as one extra-tall girl with a hooded black trench coat, also wearing solar shades.

But as soon as they got to the rope outside the Love Counseling Booth, the hooded gang was walking into it. "I'm not going in there," she said to Amos. "There's very bad vibes in that thing—place makes me ill. I'll wait out here for them."

"Okay, Gin. I'm gonna be on the lookout for the real Beth Taylor."

Virginia stood outside the roped-off line, waiting for them to come out.

The whispers silenced when the group entered the small tent, and a white cyclone of light particles took form. He stretched out his arms and wings. "Ah! Team Save the Planet and True Love is here again! Please tell me you have come to bring me great news."

"Korbin is getting flight lessons."

"Approved by administration."

"And his father."

The Dutch's black eye holes turned to a glowing red. He looked at his arms and torso and became silent until the red-black holes disappeared. "Many are gaining on us. We must get control of this situation immediately."

"It's only about a week until my cousin comes in to meet him."

The Dutch spun around and stared the extra-tall boy in the eye. "Only a week? In a few more sols, with flight lessons, being out there in space, he could remember... My fate—your fate—is on the line, the fate of all Royal magic is on the brink of becoming extinct. Which do you want?" He spun around and looked each person in the eye. "It only takes us, as a team, bringing one who has died and come back to life to his Royal Union. And it is not the foreign girl." He straightened his back perfectly upright and puffed out his chest, gaining composure and calm. "His Royal match is out there—hopefully it's this girl you are bringing in. We will get her in the booth, find out for sure if she is the one for him. If it's her, then I get released from Anywhere, with the power to give you your Royal powers."

"We should probably just get him out of the ports altogether, at least until my cousin arrives next week."

"My mother and father manage the setup of the Unity Dinner and Dance. I can tell them that Korbin wants to help."

"Yeah. My aunt always needs help in the bakery. I'll tell her he needs a job. He's notorious for being helpful—we can at least keep him so busy he won't have time to talk to her or anyone else," a voice agreed.

The Dutch grunted through his smile, and as the group whispered to each other, his form dissolved into trillions of tiny light particles and his image was gone.

The hooded group exited the Love Counseling Booth. Virginia, who looked exactly like Beth, waved to the extra-tall boy. "Where were you? Why are you out here?" he asked.

She didn't know what Beth would say, so she just shrugged and smiled with her lips pressed tightly together. The rest of the hooded group joined them at the rope. She listened closely as they began whispering.

"I don't know what craziness the Dutch is talking about Korbin remembering anything out there in space."

Virginia checked herself to make sure she wasn't showing shock and curiosity on her face. *They were actually in there talking about Korbin? He must be important.*

"He's getting flight lessons, but it's not like she's giving him the lessons. He's not even going to have a spare minute to see her," one whisper said.

If they were in there talking about me too, we must be really important, she thought, swallowing the air that she'd forgotten to breathe.

"Yeah, it's not a big deal."

"It's just a week. There's nothing that could happen in a week."

She watched as the group dispersed, considering how to make her own exit.

"I'm hungry. Let's go grab a bite," the extra-tall boy said to the girl he assumed was Beth. "One thing's for sure... when the Dutch gives me my Royal powers, I will be having fresh-cooked meals delivered to my apartment all sol long."

"Your Royal powers?" Virginia noticed him looking at her. "Great idea. I'd probably make new bread spreads appear," she said, laughing nervously. She'd lose him in the cafeteria crowd and take off the glasses where no one would notice.

What on Mars could happen in a week? I have to figure out what they're up to. What if they're planning to take him away? she thought as she stepped away to return to her own form.

"All the art of living lies in a fine mingling of letting go and holding on."

~ Havelock Ellis

CHAPTER 12

There are canyons, volcanoes, and craters seen on Mars, along with what could very well be evidence of past water features like ancient riverbeds and lakebeds.

In search of some answers, she went to Farro's office. "What's troubling you?" he asked Virginia, who sat on a stool at his cluttered worktable, arms tightly crossed with a furrow between her brows.

"Professor, you said something—and I think my grandmother said something—about 'the evil one wants us separate.' Assuming that it's me and Cha… er… Korbin, that's at risk of being separated, who is the evil one, and could the evil one actually be several people?"

Farro smiled and after a pause said, "You're a smart girl. You have discovered the tools he uses since he can't take form."

"Iris and this black-coated group are trying to keep me and Char… eh… Korbin apart. What do I do to make them stop and get Korbin to remember me? I only have five more weeks to Unite, and I need to—"

He interrupted her. "You don't need to do anything, girl, just choose." He walked away from the worktable, stopping in front of the sink and connecting the water hose to the spigot. She refused to watch him too closely, afraid that she would see something in the mirror again. "Professor Farro? Is there anyone else besides you and Ms. West and Grandmother and the Unity Administrators who know about Korbin?"

He pushed his glasses higher atop his jolly cheeks. "Of course. Many do."

"Many?"

Farro chuckled quietly. "You are never alone, dear. Many are the Royal souls, hidden, working in disguise to help secure this important Union."

"Many of the Royals?"

He nodded with his usual smile.

Unsure, or perhaps holding on to disbelief, Virginia sighed aloud, staring blankly toward the sink, where water was being shifted through the hose that Farro used to water his plants. Her gaze inevitably drifted toward the mirror, where she couldn't help but notice a reflection that wasn't hers. She moved in closer to find Korbin's face staring back at her with the same look of confusion and uneasiness that she felt inside. She tried to turn around and leave, but her feet wouldn't budge.

She looked to the left—and Korbin did too. She looked to the right—Korbin did too; she waved with her right hand—Korbin did too. She hopped up—Korbin did too.

She leaned forward and whispered, "What are you doing?"

Korbin leaned forward and whispered, "I'm following you."

"Professor Farro!" Virginia yelled and stepped away from the mirror. She looked back, waiting for his reply, but Korbin was gone.

Professor Farro walked over. "What did you see, girl?"

"Korbin—in the mirror. Copying everything I did."

"The girl always leads. He is your mirror. That's why you must make a choice. A tough one, so that he will follow and Union will prevail," Farro said with an easy smile.

"What kinda choice?"

"One that defies logic. A choice firm in belief, that will bring his road back to you," he said, flashing his normal jolly face. "Don't worry, girl. Your soul will choose the right numbers—which do not include eight, by the way, definitely not the eight—and then all of the others will come to aid you two into Union."

She spotted Korbin working in the port, but without enough time to chat him up before the game, she dashed into the locker room to change into her flight suit. She stopped to examine her face in the mirror, zooming her focus into her freckles and thinking of Grandmother's words. *"His brain hinders what his soul remembers."* Her freckles disappeared, and her elegant reflection was replaced with the thoughts in her head:

If his soul is really Charles's, then he should sense who I am when we're together!

What choice is Farro talking about?

My mirror?

I must get him to remember me soon, before it's too late!

The numbers? But not the eight?

What time is it, I wonder?

The blur in the mirror transitioned to numbers, large and small ones, numbers inside its depths, numbers that escaped the confines of the glass, changing shapes, flashing, moving around. Farro's voice ringing: *"You'll see the numbers... not the eight."* Curious, she leaned forward, allowing the numbers to entrap her in their chaos.

She became lost inside the mirror, somehow walking through the numbers that consumed the vast majority of the unknown space around her. She pushed them out of her way as she moved deeper into the entangled mass.

She moved zeros and ones that floated effortlessly like balloons out of her path, to continue forward, where twos swirled around her like a flock of birds. Frustrated, she swatted them until they flew away; nines and sevens began appearing, pulsing, expanding and contracting in the rhythm of a heartbeat. She dodged around the nines and sevens when they contracted, finally arriving in an amber-colored space with only a few fives, fours, and threes, which changed in various shades of reds and yellows, appearing as fire and disappearing in a cloud of smoke. She hurried through the burning threes, fours, and fives, but nowhere did she see an eight. She looked right and left and still did not find the number eight. Only more of every other number.

She turned around to look for the locker room, panicking when she could see nothing but more numbers moving toward her, swallowing her up.

"Virginia? Virginia?" Nicolette stood over her slumped body on the floor.

"I'm fine," Virginia grumbled.

"No, you're not. I'm gonna call the aid."

Virginia forced her eyes open and grabbed Nicolette's arm. "I'm fine. Just sit here with me for a few minutes."

She looked at her transmitter. 4:09.

Nicolette huffed and turned on the water. "You look like you're sick. Put some cold water on your face and then tell me what's going on."

Virginia took the cool cloth, avoiding eye contact with Nicolette and allowing a terribly evil but necessary plan to form behind the washcloth. *If Korbin was out in space with me, surely his soul would remember me. If I could trap Nicolette in here and take Korbin as my copilot tonight, then everything would make sense to him. And me. Then we could move on with our lives.*

After too many moments had passed without any explanation from Virginia, Nicolette spoke up. "You're not okay. I need to tell Coach Matz what's going on and get you an aid—and get a replacement pilot for our ISV."

Virginia snapped to her feet. "Look at me. I'm fine. Nervous about tonight, that's all. We're playing against my home team. I need to talk to you about it, but I, uh... need to stretch my legs and get the new lock to my locker that I left in our ISV. Will you wait here with my bag, then we can talk when I get back?"

With doubt strewn across her face, Nicolette agreed with half a nod, her broad shoulders softening. Virginia hurried out of the locker room and found Amos. "I need you to go do some damage control."

"Huh?"

"Yeah. In the girl's locker room. But whatever happens, don't let Nicolette call anyone or leave that room!"

He raised his brow and looked at her out of the tops of his eyes. "And Sofia turns me into a Rock Friend for kidnapping while you're out there playing Spaceball?"

"I've gotta get Korbin up in space tonight, and you owe me."

"Touché," Amos said and hustled to the girl's locker room, not noticing Virginia behind him.

As soon as he went in and the door closed behind him, she shorted out the door lock control panel with the water in the vial that Farro had given her. She hurried through the rows of ISVs and found Korbin wrenching on one not far from hers. The ten-minute launch alarm sounded.

She was nervous, unsure how she could get him to be her copilot. Without much thought, she decided that trickery would be her best bet. "I need to show you something on our ISV."

"Uh, Virginia, we have to prepare for launch. You can take this one if you don't feel safe in yours."

"Just check it. It'll only take a minute. Hurry, 'cause I'm taking mine."

As soon as he put his tools down, she grabbed his hand and ran with him to her ISV. "It's my manual steering handle," Virginia said, leading him inside the ship.

The five-minute alarm sounded.

"Oh, Gin, I can't. I have to go. And so do you and Nicolette," Korbin said, panicking.

"Nicolette isn't here. You have to be my copilot."

Korbin fervently shook his head. "As much as I totally want to fly, I could lose my flight sponsorship with a stunt like that," he said, shifting his gaze between the door of the ISV and the flashing yellow light above the port gate.

Virginia sat in the captain's chair, strapped in, and closed the ISV door. "C'mon, copilot. We launch in seconds!"

He exhaled loudly and sank into the copilot's chair. "We are going to be in so much trouble when we get back."

"Don't worry, I'll take the heat. Coach Matz and Farro are friends. If she doesn't understand, Farro will help her understand."

"Gin, I've only read the training manual twice and had two space flight lessons. Why didn't you just ask Coach Matz for a sub?"

"Because I'm hoping you'll regain your memory out here."

Korbin narrowed his eyes, drew down the corners of his mouth. "My memory is fine. What are you talking about?"

Virginia sensed that he was likely annoyed and spoke softly. "The memory of your soul. That little voice that makes you interested in something that makes no sense."

He shook his head and huffed. "Yeah. Like not running like hell after that alarm sounded made no sense!"

Their ISV shot off the launch assent ramp, catapulting them into the darkness of space. The two floated around the vastness in silence, waiting for the remainder of the team to enter space with them.

Korbin sighed, staring out the window. "Like the little voice that says I've been here with you before. And that little voice that told me the first sol in class that I've met you before?"

She couldn't believe her ears. "Yeah. That voice."

He chuckled. "I really do like you when we're together, Virginia. It just doesn't— "

"Hey, Korbin." Virginia interrupted the negative narrative she sensed he was about to spew from his senseless mouth. "The rest of the team is here. You shouldn't have to talk to anyone, so don't, and hopefully we'll end up back in the port undetected. We don't fire any shots—strictly defense tonight."

"Why? You're one of the best shots on the team."

"I don't want to take shots on my home team. We practiced so I wouldn't have to. I'll be maneuvering the vehicle in defense, and basically it will be your job to steady us with the wheel."

Korbin grasped the wheel tightly with both hands.

"Allow movement, but not a shift," Virginia instructed.

The first play went into motion. They blocked one of Alcetra's ISVs when it had a shot and rolled over the top of a neighboring ISV, distracting the captain from taking a shot. They worked together silently, as if they'd been teammates forever. After a few short hours and without much effort, Nos won the game with a 3–2 score.

"Has your city's team always been bad?" Korbin whispered to her.

He's out here in space with me—and playing Spaceball! I should just tell him who he is, what happened to him during his accident.

Virginia looked at Korbin, who was too silent for too many moments. "What's wrong?" she asked, noticing he was grasping his head.

"I don't know. My head just started ringing."

Her teammates flooded the open radio channels, cheering for each other and discussing the highlights of the game. She remained silent, trying to think of anything else she could say or do to get Korbin to connect more to the memory of his soul. *If he even has Charles's soul, and I'm not just crazy.*

"Virginia, you and your copilot will need to see me in the port master's tower as soon as you two dock your ISV," Coach Matz said into their radio.

"Did you hear that?" she asked. His headset was on his lap, and he was staring out the window. "Hey, Korbin," she said softly.

He looked at her.

"We've been found out. Matz just instructed us to meet her in the port master's tower."

He sighed through his gaze out the window. She wondered what he was thinking as they sat among the stars, hoping he was remembering something.

The port master broke the silence inside the cabin. "ISV 11, return to port."

Virginia set the coordinates for their descent. Before the ISV began catching speed toward the red planet, she said to Korbin, "I still want you to test the metal of my pendant. It's important to me."

"That's right. I totally forgot. We'll do it this week. We'll find out just exactly what that pendant is made of."

"Thanks, Korbin. I just know it holds some information that we both must see."

Maybe he is sensing his soul right now and he just hasn't said anything. And maybe when he realizes that my pendant is made from the same element as the Unity Stone, he'll put all the pieces together. And then we can finally live happily ever after—again.

Virginia and Korbin made their way to the port master's tower, passing the vending machines, where Amos was soothing an upset Nicolette.

"Amos told me what's going on," she said quietly. "Just because I didn't say a word to anyone doesn't mean that I'm not mad at you for not just being honest and asking me to join your mission. You forced me into it instead."

Virginia hung her head. "I'm sorry. It didn't even cross my mind to trust you."

They met their doom at the top of the port master's tower, where he and Coach Matz were sitting there waiting for them.

"I thought something was wrong with my ISV, so I grabbed Korbin, and Nicolette was nowhere..."

Coach Matz held up her open palm, and Virginia stopped talking. "I know everything that goes on with my team." She nudged the port master with her elbow, and he placed the fried electric panel from the locker room door on the table in front of him.

Virginia could feel the heat from Korbin standing next to her. The lie she had convinced herself to be true wasn't going to hold up.

Coach Matz broke the uncomfortable silence. "Korbin is on our team's support crew. He is not on the flight team and is many exams away from having a license to fly in space. You two and whatever you're up to made your team's win tonight null and void. The consequence for your actions is to relinquish your win."

"But tonight's loss will—" Virginia began to argue.

"Okay, Coach Matz," Korbin interrupted. "This is a generous punishment for our wrongdoings. Is there anything else?"

She stared him in the eye. "I think the embarrassment of you two going to the Main Conservatory and giving your team's award to Alcetra will be enough."

Korbin sighed in relief as they walked down the stairs.

"The team is going to hate me," Virginia said.

A small string band in the conservatory's center was winding down the evening, ushering the Singles to head home for the night, as the two teams began to take their seats at their designated tables for a late dinner.

As soon as Heath sat down, Virginia whispered in his ear a brief version of what had happened and what she was supposed to do.

The disappointment on his face was heartbreaking.

"I want to scold you, to tell you how terrible you are for doing this. But I'm sure you already know, and how the rest of our team will see you moving forward is punishment enough. Whatever reason you did this, I hope it was worth it," he said.

Amos strolled in with cameras blazing. Virginia flashed him the shame in her eyes and asked him to turn all his cameras off. She stood in front of the Alcetra team captain, waiting with dismay for the remainder of her teammates to arrive, so they too could know what a terrible thing she had done.

"I loused up," Virginia said once all her teammates were seated. "I employed an unlicensed pilot as my copilot, which in turn voided our win. I'm required to give our award to Alcetra."

A few Nos team members snarled and complained. Heath smiled sympathetically at her, and Nicolette and Amos got up and hugged her.

Nos's co-captain handed Alcetra's team captain the blue-lit glass trophy, then turned to Virginia and snarled, "I hope you're happy with your selfish little stunt to make sure your home team won."

The energy at her table was hostile, and she was embarrassed, but Korbin stayed next to her throughout dinner, talking incessantly, leaving her little space to feel bad. "Hey, how about I walk you to your room tonight," he said after her peach pie had sat uneaten for twenty minutes. He looked across the table at Amos, who was roaring with laughter with Heath and the others, who were beginning to forget Virginia's betrayal. "That way your roomie can stay late for more of whatever they're laughing at."

It was an hour past curfew for everyone who wasn't volunteering to clean up the conservatory or wasn't with one of the Spaceball teams, leaving no competition in the Main Hall for a conversation to be heard. "I know that you got all the embarrassment tonight and I had all the fun. Is there any way I can make it up to you?"

"Yes. Let's go test the metal of my Ananta."

"Right now? Virginia, I... er, we could get in serious trouble if we get caught down there this time in the morning."

She dropped her head and continued walking to her room. "How about in the morning then?"

"Of course," he replied.

"Korbin, do you ever see certain numbers? Like the same ones all the time?"

"Oh my! Yeah. The number 211 has been following me around since about a week before my accident. Seems like no matter when I look at the time it's 2:11 or 12:11 or 1:22. Why do you ask?"

"Really, 2:11?" She looked at him strangely, trying to remember all the places she'd seen the number 211. "I see a lot of numbers too—it's like they're following me."

They arrived at Virginia's suite, and Korbin laughed. "Door 211. Would you believe that!"

She was shocked. "Wow," she said, smiling with a contented breath. "Maybe they do guide us to where we need to be."

"No one is actually dead until the ripples they cause in the world die away."

~ Terry Pratchett

CHAPTER 13

The autonomous helicopter Ingenuity, which arrived on Mars in February 2021, attached to rover Perseverance, flew for over 1000 days, until it retired in 2024, proving that flight is possible in the thin Martian atmosphere.

"Where ya going?" Amos asked Virginia, watching her fasten her boots on the bench next to the suite door.

"To sit with Korbin in Port 1. He was supposed to test my Ananta on Monsol, but his father was in the lab all sol and night, so he promised me he would test it this sol, while his father is traveling. I'm gonna wait with him there so he doesn't forget."

"Do you think you two are close to courting again?"

"I hope so. Soon. Right now, though, I think we're in the just-friends zone. My only hope is he sees that the metal of my pendant is composed of the same thing as the Unity Stone and realizes that we are..."

"Destined? A Royal Union?"

She tried to hide her sadness, faking a smile. "Of course! If this is all real, that is. If Grandmother's clues and Farro's clues and Mister and Missus's clues aren't all just a figment of my imagination."

"Ah, don't worry. It'll work out. And if it doesn't, you have Frankie—and of course, you have me!" He flaunted, lifting his chin with the top of his hand. "Who is about to go make some crazy news so everyone will stop talking about the Nos forfeiture to Alcetra last week."

She smirked away her shame.

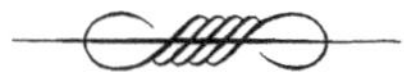

Korbin seemed happy to see her. Virginia sat on the ground next to him while he wrenched away, listening to him explain the engine system in the courier plane he was working on, a plane needed in a few hours to transport supplies to the city of Hydra, only a few hundred kilometers away.

"What time do you think you'll be done so we can go test the metal of my pendant?"

"I came in early this morning to work on this plane so I could leave early to do just that!" He slid out from under the plane and flashed her a reassuring smile.

Time passed as she handed him tools and they chatted about everything and nothing at all. Virginia was drawn to look at the time on her transmitter. 12:09.

"Hey Korbin, I'm going to go up the hall and get a snack."

"I'm done with this. I'll meet you there after I clean up."

Hall 2 was filled with older citizens leisurely strolling between the old shops and eateries in the Galleria and families with older children pacing around the aid station, likely concerned for an elderly loved one. Virginia felt around inside the depths of her pocket for one of the coin storage units Ms. West had given her. She went straight to the pretzel stand and bought a fresh-baked pretzel with a warm creamy dipping sauce for herself and Korbin, then took a seat on a bench and people-watched as she waited.

Within moments, he arrived with his head hung, pushing his hair back as he walked up to her. She handed him his pretzel and drink. He drank like a parched camel and looked at the pretzel bag silently.

"What is it?" Virginia asked, sensing there was some bad news on the way.

"I got called to Port 3. I have to help unload the freight vehicle." He turned his gaze and a hopeful smile toward her. "But it won't take long, and as soon as I'm done, I'll go straight to my father's lab and call you when I'm on my way." He pointed toward Extension 220.

"Your father's lab." She whispered because it would be a horrid show to release the screams of disappointment and betrayal that were breaking her heart. "Okay. Later then."

Virginia watched him walk away, assuming that he would never test the pendant, never know what exactly had happened with his accident, and never get to see her whole life coming together in one moment.

She allowed time to pass as the sadness, that was as an angry Martian windstorm inside her body, settle.

She answered a call from Heath. "Virginia, we are doing a safety inspection on your ISV. Can you get here to discuss performance of the vehicle from your last flight?"

Standing in front of the doors to Port 3, she hoped that Korbin wouldn't think she was following him. She looked at the time. 2:11. *Hmmm... Korbin's numbers. Maybe I'm supposed to be here.* She walked up to the viewing tower to find a way to avoid being seen by Korbin. Instead, she was fixated on the Dot freight plane that had just arrived.

The extra-tall guy, his face shadowed by his hood, and Korbin stood at the door of the large Dot plane. She watched the fat-bellied Mr. Dot, the owner of the one and only galactic freight company, exit the plane, and the extra-tall goon almost immediately introduced him to

Korbin. Curiously, Korbin didn't join the group unloading the freight, but rather stayed and conversed with Mr. Dot.

Next, a terribly ordinary girl exited, wearing the same brown zip-up pantsuit that every other Upper Ender on Alcetra wore, with long straight brown hair and straight eyebrows and lips and a figure that were just as straight. Virginia recognized her at once. Known in Alcetra as the daughter of freight, Jayne Dot stepped off the plane and greeted Korbin. They didn't hug, but nor did they stand awkwardly next to each other like they were strangers—they had definitely met before.

Is this why he just ditched me? They've been talking. They know each other. Why?

Her hopes of ever being happy again began leaving her body like a flock of birds. Virginia had to stop watching after the Dot girl's round mother hobbled off the plane and introduced herself to Korbin. She took a moment to use the pain to imagine something lovely. All she could picture was Charles's smile, all she could remember was his laugh as their untethered limbs floundered in the weightlessness of space in a flight simulator.

As she began to walk away from the window, she sensed something familiar and looked back to see her best friend bounce off the plane, excitedly swinging her long silky black hair behind her back and grabbing Frankie's brother's hand as he exited with his twin.

"What? Frankie's here too! Did everyone know about this except me?"

Relief and disappointment battled each other in her head. Confused and frightened, Virginia just began running, trying to escape the emotions that were spinning feverishly inside her body. She ran up the Main Hall, through the conservatory where the Uniteds were preparing for the night's dance. Without thought, she headed toward Conservatory 5.

Just inside the connector, Mister stopped her. "Shouldn't you be getting ready..."

"...for the big dance tonight?" Missus finished his question.

The rest of the planet stopped moving, and only the three of them stood animated in the connector between Conservatories 6 and 5.

"Why are you here? And right now?" Virginia asked the pair.

"We just wanted to let you know..." Missus began.

"...that we are here for you," Mister continued.

Puzzled, she looked around, but the conservatories in front and behind her were blurry. Mister and Missus were the only thing that was clear. Virginia lifted her hands to her face. "Is it all over? Did Korbin make his choice?" she cried into her hands. "Am I supposed to go home with Frankie and Paden?"

"The boy mirrors the leader," Mister said, moving closer to Missus.

Virginia looked up, scrunching her face. "A mirror... I saw that before. But what does it mean?"

"It will be fine," Missus said.

"Once you make your choice, *many* will come to aid in the Union," Mister added to his original statement.

"The energies of the Royals are many," Missus whispered and winked before she pointed toward the Main Conservatory's dome, which was barely visible from where they stood.

"I think I've heard all of this before," Virginia mumbled.

"You can only believe in one truth," Missus said.

Virginia looked down at the floor, processing what she knew they were telling her. "Like the choice of magic or the choice of safety."

"Exactly. One is the truth, and the other is a lie," Mister said.

"And we can only serve one master," Missus added. "But you must hurry, girl."

"His future roads are building as we speak," Mister added in a whisper.

Virginia found herself sitting comfortably at the same Unity Festival table where she'd sat with her friends since the first week she arrived. Tonight it was decorated brightly in the Unity color of purple. She looked above her at the Ananta, a steadfast beacon of hope for the Singles hoping to Unite Royal. Thoughts of Korbin filled her head. *Were the clues Grandmother, Farro, and Mister and Missus told me true? Or did I only interpret it all to mean what I wanted it to be?* She stared at the slight flickering in the glowing symbol, trying to put together pieces, discover which was the lie and which was the truth.

The lines thickened at the vendor tables, while the Uniteds happily filled the cups in front of everyone at the table with fruit, likely brought in from Alcetra. She was relieved when Jeremiah and Ellis showed up with their regular low-key smiles to interrupt her heavy thoughts. Next, Amos arrived with a camera held up high, recording her. She forced a smile and waved, stopping when a soft pair of hands that held a familiar scent covered her eyes. "Paden?"

"Yep! And Frankie's here too! And of course *my* true love, *Jaaames...*"

She looked behind Paden. "Where are they anyway?"

"They went to the observatory. Did you know they have one here? You and I are on our way to meet them there," Paden said, pulling out Virginia's chair.

James and Frankie were exiting the planetarium as Virginia and Paden neared the doors. As they walked toward each other, Virginia admired Frankie's stature. He was strong, graceful, and confident.

She blushed, taken aback by his perfectly peach lips, glowing caramel complexion, and bright white teeth, his perfect smile taking center stage in front of his long wavy black hair, pulled tightly behind his head in a ponytail. Dread flooded her bloodstream—soon she would have to make a final choice.

"All the telescopes are taken," Frankie said, pointing at the observatory behind him with his thumb.

"That's okay," Paden said. "They'll be serving dinner soon."

As they walked side by side back toward the conservatory, Frankie didn't have anything to say, and the entire walk down the Upper End Hall was cumbersome as Virginia's thoughts raced anxiously. When was he going to ask her to court officially? Or go home with him? How would she reply?

She was relieved as soon as they stepped into the noisy conservatory, filled with happy people and fiery music. The only way he could ask anything through this noise would be to pull her to the side or even back to one of the halls, and that didn't seem like a move Frankie would make.

"How did the Dot girl get seated with Korbin tonight?" Amos whispered to Virginia when he took his seat like a plane crash landing.

She looked in the direction he was pointing to see for herself, and something between anger and sorrow built up inside her. She took a quick breath in through her nose and a deep exhale, to keep from imagining any harm with her incomplete powers.

Frankie's here. I'm okay. Everything is going to work out great.

"I think those two would make great news. Nobody really likes her, and he's kinda popular around here," Amos whispered.

Dinner came, and Virginia managed to keep an eye on Korbin, who didn't appear to be comfortable. He kept his hands under the table and his shoulders drawn into his chest while the Dot girl smiled as if she'd just captured a herself a mate.

Jeremiah and Ellis were the first on the dance floor. After three songs, Paden and James finished feeding each other cut fruit pieces with their fingers and made their way to it too, leaving her and Frankie with nothing other than each other.

During each song, she filled Frankie's ear with as much useless information as she could, keeping him from asking her any important questions she wasn't ready for.

Finally, a slow song came on. "Will you dance with me?" Frankie asked.

She didn't want to. Korbin was dancing with the Dot. *Maybe if he sees me dancing with someone else, he'll realize his soul is telling him how wrong it is.* Maybe it would be a good opportunity, within the safety of Frankie's presence, to ask Korbin about testing her pendant again, since that seemed to be the last and only chance she had at him realizing who she was. "Yes, of course. I love this song."

She danced silently with Frankie, reveling in the idea of using her powers to dissolve Dot's dress until there was nothing left or to put a swarm of invisible flies by her ears and watch her shoo them away like a mad person. Virginia didn't even realize she was smiling until she heard Frankie say, "I didn't know you like to dance so much. I'm glad you had such a good time."

Before she had a chance to ask Korbin about testing the pendant, they were leaving the dance floor, following Paden and James, who were following behind Jeremiah and Ellis. The announcer was giving instructions for the end-of-the-night exits.

"I'd like to walk you to your room," Frankie said.

Great. Here it comes. I'll have to decide. She swallowed hard, nodding in agreement.

She walked next to Frankie with her gaze in front of each dreadful step she took closer to her suite. She tried to listen to the conversation Paden and James were having behind them, but their words were inaudible. Sensing Frankie looking at her, she looked up to meet his gaze with an efforted smile, wondering what he was thinking.

"My suite is down here," Virginia said, pointing to the extension on the right as she began making the turn toward it.

Paden ran up and whispered, "Gin, I'm staying with you tonight. I'll come down as soon as Frankie walks you to your room."

The walk down the extension was more uncomfortable than any other conversation or moment she'd had with Frankie. *Will he ask me to come home now? For an official courtship? For a kiss?*

In the last couple steps of silence before they stopped in front of her door, she tried to make it as simple as possible in her head: *Being with Korbin does feel as easy and natural as it did with Charles. What I wouldn't do to Unite with the joy of my soul. But is it really all real? If it was real, he wouldn't be with that Dot.*

If I Unite with Frankie, I'm safe, with my plant DNA work, with my best friend, in the city I grew up in.

What a dilemma. I need a sign!

They finally reached her door. "Suite number 211, eh?" Frankie said.

Virginia smiled. "Yeah. Good ole 211. What suite are you and James in?"

"Suite 88 on Extension 8, of all places." He laughed.

Tension released its tight grip on her muscles, and she exhaled with a smile. "Frankie, I just can't do it. I'm so, so sorry. You are sweet, kind, charming as can be, and heavenly to look at too. But I cannot court you. I cannot Unite with you. My path is to believe, to have faith that the soul of my true love has found his way back to me. And I'm sorry, but I believe that Korbin is, oddly enough, the one I need to Unite with."

The expression on Frankie's face was like he'd just been punched in the gut. "I don't understand."

"Yeah, me neither." She frowned and furrowed her brows. "You are more of a prize than I could have ever hoped for. Part of me can't believe I'm making this choice, off of a little voice in my head telling me that someone else is the love of my soul." She hung her head. "Perpetual love even."

"A little voice in your head," Frankie repeated. He covered his mouth with his hand and shook his head, silent.

He looked disgusted.

"Virginia, I think you're going through something right now. I'm going to give you a little space, but I'll be here for you," he said and pulled her into his embrace.

Although she found comfort in his warmth, she remained confident that this decision was not one that would ever lead her back to him.

"Death is a reminder to live fully."

~ Ram Dass

CHAPTER 14

The Martian atmosphere is about 100 times thinner than Earth's, composed mainly of carbon dioxide with very little oxygen. Humans couldn't breathe in the open atmosphere.

Virginia came in hot, her eyes blazing flames, as she slammed her bag down onto the table where she found Amos eating a snack from one of the only eateries open late at night in the Lower End cafeteria.

"Nice to see you too!" he teased.

"Everything was supposed to change after I made my 'choice.' But nothing has changed. *At all*!"

"It's only been a week."

"I'm scared, Amos. I don't know why I did this. Only four more weeks left of the Unity Festival. I thought it was gonna be easy. Mister and Missus told me once I made a choice, he would 'be on the path to truth'! Some path to truth. That yellow-bellied boy wasn't working on our ISVs this sol—he was sitting at the table gettin' cozy with that scrawny, stringy-haired Jayne Dot. Now Frankie's gone, along with my promising future as Alcetra's plant

DNA scientist, if Korbin doesn't realize who I am. I'm sick! It's like it's all a nightmare." She dropped her head into her hands.

"What else did Mister and Missus say?" Amos asked in between bites of his hot veggie hoagie.

"Ugh! I don't know," she replied from her buried head. "Something about numbers, of course, and many helping or something. Nothing that made any sense."

Virginia looked at the time on her transmitter. "Oh look, it's 10:09. There's always the same numbers around, since before I left Alcetra. More nines than I can count. I have to go find Mister and Missus. Ask them what is going on with my choice."

"I'll come too. I need to find a new news source since the Big Dot threatened my new streams of income if I ever put his plain Jayne daughter on my news channel again."

"What?"

"Yeah. I followed Korbin and her around the other sol, and Alcetra gave her a bunch of disapproving comments. Big Dot no-likey. And honey, there ain't no way I'm gonna risk my money or my career over that girl. She doesn't even look good on camera."

Inside Conservatory 2, on their way to the administration offices, they noticed Professor Xander walking toward the shadows of the connector to Conservatory 1, which they knew was closed off and prohibited, along with Hall 1.

Amos and Virginia locked suspicious eyes.

"We have to see. Do you have your glasses?"

She pulled them out of her pocket and put them on.

"Be Sofia."

"No way, those two have been seen together far too often. She could be over there," Virginia whispered and looked around the conservatory, where she saw a Rock Friend rolling toward Hall 2. She grabbed Amos's hand. "We'll be a Rock Friend."

They transformed instantly and rolled their way toward Conservatory 1, posting up at the opening of the connector, just like the other Rock Friends.

Xander had just finished a call with someone on his transmitter. They listened to him grappling with the locked door to the conservatory, holding their breath until the door creaked open and the click of Xander's walking stick faded. She took off her glasses, and they rushed to catch the heavy closing door. She grabbed it and took a deep breath, opening it just enough for her and Amos to peer into the conservatory behind it.

"I don't see him," he whispered.

The pair slithered through the partially open door into a conservatory jungle. Unmaintained trees and vines blocked out the light from the setting sun. They stood silently in awe with their backs against a dark wall of overgrown flora.

Amos nudged Virginia. "To the right," he whispered.

They peered at something moving in the shadows where the Upper End Hall came into the conservatory and watched closely as the movement revealed a human form, preceded by Xander's walking stick, followed by his cape.

PSSSHHHHEEW!

An echoing sound filled the conservatory, followed by waves of red fire—like a glow emanating from the ground. Xander was stepping on something atop the glow, heading in the direction of the Upper End Hall.

The pair hugged the shadows of the wall, scurrying toward the spot he'd left.

"Lava," Virginia whispered. Underground lava kept the city warm, through tubes under the halls and extensions, but most civilians never saw it.

Their eyes followed the flow of lava through the center of the conservatory, tracking the tall, narrow silhouette of Xander, walking stick in hand, as he floated down the hot, hot lava stream, clearly atop something cool enough to stand on.

"Whoa. We gotta follow him."

Virginia shook her head. "No. I gotta go find Mister and Missus. I need to get United, not discover what Xander is doing sailing along an erupted lava tube," she argued.

"But it's like eleven p.m.—Mister and Missus are probably in their apartment, not their office."

She looked at her transmitter. 11:18. "Yeah, okay. You're right," she capitulated, and they both searched the ground for something that looked like whatever Xander was standing on.

"Rocks, some piece of an old hyperwalk..." Amos mumbled.

Virginia waved her hand in disagreement. "They'll all get hot. Maybe the lava rock won't get too hot, but—"

"What if this isn't just any ole lava rock? What if it's one of Xander's 'rock experiments'?"

"What if it's not, and our feet start burning halfway down the lava flow?" she argued.

Amos rolled a large rock over to the lava tube and tipped it in.

PSSSHHHHEEW!

The rock bobbed up and down on top of the lava. He touched it gently with his fingers. "It's not hot."

"Yet!"

"It'll be fine. We can stand on our coats if it gets hot or jump to the side where there's higher ground– along the domes foundation," Amos said and stepped on the rock as it slowly began to drift toward the darkness of the Upper End Hall.

Virginia found her own rock and plunked it into the flowing lava stream. Before she stepped on it, she noticed Amos, ahead of her, was dancing atop his rock.

It's getting hot.

He was floating in the middle of the lava stream, the metal bar he'd found to use as a paddle unsuccessful at directing him to the side.

She ran to the end of the path and tossed him a vine that hung from above. He couldn't catch it. She grabbed a fallen tree branch, stretching it far into the hall, but it was still too far out of his reach.

Out of nowhere, Sofia floated by on something shiny that looked very different than a rock. She was moving quickly, clearly in a hurry toward Amos, but she pointed deep into Virginia's already frightened face, the snakes atop her head hissing angrily, extending inches from Virginia's eyes. "My office—immediately."

She took a few steps back and watched Sofia ride swiftly atop the lava until she caught up with Amos, finally relieved when she saw their silhouettes jump to safety.

Virginia hovered outside the office that could quite possibly be the most dreadful place in the city, wishing that Korbin would show up with some brilliant plan and rescue her again. Wondering if Amos was injured, knowing that she needed to quickly come up with a great excuse for being in Conservatory 1. Worried about her future and toying with the idea of hijacking a plane out of Port 1 and going home to Alcetra.

She looked down at the clock. 11:36.

The nine is still here.

She spun around, deciding to go to Port 1, to at least attempt an escape of some sort, maybe stow away on someone else's voyage. When she neared the end of the extension into Hall 2, she had a strange urge to look behind her, but saw no one when she turned around. Curious, she continued on, toward the end of the extension, which seemed to stretch in complete silence for an eternity. The eeriness grew stranger when a purple spark of light up ahead caught her eye. She followed it to where it disappeared—in front of the last door on the extension. Mister and Missus were standing in the doorway of their office, shining their bright, welcoming smiles. *That's weird. What are they doing here?* They looked as if they were waiting for her. Did they know what was going on?

"See the clock," Mister said.

Virginia looked at the time on her transmitter. 11:54.

"The nine shows the way to completion," Missus whispered, ushering Virginia into the dark room, only a dim purple light flickering behind their shadows. Missus tapped the transmitter in the center of the round table and sat down. "Sit with us. You will meet the Legends now. They have to test you because..."

"...the mission is dangerous, in a battle against he who benefits in keeping you separated," Mister finished.

Virginia suppressed a shiver. The air was heavy, the darkness mysterious, but she trusted Mister and Missus. Something important was going on here.

From the depths of the dark walls appeared an orange hologram, and then another. A man and a woman smiled and sat at the table opposite Virginia, images of people she had never seen before.

"Orange holograms?" she whispered aloud, remembering the orange glow in her pendant.

"Their powers go beyond our universe," Mister replied softly.

"Greater than Royal powers because they are like you and the soul of Korbin..." Missus continued.

"...meeting again in the same lifetime," Mister finished.

Overwhelmed, Virginia remained silent, her heartbeat heavy as more glowing orange holograms emerged from the dark wall; a total of twelve sat at the table when finally a purple hologram danced out of the wall with her banana cane overhead. Grandmother did not sit down, but instead stood behind Virginia. Thoughts went around in circles in her head. *Are they people who are dead like Grandmother?*

A hologram of a tall and strong elderly man spoke up. "Virginia, the boy's future begins with you." *He looks like Mr. Bryant, if Mr. Bryant was eighty-five years old.* She narrowed in to pay close attention to him as he continued.

"But the boy's future has gotten out of control, and for you to Unite with him in time, you will need to cross through the portal into Anywhere and eliminate the roads of his future that are being created as we speak."

She rolled her eyes and took a frustrated breath. *Great, a portal to anywhere? Is this like a black hole to my own death? Does this guy even know what he's saying to me?*

An older female hologram spoke. "There is a powerful force there who cannot take form, but he is very angry that you two are so close and has much to gain if you don't Unite with the boy. We have everything to gain when you do."

More holograms talking in clues. I hope they figure out how to tell me things straight, she thought, her eyes squinting at their images, trying to decide where they came from.

The hologram of another man who reminded her of her father spoke next. "If you do not take the mission, you and the boy are bound to an unhappy life—and if you do not finish the mission, you will be bound to Anywhere until you gain enough power to return to human form."

Frustrated with all the riddles, Virginia spoke up. "I don't even know who you all are or what you're talking about—anywhere, mission, portal!"

"Virginia, dear, Anywhere is where souls wait until space is available for them to have a new form. The Dutch, a formless yet powerful soul, can only be freed when he keeps two souls who find each other twice in the same lifetime apart. He will be there, fighting. You must defeat him by completing the mission. If you fail the mission, you will take the place of the Dutch and be trapped there."

She looked at them with concern. "You're telling me to risk my life in the great unknown and fight some angry soul who has been bound to some strange place in another universe? I think I should just go live on Earth with my aunt!"

"Your soul will grieve without him," another orange hologram said.

"Or the boy—he is the other key—he could take the mission," blurted out a gentle voice. It was a hologram of a girl with a kind and compassionate smile who looked like she was the same age as Virginia.

She laughed to herself at the thought of Korbin taking some strange mission because a bunch of orange holograms told him to. "Yeah, so it would be me taking this mission to make sure that the soul—presumably of my deceased boyfriend—and I get to spend forever together."

The young girl spoke up gently. "Love never ends. You must believe."

Virginia stared at the kind-faced hologram with her mouth open.

"Because this mission puts your entire life on the line, requiring the greatest resilience, you must first pass our test, a brief preparation for your purpose ahead, so we will know you are of sound mind and body to go on the mission, to change the future that the boy is currently creating," the hologram who resembled the elderly Mr. Bryant said.

"Whoa! No way. I'm not changing someone's future." Virginia drew her mouth down. "And if I have to put my life on the line for someone who I believe has the soul of my true love but doesn't even recognize my soul... I think I just need to accept my Earthly fate." She stood up from the table.

The young girl's hologram got up and moved toward her. "Wait," she pleaded with Virginia, who was searching for the exit. "You won't be alone out there. You've never been alone." She drew a glowing purple Ananta in front of Virginia's face. "Many are here, everywhere. Their powers are great enough to protect you—even in Anywhere."

Virginia shook her head. "I want to. Well, I did. But I'm tired of believing in what I can't see. And all this has just gotten a little too serious for me."

"Look," the girl said, pointing toward the hologram scene that was taking shape in the center of the large round table.

It was Korbin and the Dot girl. They were together, but he wasn't smiling. He was just there. He had a job working in an office where the Big Dot stood behind his back. He had a son, who died, and as he aged, Korbin became thinner, his back more hunched and his countenance more heavy.

"But this is against his will—shouldn't he be choosing me?" Virginia muttered.

"Does this look like a future that Korbin would love? Wouldn't you breathe in someone's mouth if they needed air to live?" one of the holograms said.

The hologram image in the center of the table changed to a scene of an aging Virginia watering her plants on a rooftop in a city on Earth, caring for her bedridden aunt in between. She too looked sad and frail as time went on, aging with the little world around her.

"Can I just change *my* future?"

"You two are bound. You can only save each other, not yourselves."

"Bound." She exhaled the word. Virginia dropped her head and shook it as images of Charles's face and the moments they'd shared played like a movie in her head. "I want to be happy again too—and if I disregard all these clues and holograms and magic coming to tell me what to do, neither of us will have a chance to feel joy again."

The older version of Mr. Bryant spoke. "You're here because you are worthy of happiness, because you are pure—because your purpose is more grand than you can see from these small trials."

The young hologram girl walked to the other side of the room, where a doorway appeared. "Begin the journey here. Everything will be fine. Just know."

Grandmother crossed over to her and laughed toward the sky. "Fear is only an illusion. You have already been given all the gifts for success!"

Virginia walked toward the open door, which led into a dark, unknown abyss. She wanted to cry. "Can I die in here?" she asked the girl.

"Never alone. You are always safe," the orange hologram whispered.

As soon as the door closed behind her, all light faded, leaving Virginia in an eerie darkness. She could feel fear traveling through the blood of her veins. She was angry that this was her path—that her path to a love that lasted forever couldn't be an easy one. As soon as the anger that had surfaced like boiling water subsided, she reached behind her, feeling for the door she had just come through. Nothing.

She reminded herself of the words from the hologram girl with the kind and compassionate face. *You're safe.*

She took a deep breath and said aloud, "Fear is only an illusion. This is just a test. A preparation. Grandmother is right outside the door. Unfortunately, it's also the door that you can't find. But just breathe anyway."

Whumpf... whumpf... whumpf.

The sound of something heavy falling through the air startled her.

Whumpf... whumpf... whumpf.

The sounds were coming closer. She began scooting backward.

Whumpf... whumpf... whumpf.

Whatever was falling was moving faster and getting closer. She scooted backward more, hoping to back into the door she'd come through.

Whumpf... whumpf... whumpf.

She moved herself backward , becoming still, remembering to breathe. Waiting for more of whatever was falling.

A dozen more deep breaths and still nothing. Whatever it was seemingly stopped. A dim yellow light in the far distance became brighter, revealing twelve golden swords hanging from a black abyss right in front of her. They began to slowly sway, one in front of the other, forming an *X*.

What am I supposed to do with this?

A dim image of Charles passed in front of her—he was smiling, and she smiled back. He suddenly vanished and came back again, standing in front of her, smiling, his hands fiddling in his pockets, right before he turned around and made his way through the swords—unscathed.

He's trying to show me something, she thought and reached into the depths of her pockets. She pulled out a handful of little things, but the twine that she'd recently used in the lab with Farro caught her attention.

She made an attempt to toss the twine into the swords, to determine if they were as sharp as they looked, but the twine itself wasn't heavy enough to reach. Finding nothing else in her pocket that she could part with if it were cut, she took off her sock, rolled it up, and tied it to the end of the twine, then tossed it into the swords.

When she pulled it back, the sock remained on the end of the twine. Her heart pounded.

It's definitely heavy enough to reach, but I better try it again.

She moved herself closer and swung the sock on the twine into the swords again. Still, nothing was cut.

What if it wasn't cut because the swords weren't crossing at the exact right time? I should try again.

Again, the twine remained uncut. "Fear is only an illusion," she whispered.

As she stood looking at the swaying swords, she noticed Charles's shadow moving farther away.

Wait. I need you. Don't leave, she whispered with sorrow in her mouth.

She looked down at the ball of twine in her hands and ran toward the swords, running between them as soon as they opened. Holding on to the remaining sight of Charles's shadow, she ran through the next row of swords as they opened. And then the next... and then the next... until at last all six rows were behind her, and Charles's shadow was nowhere to be found.

She could hear the swish of the swords slowing behind her.

"Charles!" she cried out. She walked forward, searching for his shadow, trying to catch the echo of his fading laugh. "I really miss you," she said softly as her eyes released the heavy grief in her heart.

Virginia stood still, disappointment, loneliness, and sadness wrapping themselves around her, comforting her in the dark, until whispers of a multitude of voices finally broke the silence.

She yelled into the black space, "Who's there? Hello?"

There was no response, just the faint whispers of the unseen voices. She started to feel a heat rising from below. It became hotter, but it wasn't too bad. She walked around, looking for a cool spot, only to find it getting hotter under her feet. She became annoyed. There was nothing she could do to stop it.

"What's going on here!" she screamed to the unknown voices, hoping for a reply.

Nothing.

The heat finally became unbearable, so she took off the coat that Amos's mother had made her and put it under her feet. *I feel like I'm in a nightmare. And I chose it*, she thought as defeat began to creep into her head like a disease.

And along came anger, quickly heating up her head. Had Korbin any sense, she wouldn't be in this torture. Rage had taken over, and she began to cry.

Something inside her told her to look up.

There was a small fire in the middle of the blackness. Panic rushed in, heating her skin, and she ran away, but more fires began erupting throughout the floor, then growing bigger.

An image of her mother and father appeared in front of her, and she stopped running.

"Try breathing," her father said.

"Papa?" she asked.

"Yes, darling daughter," he whispered gently. He took a deep breath in, and she took a deep breath in with him. He exhaled all of the air, and she did too.

She could feel the panic slowly exit her body.

"Water," her mother whispered.

"Water?" Virginia turned to her mother, who did not reply. She looked at her father's gentle smile and kind eyes.

"The solution can only be understood during calm," he said.

WATER!

She reached into her pockets, watching the items move around through the fabric of her skirt, thinking about the little item she was searching for. "Aha!" She pulled out the little bottle of magic water that Farro had given her. She held it up, looked for her mother and father's approval, but they were gone.

Disappointed, she dropped her shoulders and hung her head, holding the bottle upside down and shaking it as she walked forward. Steam came up from the floor, and as she walked, the fires around her went out.

An orange light caught her eye. She looked up to see all twelve of the holograms clapping and congratulating her.

"Although that space could not take your life, only test your determination, you can now see that you have everything it takes to overcome fear," the hologram who looked like a much older Mr. Bryant said. "You also have the help of Many that you need to win in the place beyond the portal that could take your life or save so many."

Virginia was too overwhelmed and too exhausted to ask any questions.

The hologram of the young girl began to speak. "You see, a portal to another time or place can be found with the right coordinates and the right speed on your ISV. That's how you will get there. That's how the Dutch got to Anywhere, where he went to bring back his wife.

"The gatekeeper, Hadley, has rules though. She will let you into Anywhere to find the soul you're looking for, but you have to finish what you start. The Dutch broke Hadley's rules when she instructed him to wait at the gate for his wife's soul for thirteen months. Because he broke her rule and went to search for his wife after ten months, he lost his true love, and Hadley punished him and banished him to Anywhere—until someone else comes to take his place."

"And if I don't finish changing Korbin's future, I'll be taking the Dutch's place in Anywhere?"

"Well, Korbin holds the other key. He could finish the mission if something were to happen to you, before you lose your chance to Unite on the last sol of the Unity Festival. But by then, the Many, the energy of the living Royals, will be made strong enough to protect you."

"And if something happens to Korbin?"

"Then the Dutch will have succeeded in keeping you two separated. Korbin will be stuck in Anywhere, and so will you. The Dutch will be released with powers like ours," one of the orange holograms said, looking at all of the others at the table.

"There are only a few of us who have found each other after death in the same lifetime, like you and Korbin, who have these powers. More powerful than any other. Powers that can move planets and create planets. Powers that let us access various galaxies and lifetimes and even alter time and space. But if the Dutch attains these powers, he will likely use them for his own gain."

Virginia folded her face into her hands as the group of holograms whispered among themselves. After many minutes of being lost in her thoughts and fears, she lifted her head. "I don't even know who you are, just a bunch of holograms, and you're telling me that I'm not only responsible for a reunion with my soul's true love, but now I'm responsible for the fate of the universe as we know it."

"The powers of the Royals, the powers of the Legends, will not let you fail," the young gentle-voiced girl said.

Grandmother Blane moved toward Virginia and smiled a devious smile. "Just know."

"Just know," Mister and Missus whispered.

"Believe," another hologram said.

"Just know" echoed in whispers around the room.

Virginia laughed out an overwhelmed breath. "Yeah. I *just know* this would be the craziest thing I ever did. Do you mind if I leave, take some space to think about what's going on?"

She was relieved to see Amos working at his desk inside their suite. "You're alive and not a rock!"

"Yeah, after Sofia saved me from burning to death, she threatened me, and then she jumped back on top of the lava and floated in the direction of Xander. That was it! I'm also surprised to be here. But now I'm really curious about what is going on in Nos's Conservatory 1."

"Yeah, what is Xander doing there?"

She told him where she'd been, everything about the orange holograms, the test of swords, the magic water, the mission to Anywhere, and about the Dutch.

"Sounds like you have a big choice to make, Virginia. What are you gonna do?"

She exhaled as much air as she could. "I don't know. I want to be as happy as I was before. I just have to decide if I want to..." She remembered Farro's clues. "Pay the tax to have it."

"Whenever sorrow comes, be kind to it. For God has placed a pearl in sorrow's hand."

~ Rumi

CHAPTER 15

NASA's InSight lander, which operated on Mars from 2018 to 2022, collected data using seismic waves generated by marsquakes, revealing a layer of fractured igneous rock saturated with liquid water, suggesting the planet's water did not escape into space, but instead filtered down into the crust.

Virginia opened her eyes to look at the time on her transmitter, sitting on her bedside table. The time read 5:00 in pale green glowing numbers.

Wondering why she was seeing a 5, she attempted to go back to sleep, but the decision to risk her life for happiness was as heavy as a Martian boulder resting on her chest. *How will I tell Paden that I chose Korbin? She is going to be heartbroken if she never sees me again.*

Why couldn't he have just tested my Ananta for me—then all this wouldn't have to happen. Maybe I should ask him one more time.

Daylight finally came, but her thoughts were still heavy. So heavy that she found herself in the Upper End cafeteria, standing in front of a coffee shop and breathing in the rich aromas of comfort. She walked up to the barista at the counter. "A sweet Neptune Café, please."

The barista handed her the hot drink with a puffy white cluster of sweet cream on top. She sat at a table with her extravagant drink cupped in her hand, sipping it slowly, when she saw Korbin and Jayne Dot walking nearby, looking cozy and close.

Guess I won't be asking him again. I've got to tell Mister and Missus that I'm ready to take the mission now.

Inside the room of the door that wouldn't close all the way, the Dutch was grinning from ear to ear. "Well done," he said to his group of helpers. "I believe this girl could be the one. Get them in the booth tonight, and I will test them for their Royal powers. If they test Royal, we will all have extraordinary powers to live the rest of our lives with."

The group began talking among themselves excitedly.

"I'm going to be mayor of Erbos and have new stuff show up at my door every sol," one whispered.

"I'll build my own spaceship that I can live on the rest of my life," another said.

"I will spy on everyone in the city and blackmail them with all the information I collect," another said. "Everyone will bow to me!"

Virginia looked at her classmates outside the lab, waiting to go in for class. But she couldn't. She had to make a move. At least try to save their love, their lives. She spotted Jeremiah and hurried to him. "If Farro asks... I'm not in class because I... I'm sick."

"Okay. Sure, Virginia, but what's going on? You don't look good."

Their classmates began strolling into class behind them. Virginia swallowed hard. "I may be dying this sol."

He drew back, his face shocked. "That sick?"

"Maybe. Well, no, hopefully not," she said, not wanting her friend to worry. "I'll be fine. Thanks for your concern." With effort, she flashed Jeremiah an encouraging smile, then hurried toward Mister and Missus's office.

They were standing in the doorway like they were waiting for her. "Are you here to see us?" Mister asked.

Virginia looked around, dreading the conversation that was about to happen. "Yeah, I am." She'd hoped they would invite her in to talk privately, but they didn't. They just stood there, smiling. "I'm here to ask you how I'm supposed to get to Anywhere... you know," she said with her eyes pressed open.

"There's no how, girl," Missus said.

"The numbers will lead you there," Mister began.

"I've been seeing a new number lately, five..." Virginia said. "But how is a number supposed to take me somewhere—er, Anywhere?"

"Five is the number of the future. Just follow..." Missus began.

"...your happiness," Mister finished.

She had come for answers and was frustrated that they wanted her to find happiness when her life, and the lives of Royal Uniteds, were on the line. "Happiness?" she asked, rolling her eyes unashamedly.

Mister raised his chin and laughed into the air. "Answers cannot come to you when you are worried, angry, or in any other negative place."

"The solutions make their way when you are thankful, generous, calm, and when you believe—when you are full!" Missus said, pointing to the space between her eyes, which was also known as the seat of the soul.

"Happy," Mister added.

Her brows raised, Virginia asked, "So the answer to going on a life-threatening mission to reunite with my true love is to get happy?"

Mister and Missus confirmed, nodding and smiling.

She walked away, confused and a little angry that they didn't have a solid plan for her to follow.

Get happy—then I need to spend time with Amos. She called him. "Where ya at?"

"Port 2, of all places," he replied.

"I can't get in there."

"Sure ya can, I'll tell them you're my assistant."

Virginia started toward Conservatory 3, where she could ride the hyperwalk down Hall 3 to Port 2, while having a few moments to get calm. She took a giant deep breath in through her nose and pushed a strong exhale out through her mouth. And continued repeatedly until she found herself very relaxed on the southbound hyperwalk.

Wow. That was GREAT. Now to be thankful. I'm thankful for my sweet dog at home, she thought, taking some time to remember little Ridgley, until she noticed a tingling sensation throughout her body. *Ms. West, Paden, Amos, my grandmother, my smarts, my clothes...* She thought about each until she felt the sensation again.

Suddenly, the hyperwalk ended and there was a long stretch to the doors of Port 2, along with a bright and exciting energy rising inside her.

Generous, she said to herself, looking around for an opportunity to be generous before she entered the port. She pulled up all the joy she'd ever experienced and with ease released a smile at the small children and teenagers who were entering the northbound hyperwalk next to her.

Time had vanished; space became merely a concept. The doors to Port 2, now directly in front of her feet, became blurry, dizzying even.

Come, girl, she heard the voice of her grandmother say, and she opened the doors into a blurry port. She searched through the haze for Amos's tall, lanky form, but distracted by a small flashing purple light in front of her, she took a step toward it, and then many, many more steps.

"Aah!" Virginia screeched, grasping her chest. Coach Matz was silently standing in front of her, next to an ISV—and the blurriness had disappeared.

Coach Matz chuckled without glee. "I'm just here to help," she said without moving her thin upper lip.

"Help with what?" Virginia was confused.

"To get you out in space so you can get to that portal. You'll take this spacecraft here," she said, tapping the stealthy matte-black Planet Protectors ISV behind her.

"You're in on this too?"

She nodded with lips pressed so tight they disappeared. "More than Many are helping the important couple, for the fate of all Royal Unions. You've never been alone on your journey. And you won't be alone out there either. I'll be on the radio, guiding you each step of the way. Now check your machine for safety and get strapped in. You leave to search for Korbin's future box on the green light," she said, then disappeared before Virginia could ask anything else.

She stood in front of the massive Planet Protectors spacecraft, double the size of the ISVs she was used to captaining. *I don't know anything about these space vehicles.* Thoughts of defeat began knocking. *Nope. Now's not the time. I can do anything, and that's exactly what I'm here to do.* She began to check the vehicle's wires and tubes and plugs for sound energy connections and wheeled under the carriage, checking the tightness of the canisters.

Without asking permission to board, Amos slipped onto the vehicle as Virginia put her tools away. The yellow port light started flashing, and she hurried into the ISV, locking the door behind her.

He hid himself in the mechanical closet behind the second row of empty seats.

Ugh. At least I can finally get this over with. Win or lose, either way, now life will go on. Or maybe not. Virginia mumbled to herself as the port doors opened and she drove the ISV onto the launch ramp.

The spacecraft shook, heating up as it was expelled through the atmosphere. *No turning back now.* She closed her eyes, replaying memories of her life in Alcetra with Paden and Charles until, at last, she recognized the ease of floating free in the endlessly deep star-studded sea. The calm of space.

She exhaled. "Now what?" she said into her radio.

Coach Matz replied, "Use 0101 before Korbin's safety coordinates, and autopilot will take you to the fifth, Korbin's future. Your safety coordinates will bring you home."

"Are his safety coordinates his birthsol, like mine are?"

"Ch... re... be... re... che... meh... sss." Coach Matz's broken words came through the radio.

"Coach, you're breaking up. What's his birthsol?"

"Be... th... che... se... torrid cannons."

"Coach! What are you saying? Coach Matz, I don't know Korbin's safety coordinates. I need you to tell me! Ugh!" Virginia yelled, angrily hitting buttons in more failed attempts to reach her.

"I know his safety coordinates!" a voice yelled.

Sounds like Amos. I sure do wish he could be here on this mission with me. She turned to see the door of the supply cabinet spring open, a clatter of mess falling out.

"Amos? Is that really you?" Her friend slowly wriggled his way out of the cabinet. "You can't be here! Why—"

~ clunk ~ smack ~ crack ~

Air tanks and helmets and wrenches tumbled to the floor after him. "Yeah. I'm here!" Amos shouted. "Lighten up, Ginny cakes," he replied to the furrow in her brow. "Friends don't let friends travel to just Anywhere alone."

"Amos. This is terrible! You're risking your life being here. I don't know what will happen to you if you take this mission with me!" Virginia was upset. "I—eh, well, we—may not even come back from this mission."

"You have a better chance of coming home if you have a copilot," he argued.

She rolled her eyes and nodded toward the empty captain's chair next to her. "*If* we come home, copilot," she said and again tried to make contact with Coach Matz. "What a nightmare!" she yelled. "I don't know what to do next. I still need Korbin's safety coordinates, and she said something about the torrid cannons."

"Safety coordinates are someone's birthsol right?" Amos asked. "Because I know his birthsol—he told me when I interviewed him, and I remember because he shares my sister's birth date."

He stood up and reached inside his pocket. "Let's get Grandmother in on this," he suggested with a sly smile, holding up her transmitter.

Grandmother's hologram quickly appeared, her hand on her hip, shaking her banana cane at Amos. "Only two hold the key. Number Three must remain or be lost completely."

"See? Grandmother's worried about you not coming home either. You really put us in a bad place, Amos."

"Hey, Ginnycakes! This is what friends are for," he said with conviction. "Now let's get this show on the road. Grandmother, can you tell us what we're supposed to do next?"

She pointed her banana cane at Virginia. "You were told."

Amos looked at Virginia. "What else did you hear Matz say?"

"Mmmm... she told me to use autopilot with 0101 in front of Korbin's safety coordinates and use mine to return. She said something about the torrid cannons, preceded by a bunch of static."

He tapped his foot. "0101?"

"Launching to five," Grandmother chimed in.

"The torrid cannons, what do they do?" Amos asked.

"They heat up the space around our spacecraft. Hot enough to disintegrate anything within miles."

Grandmother interrupted their conversation with boisterous dancing.

"That's it!" Virginia blurted. "Danny, safety coordinates 0101... Amos," she whispered. "Tell Danny Korbin's birthsol."

"12013079." He spoke loudly so the Planet Protector Vehicle computer would translate accurately.

Danny repeated the safety coordinates.

"Danny, torrid canons on," Virginia commanded.

"Why do I sense that I missed something?" Amos asked.

She shrugged and exhaled a laugh. "That's all we have to do! What I was already told!"

The hum of the machines beneath their feet was heavy. "So where are we going?" he asked.

"Into a black hole, I think." Virginia sighed.

The velocity threw the pair back in their seats, yet the spacecraft held smooth and steady, as if they weren't moving at all. Time stood still, with no point of reference except the sensation of the machines, which had begun to quiet, and soon Virginia and Amos noticed the torrid cannons had completely stopped and they were no longer nestled amid the comfort of their stellar companions, but rather sitting in a black abyss, completely devoid of light or stars or moons, or movement or life of any kind. Somewhere where lives could be lost or gained.

"Ugh. So dizzy. Did we just spin our way here?" Amos complained.

"Quite possibly. My stomach is churning like a blender."

Virginia pointed to a pin-sized white light in the corner of her window. "There's something." She studied their current coordinates. "0000," she read out loud. "We could be spinning, but there's not one solid point to give us a clue. Now 0001... But we are moving somehow. 0010..."

"Hey look!" Amos said, his finger on the glass, pointing to something in the dark. "I think we're getting closer to something."

She leaned toward his window. "I wonder if that's the same light." She looked back at their speed and coordinates. "We're moving at hyperspeed. 010—"

"Ugh!" she and Amos yelled together, covering their helmet viewing panels.

"Danny, UV shield high!"

"UV shields on high, Captain," Danny confirmed.

The two friends released their hands from their helmets and squinted their eyes open.

"Where are we?" Amos asked in awe.

"The coordinates are holding at 0101," Virginia said. She looked at the reverse camera, revealing the black abyss behind them. "I think we're here. This is Anywhere."

The space around them was intensely bright white with no ceiling or floor. The pair watched out the front window as they coasted down a long, straight, narrow path, which was divided by hundreds of other straight paths with bright boxes, each about the size of the Planet Protector ship, lined up along each side. Some boxes emanated a bright white light, while others were the various colors of the Uniteds.

"I wonder if all these boxes represent someone's life," Virginia said. "Since we are here to change Korbin's future."

"How are we supposed to find what we're looking for?"

She glanced at their coordinates. The 0101 held steady, and the following numbers changed without slowing, without showing similarities to Korbin's birth date. The spacecraft continued slowly forward, finally stopping at a brightly lit white wall with only two options—a path to each side. "When in doubt, go..." Virginia said.

"Left!" Amos eagerly replied.

She maneuvered the spacecraft to the left, where brightly colored boxes lined only the left side of the straight path that the two friends slowly and steadily rode along.

"I don't know what I'm supposed to do here other than change Korbin's future and finish what I start," Virginia said. "Where's Grandmother?"

He looked down at his empty hand and replied, "I think I lost her. When we... went through... ehh... whatever happened that got us here."

"Ha!" A laugh eventually came from an unidentified location, breaking the silence.

"There she is!" Virginia cheered.

"Darkness," the voice replied.

Amos got up to look for her, rummaging under the seats.

"Seek and you will find," Grandmother said after Amos had found her hologram transmitter in a dark crevice.

"Grandmother?" Virginia asked.

"Trust your power of sense."

"Ugh! If I had any sense I wouldn't even be here!" she yelled in frustration.

"Aware! Another is close," Grandmother warned.

"Well, that doesn't sound good," Amos said.

"I hope she's not talking about this Dutch that I've been warned about. We haven't even found Korbin's future box."

Before they could ask Grandmother any questions, she turned herself into a bright purple Ananta and emitted quiet, soothing piano music.

Amos shook his head. "She's probably trying to keep you calm. Just keep moving. Stop when your superhuman senses make you curious about something."

"Great plan," she replied sarcastically.

The path came to an end. With nowhere else to go, she turned the spacecraft around and continued back the way they'd come, the same boxes now on the right.

"Gin, look at that purple box," Amos said, pointing only a few boxes forward.

She stopped the spacecraft in front of it. "The light is flickering."

"It's a sign!"

Virginia made sure she showed him the disbelief in her eyes.

"What?" he argued. "It is a sign!"

She moved the spacecraft to hover above the flickering purple glow. Both friends looked outside, down into the box. "Looks like a layered maze," Virginia said. She adjusted the spacecraft's external cameras to zoom in.

They each leaned forward, looking closely at the screen that captured the maze. Many small and large roads atop each other, colliding, merging into each other.

"Look, Gin! There's people on those roads! Zoom in more."

She adjusted the cameras, and they narrowed their eyes to make out who the people were.

"It's him." Virginia sighed relief that she'd found him and could begin doing what she'd come to do.

"Gin, look!" He pointed at the control panel, which was lighting up sporadically. "What's going on?"

"It's all the tools. The planet protection tools. The laser cannon, the X-actionator, and the..." She reached under the three corners of her seat. "...ray guns."

"It's another sign!" Amos said. "Maybe a sign to blow up Korbin and the Dot girl."

"She's down there too?" Virginia paused, feeling her stomach turn over, and looked closer at the images on the screen. "Yeah. Just like the Legends told me," she whispered.

She remembered their words before the test of swords: *"His future begins with you."*

"I have to remove some of the roads. Cut them off. And I have to use the planet protection tools to do so."

Amos grinned and replied, "You got your senses back."

"Maybe I've just had a lot of help along the way."

Virginia commanded Danny to engage the laser cannon. She leaned into the camera screen and analyzed it thoroughly, her heart racing faster than the speed of light. "If Korbin's soul is the joy of my soul, then any road without me on it is one that has to go. That's the right move."

"Great idea. Let's do it!" Amos said, leaning in to analyze the screen with her.

"Right here," she said, pointing to the first road at the top of the maze. "I'm going to cut it right to the wall so it will fall off and I can see clearly what's on the road below it."

She locked the laser cannon on the location and commanded Danny to fire. They looked at each other, flushed with surprise, when the road disintegrated and revealed the next road below.

"Get this one, right here," Amos cheered, pointing to a road that appeared to be a big giant party.

Virginia cut it with the laser cannon, and the two friends breezed through the task of cutting more roads. A long straight road, with innumerable small roads connecting to the wall, stood out. She knew it was an important road, knew who the three people on it were. It was exactly what the Legends had shown her of his future.

He'll never understand why he's so sad if I don't do it. But before she could finish severing all the roads from the wall, a dark fog engulfed the spacecraft.

She looked at Amos, her eyes wide. "What—is this?"

"Uh... looks like we have company," he whispered.

"Yeah, and it's covered the cameras!" Virginia panicked. "How am I supposed to finish cutting Korbin's roads with this thing blocking my view?"

"It can't stay forever," he encouraged her.

They waited, silently watching the screen for a change in the view.

"I don't know what to do. I don't even know what it is," she complained.

"'He who gains from keeping you separated cannot take human form.' Er... something like that is what Grandmother said. Remember?"

"The Dutch?" Virginia pulled her hair back, her palms sweaty. "If this is the Dutch, he wants to kill me—us now."

"Oh boy." Amos shook his head.

"I could, uh... try the atmosphere reentry shields. They lower the temps surrounding the spacecraft." She looked at him for encouragement. "If it's freezable, the shields will freeze the fog, and it would likely shatter."

He nodded and shrugged.

"Danny. Atmosphere entry shields on," she commanded.

The spacecraft's computer counted the level of power in the shields aloud. They watched the camera screen closely, hoping for a change in the black fog. "Shields one hundred percent," Danny confirmed.

The two friends looked at each other with dismay—it was still as black as ever. Worry ignited Virginia's rage. "This is bull!"

"Maybe Grandmother will give us an idea," Amos said, reaching in his pocket for her transmitter. "Wait. Gin, is that a crack in the fog?"

They watched the screen together, amazed how one crack split the entire fog into little pieces that disintegrated, each fissure revealing more of the roads in the purple box below.

"Wow. It worked!" Surprised, Virginia clapped her hands. "I'm gonna finish cutting these roads so we can get out of this nightmare," she said, more determined than ever.

She locked the laser cannon on one of the last few small roads connected to the large road that had begun falling away. "Danny, fire laser cannon," she commanded and watched the road begin to separate from the wall—when, again, the black fog appeared in front of the spacecraft. This time it was moving, circling them again and again. The ship began to rock from side to side.

"What's going on?" Amos asked.

She shook her head. "It's creating some type of wind. I think."

The spacecraft began tipping harder to each side as the fog became darker and stronger. "The ship won't stay steady long enough for me to get a laser cannon locked on the road!"

"Yeah, and I think it wants to tip us upside down," Amos said, grasping the handrails above his head.

"Danny, prepare the X-actionator," Virginia commanded.

"Wha... whaaat are you fixin' to do, Gin?"

"I think this could be the last road to eliminate—or maybe one of the last ones. I just need a glimpse of the road, for a split second, to lock onto it," she said, her hand flailing around the screen with the turbulence of the spacecraft. "I'm gonna wipe it out so we can get out of here."

"Captain, I could not power up the X- actionator," Danny said. "Diagnosis reveals a fiber disconnect at the power source."

Virginia mumbled complaints as she unbuckled her seat belt. "This will only take a second," she said, easing herself to the back of the spacecraft, holding on to anything she could to keep from tipping over with the ship. She opened the control panel to the X-actionator in the floorboard.

~Ssshhwooooooosh~

~Thwack~

~Doink~

"Gin. Gin. Wake up," Amos said, hovering over her and patting her face with his hand, wondering if she was going to die right in front of him.

Virginia cracked open her eyes. "What?" she mumbled, lifting her head from the floor. "The spacecraft isn't tipping over anymore." She massaged her forehead with her fingertips.

"No. The force from the Dutch, er... that black fog flipped the ship upside down when you were fidgeting in the control panel. Knocked you unconscious," he explained.

She sat upright. "Right. Help me back into my seat, would you?"

"We gotta hurry and get this done before he—whatever the evil force is—comes back."

Virginia rubbed her eyes, reaching for her seat belt. "Amos. I'm dizzy. Will you help me strap in?"

~ Pssheeewwwww ~ Ssshhwwoooooosh~

The black fog flew past the spacecraft so fast it spun them in a full 360-degree circle.

Amos stared, dumbfounded, at Virginia's head—which lay limp where it had smacked against the window during the spin. He reached for her hand. "Virginia, are you okay?" He got out of his seat and grabbed the first aid bag and put the vitals tester on her finger.

"The captain's heart rate is slowing. I suggest you seek medical attention immediately," the computer said.

"Okay, Danny. Take us home. Safety coordinates 02143079."

The spacecraft's torrid thrusters turned on automatically, quickly propelling them out of the bright white space of Anywhere and back into deep blackness. Amos's stomach tightened. What would happen to Virginia since she hadn't finished the mission?

Out of the darkness appeared the head of a man, with a chest like Zeus and the wings of an angel and long hair blowing back, glowing gloriously in a white fog, which the spacecraft passed right through.

Amos could not process what he'd just seen. What he'd just experienced. He turned off his brain and closed his eyes, so that fear could not penetrate him—if death were to be his fate.

"Tears are words the heart can't express."

~ Gerard Way

CHAPTER 16

NASA's Curiosity and Perseverance are the two operational rovers studying Mars as of 2024. Sojourner, Spirit, Opportunity, and Zhurong are inactive rovers on Mars.

The PPV returned them to Alcetra. Amos paced the aid station floor, thinking about everything he'd seen in Anywhere, while Ms. West and Paden discussed Virginia's medical condition with an aid.

"There's swelling in her brain. Once the pressure is released, she will regain consciousness," Paden finally explained. "What were you two doing out there anyway? Joyriding for like a week? Didn't you get hungry? What kind of friend are you, to allow her to do something so crazy!" Her furrowed brows and sad eyes said that she was more than worried about her best friend.

He was defeated, disappointed that he couldn't keep his friend safe from harm. He gripped his forehead with one hand, exhaled and apologized, said a few words to relieve some of Paden's worry.

Virginia's in a lot more trouble than this.

Once Paden had calmed down, he left Virginia's room, Ms. West shuffling her feet as she followed him into the hallway.

"A Healer has seen her, not to worry, boy," she said, addressing his troubled face.

"I'm sure, but... Ugh. It's way worse. Virginia and me, I think, are in big trouble. She's got to get out of here. Before it's too late." He clenched his head in his hands and sighed.

"You need to get the other key," Ms. West whispered.

Amos tilted his head, looking at her, wondering how she knew. "That's right. Two hold the key." He smiled. "Korbin can finish this mission!"

As he waited for her to say something, Mr. Bryant casually walked toward them, his hands in his pockets and a cool expression on his face. Amos attempted to replicate his untroubled demeanor, but it quickly fell apart when Mr. Bryant greeted him with a comforting hand on his shoulder.

"Mr. Bryant! You gotta—" he blurted with distress but stopped when Mr. Bryant just nodded in agreement. He looked at Ms. West, who was silently in on the conversation. "You know too, don't you? You have to take me to Nos to get Korbin. I don't know how I'll convince him, but I will."

Mr. Bryant chuckled coolly. "Don't fret, boy. I'll take you back to Nos. As soon as I say hello to Virginia."

At high speed, Mr. Bryant and Amos panned over the red mountains in one of the newest ultra-maneuverable planes designed specially for the Planet Protectors ground support crew. The sun was bright, disguising the cold planet with warmth. Amos questioned him about his knowledge of the situation they were in. Mr. Bryant pulled a chain out from under his shirt and held the pendant in the palm of his hand for Amos to see.

"It's the same one Virginia has. Does it mean you're a Royal?" Mr. Bryant didn't reply. "Do all Royals have that pendant? Do all the Royals know about what's happening with Virginia?"

"Perpetual Love—as it was called way back when there was no Unity Festival—love that Unites the same souls in the next lifetime, is what you know as Royals. Our ancestors, who were the first to discover the great powers of Perpetual Love, passed down these pendants, which were carved from the Unity Stone. They were said to keep them safe from the ones in the center of the planet who were searching for the stone that Sofia took to the surface when she was banned from her world."

Stunned by the new information, Amos's voice cracked when he asked, "The center of Mars?"

Mr. Bryant smiled from the side of his mouth. "Oh, you don't know. I'm sorry, boy, but yes, our planet has many hidden secrets, that now you also must keep. Including the great battle against the one who fights to end the powers of Perpetual Love—or Legendary powers—that has been destined for thousands of years. The battle that you and Virginia have begun." Mr. Bryant took a long pause, looking out the window. "I never imagined it would be the soul of my son who would fight him."

"Is the image I saw out there the Dutch?" Amos asked. "What... eh... who is the Dutch anyway?"

"Once a well-respected scientist on Earth, who discovered many important chemical combinations—one of which accidentally killed his wife. He was devastated."

"He was human?"

Mr. Bryant confirmed with a nod. "Conrad Dutch, yes. His grief drove him insane. In search of a way to bring his wife back, he and a physicist friend experimented for decades until finally he discovered a portal inside a black hole where he could bring his wife's soul back to Earth."

"Whoa! That's wild. Did she come back with him?" Amos asked.

"No. Hadley, the gatekeeper of Anywhere—the space between life and death, the space where a person's future lies—had a rule that Conrad had to agree to. And he agreed, but didn't follow the rule."

"Is that where we were? In the space between life and death?"

Mr. Bryant nodded.

"So what was the rule?"

"Hadley would release the soul of Conrad's wife *only* if he waited in Anywhere for her to come out." Mr. Bryant paused, noticing Amos's intrigue. He nodded. "It was taking a long time, and Conrad went looking for her, and Hadley kept her word. She did not release the soul of his wife, and he was bound to Anywhere, a formless being. Unless he discovers the power to return to human form."

"How does he gain the power to return?"

"When souls with mates of Perpetual Love cross between life and death, he's there and entices them into his light. If both souls get caught in his energy, they miss their chance to reunite among humanity. With enough energy of capturing Royal love, he will gain human form again."

"But Virginia and Cha—er, Korbin are alive."

"Exactly. Their Union would be more powerful than Royal. He discovered how to keep Royal souls apart for many years, disguised inside the Love Counseling Booth."

Amos gasped.

"And he's attempted and failed to keep Charles's soul—a Legend, Perpetual Love returning for his mate in the same lifetime—from returning while Virginia is alive. But if he somehow succeeds at keeping a Legend Union from happening, it will give him the power to be free... power enough to return to life. And it's said that his powers would be as wicked as his anger. Powers that could wipe out galaxies. Exist in different dimensions and destroy timelines, unravel universes and ecosystems of all sorts."

"Wow. This is really serious business we're in," Amos said.

"More than serious for you, Amos. Because you were on the ISV and started the mission with Virginia, you must finish it too—with Korbin."

Looking out the window, Amos denied his angst. He took a deep breath. "That's okay. I just know we're all going to be okay."

Korbin wasn't in Port 3. Amos ran up the hyperwalk to find the one who held the key to Virginia's life—to his life, to the life in unknown galaxies. He could be in the other ports, but tonight was the final Spaceball playoff game of the season. Every red-blooded Single should be in the Main Conservatory.

He walked toward the rowdy crowd gathered around the giant hologram that was showing the Spaceball game between the teams Hydra and Tyrese. Heath noticed him and popped out of the crowd, his hand waving in the air. "Where have you been? You've been gone for like a week or something! Without even answering my calls or messages."

"I'm sorry," Amos said. "I'll explain later. Right now, I have to find Korbin Xander. Have you seen him, by any chance?"

Heath looked concerned but didn't ask any questions and pointed to the upper-level seating tier. "Probably up there with the rest of the pompous speculators."

"Ugh. Of course." Amos exhaled his dismay.

Heath concentrated on something on his transmitter for a minute, then said, "I've just sent you my family's seating passes. Just show them the code and you'll have access to the whole tier."

Korbin sat with Jayne Dot and her family and some of her father's friends, picking at spreads of food that could feed several families for sols, in a boxed-off area where the administration and the Upper End residents sat in plush seats, excluding themselves from the rowdy Singles and the United volunteers who feverishly cleared tables and tidied up Unity decorations. He watched the game on the giant hologram below, listening but not really listening to Jayne, thinking about what his life would look like working for the Big Dot and wondering if Jayne would ever be less boring to listen to if they became United. He felt as lifeless as Martian soil.

He was startled and maybe a little relieved to see Amos burst shamelessly through the door. "There's an emergency. I need to talk to you," Amos said, looking into his eyes. He gestured toward the door with his head.

With a wrinkle as deep as Mars's biggest volcanic crater forming between his brows, Korbin looked at Jayne and caught the fire that shot from her eyes. "Amos," he said slowly, afraid to exit his chair. "What's wrong? You look... scared."

"Come outside, its personal." Amos said, refusing to look at Jayne.

Korbin politely apologized to Jayne and met Amos outside the family's private seating area.

"It... it's Virginia. We were in an accident, and she's in trouble."

"An accident? Where? Is she okay?"

Amos shook his head fervently. "She saw a Healer, so yeah, she'll live, but she has to finish the mission in the portal to Anywhere, or... or, well, she and, uh, I, will have to go back and stay."

"Virginia is hurt? What mission? What portal?" Korbin was overwhelmed by what he was saying. "Amos, are you okay? Where's Virginia? What are you talking about, going back to stay?"

"You're the only one who can complete the mission and save her."

Korbin drew his entire face into the deep wrinkle and laughed. "Amos, what are you talking about? I care about Virginia and want to help, but I need to know what's going on."

"I know someone who can explain it better than me, come on," Amos said, waving him toward the exit stairs.

Korbin raised his eyebrows high. "I don't know if I can," he said, shaking his head. He looked at Jayne Dot and his empty seat next to her and then again at Amos. "Amos. I'm courting Jayne Dot for Union this week. If I don't Unite into a space flight opportunity, I'm gonna end up stuck here, training for administrator of Living Rock Sciences with my father. I want to help Virginia, but I'm afraid to mess up and lose this deal."

"Then go tell Jayne you'll be right back," Amos said. "Tell her we have to go to Professor Farro's office to help him with something real quick." Amos furrowed his brows. "Korbin. It's about Virginia!"

An image of Virginia's smile flashed behind his eyes. "Yeah, okay. Just for a half hour though." Korbin walked over to Jayne Dot, and her eyes that pitifully begged him to stay, and obliged her with a pat on the shoulder and left her hopeful.

He noticed something like relief when he left that box.

The two boys hurried through the crowd in the Main Conservatory and ran to Professor Farro's office in Conservatory 5. Amos slowed his pace to a hurried walk and finally stopped in front of Farro's silent office. "I sure hope he's here," he whispered, standing at the long workbench that was filled with Professor Farro's plant experiments.

"It looks like he recently watered these," Korbin said, catching fresh droplets of water from a vanilla bean plant that gracefully climbed a conservatory support beam. Amos disappeared to check the black laboratory for Farro, who was nowhere to be seen.

Korbin found himself staring into the mirror above Farro's wash sink. He saw Virginia running around with Charles through Alcetra's halls. Saw images of her shining smile against a backdrop of curls, of her face in the dim light of space, her face under the canopy of banana trees. Chills went through his body, and sorrow coated his organs.

Startled by a transmitter beeping, he turned around to see Amos, a tear in the corner of his eye. "I don't know what I just saw or why I'm so sad. I don't know what it is about Virginia."

"You remember her," Amos whispered to the floor.

Neither of the boys could say anything. There was a wonder lingering between them like water evaporating under the Martian sun, until a song broke the moment.

"Hey, I know that song!" Korbin hummed with Farro, who had appeared, a tune that really had no words but echoed majestically between the dirt floors and the plants.

"It's a very old song. How do you know it?" Farro asked.

"I... I don't remember."

Farro laughed. "Maybe you're remembering that it's the song of your soul."

"Professor, Virginia needs Korbin's help," Amos said. "I told him you could explain it to him."

"Only you hold the other key," Farro said, smiling at Korbin.

"What key are you talking about, Professor?"

"The key to two happy futures," he replied from behind a large-leafed vine plant. Noticing Korbin's baffled gaze, he continued, "She is the other key. She risked her life to save you from an unhappy future. You remembered her in that mirror. Now she needs you."

"What unhappy future?" Korbin mocked. "I've never been more comfortable around a girl like I am with Virginia, but that doesn't mean she's someone I should Unite with. I'll have my interplanetary license in a few sols, and soon I'll Unite into the only freight transportation company on Mars. I'll have a career flying to Earth and the moon every sol," he replied dreamily.

"Are you sure that's what your future is, dear boy?" Farro asked.

Korbin shrugged. "I have a chance to break away from my father and Living Rock Sciences. I'm pretty sure Mr. Dot will give me a job as a pilot." His heart started racing, and he put a fingernail in his mouth to bite it. He cleared his throat. "And I can get used to Jayne, I'm sure."

"So you haven't talked to Mr. Dot about working for him yet?"

Korbin stuck out his lower lip and furrowed his brows. "Not yet—I will tonight."

Farro put his arm around Korbin's shoulders and walked him toward the mirror. "Take a look at what your future looks like as of now, boy."

Mister and Missus, dressed in orange and purple, were elated, waving to Korbin from the mirror without a sound. They walked somewhere strange, where there was a box of some sort with roads above and below and around each other. And then he saw himself—on one of the roads, he was walking onto the grassy space in the Main Conservatory. He didn't look much older; only the vertical line between his brows looked a little deeper. Walking next to Korbin was a small boy whose ears stuck out.

"Kid looks just like me! Is that my son in the future?" he asked with an excited smile.

Farro chuckled. "Yup! Just like you!"

"It doesn't seem like a bad idea... to have a kid," Korbin said, contentedness warming his whole body.

Mister and Missus stopped on a road where Jayne Dot was pointing her finger at Korbin, who received her discontent with a sullen face. They continued on what seemed to be an endless road where Jayne Dot continued to point her finger at him.

Korbin started biting his nails. "That looks terrible! Can you go somewhere else already?"

Mister and Missus held each other's hand as they stepped onto a dark road surrounded by blackness, until a stream of glowing white light from a falling asteroid lit it up. A Dot transport ship appeared in the dark sky, along with the Planet Protectors, shooting meteors with their X-actionator.

Korbin stood up straight and rubbed his hands together. "Ha! Yes! That's better! That's probably me captaining that giant freight ship!"

But the Dot freight ship docked in an Earth landing hanger, and the captain, who was not Korbin, exited, and the crew unloaded Martian metals and elements from the undercarriage. Korbin folded his arms across his chest as he followed the image of Mister and Missus, who walked into an office where a recognizably older future Korbin was planning something on a workboard. Mr. Dot came into the office, yelling at him. He watched himself drop his head, politely receiving Mr. Dot's discontent.

Mister and Missus walked a little farther, until they stopped in front of a service where the Dots and the

Xanders gathered in tears around a very small box waiting next to the embarkment door.

Korbin's shoulders dropped, and sorrow washed over his body. "Doesn't make me want to go back to that seat next to Jayne Dot tonight." Every hope for the future he'd had, hope that he'd worked so hard to build since he met Jayne, left his body, leaving him empty inside.

Mister and Missus began running as the roads behind them crumbled. They ran back to the mirror, and each held up a palm, remorse pouring from their eyes.

"That's okay." He exhaled great disappointment. "This is why you brought me here, right? To show me that my future is so fated that I should risk it to save someone I care about, someone I like?"

Instead of answering him, Mister and Missus walked hand in hand on a road that led to the Spaceball game he'd just left.

"Hydra wins? I should go back and bet on it," he said, watching them stand behind Mr. Dot as he talked to his friends. "What are they saying?"

Farro opened his hand, and the volume of Mr. Dot's voice filled the room. "...No. I have enough captains. I will groom him to take over the family business."

Korbin shook his head. "I could still go back and change things... make it all work out for me, with the Dots. But another part of me is saying no. Nothing is worth staying here and leaving the girl I've spent so much time getting to know, the girl I look forward to seeing, enjoy every minute with." Korbin took a deep breathe and the muscles in his face and shoulders relaxed to reveal a peaceful face. "Leaving Virginia in a mess so I can Unite with a girl I don't even like, but because I want a career in space flight, isn't right at all. I deserve better for myself. She deserves better. I think she needs me to start listening to that greater part of myself—the part that says no more foolishness. I gotta get her out of this mess she's in." He said with pride in his tone.

Amos smiled. "Great! Then this is what we'll do." He waved his hands in the air, saying with a theatrical voice, "We take a Planet Protectors vehicle to space, drop into a black hole, find Virginia's future box in the bright space of Anywhere, and sever any roads inside her box that don't have Y-O-U on it."

Korbin raised his eyebrows and widened his eyes at Amos. "Is that all?" he mocked.

"Nope. You gotta finish the mission, which includes fighting off the Dutch, who, although he can't take a physical form, is somehow really powerful anyway—and if you don't complete the mission, the Dutch goes free with powers that could destroy our entire universe, and we, all three of us, get stuck in Anywhere until we figure out a way to keep enough Perpetual Love separated, both

Royals and Legends, so that we can be released." Amos took a breath and shook his head with an expression of disgust. "It's a very dark plot."

"Maybe a lifetime with the Dots doesn't sound so bad after all," Korbin said, overwhelmed with the proposition of being trapped in some weird empty and mysterious space for an eternity.

Professor Farro put his hand on Korbin's shoulder. "Yes, it's a very dangerous mission that you must finish. It's the cost of changing the future," he replied with empathy. "But the army of many Royals is gathering, and you won't be alone out there. They are on their way as we speak. You should believe in your own strength and the magic powers of Perpetual Love. The Many who have the powers to save their kind."

"And we have to finish before the end of the Unity Festival," Amos added.

Korbin lifted a fingernail to his mouth and chewed nervously. "That's six more sols. And what does this army of many Royals look like?" He could feel his heart racing in his chest. "How can I know they'll be there to make sure I make it home?" He looked at Amos with his brows drawn together. "*We* make it home."

Professor Farro opened his palm, revealing a transmitter. From it rose a cloud of glowing purple light that gracefully transformed into a little Ananta, which transitioned to Virginia's face and then Korbin's, both smiling brightly. "It has already happened," he whispered.

Chills shot up Korbin's spine. "You're telling me that's the future." He looked at Farro next to him, who had his eyes closed and was breathing deep.

As Korbin also took in deep breaths, letting his eyes fall closed. He heard Farro whisper, "Once you decide, your power of sense will arrive, and with Union, you will see the truth that already lies within you. Like magic."

He opened his eyes and looked at the professor. "Virginia was the one for me all along, wasn't she?"

Farro said nothing.

"That's why you got me into your class and brought her here," he said, watching Farro smile.

Through the silence, Korbin could feel his heart beating like a drum, echoing between the leaves around him. "I could just never live with myself if anything bad happened to her. Let's get this done," he said.

Amos raised his heels and started moving. "Coach Matz set us up with a Planet Protectors ship last time. Hopefully she's there now."

Korbin followed. "Amos, we are coming back, I promise you," he warned. "My mother and sisters almost lost me once. I cannot break their hearts."

Inside Port 2, the boys walked through the aisles of the newest and most technically advanced vehicles, looking mean and ready for the toughest of missions. They stopped where Mr. Bryant was standing in front of one of the ships. "This is your ride, boys," he said, staring into Korbin's eyes.

As Korbin locked gazes with him, he began to smile, feeling the divide between his eyes softening, his whole face softening.

"I'm Charles's father," Mr. Bryant said, introducing himself with a handshake. "Now get on board, boys. Korbin will captain—use 0101 before Virginia's safety coordinates. Amos will tell you her birth date as the coordinates so you can arrive in Anywhere. Believe in yourself and the powers of the Many of Perpetual Love, who you may not see but are always with you." He gave each boy a pat on the back before he walked away.

"I want to say I've met him before, but I didn't recognize his name," Korbin said to Amos, watching Mr. Bryant walk away.

Amos shot him a devilish grin. "It will all become clear to you... like magic!"

Korbin looked at the time on his transmitter. 9:05.

Once in the Planet Protectors vehicle and strapped in, they waited for the port doors to open. "I guess if I wanted to back out, now would be a good time." Korbin looked at Amos for a reply.

He shook his head. "Virginia needs you. And I just know everything is going to work out fine."

"I hope you're right." The port doors opened, and they began their journey to the launch ramp. "I can't believe I'm doing this. This is absolutely absurd," he said, chills racing under his skin as the space vehicle hooked onto the launch ramp.

"Korbin Xander, this is Officer Vando." A smooth, deep voice came over the radio. "I just want you to know you are in my space vehicle and it will keep you more than safe. Believe in it and the computer system."

"Alright, Officer Vando. Thanks," Korbin replied, noticing a new confidence in the ship all around him.

"When you get up there, after you put in your safety coordinates, turn on your torrid thrusters. At the right time, you'll be brought into the portal." After an extended silence, Vando said, "Don't fear. There is an army of Many who will be there to help."

"Right, a portal." Korbin sighed, acknowledging all of his fears of being stuck in some unknown universe forever. *I can't go out there with doubt. I can't win with this attitude.* "Alright! We've got this! Let's get this done! Eh, Amos?" And he allowed his heart to pump the blood of determination through his body.

The space vehicle picked up speed on the launch ramp, and Korbin closed his eyes, remembering Virginia's expression when she'd tasted the tea he bought her from the vending machine. He pictured his sisters' faces as they played together and his mother's laugh. *These women in my life need me, and I will not let them down, no matter what.*

"The only thing that can even slightly relieve the pain of grief is gratitude."

~ Bee Davis

CHAPTER 17

Mars's axial tilt is 25.2 degrees, similar to Earth's, creating seasons like ours.

Korbin's thoughts were quiet as he stared out the window at the vastness of space, admiring the infinite luminous pinholes scattered throughout the never-ending darkness.

Amos broke their solemn state. "Are you ready for this?"

"Somehow, I get the sense I've been here a thousand times." Korbin looked at him, his brows drawn in by the deep vertical line between his eyes. "You know, I've never operated a space vehicle as a captain. Supposed to get my license in two sols."

"Don't worry. If I made it out of this black hole, or whatever it is, once, I'm gonna definitely make it out again—with you!"

Korbin looked at the time. 5:05. "Five, hmmm."

"See the number of the future," a woman's voice chirped.

Amos pulled a round transmitter out of his jacket pocket and held a miniature purple hologram in his hand. "By the way, this is Virginia's grandmother, Blane."

"Hi, Grandmother Blane, are you calling from Alcetra?"

"Grandmother Blane's soul embarked on her next journey about nine months ago," Amos whispered.

Grandmother laughed. "Watch them. Number codes. Directions for the driver of your body. It's fun!" she said with a childlike excitement.

Korbin was confused. "If she's no longer alive, how can she come through on a hologram?"

"I am one of many. Many who come to aid the important couple."

"Interesting." Korbin was curious.

"Grandmother knows some things we don't," Amos explained. "But generally, she's very helpful."

"Helpful?"

"Yeah. Somehow she has the answers when you need them the most." Amos put her transmitter inside an empty cavity on the PPV's dashboard. "Keep her here so you can call on her when you need her."

"Hey Korbin, when you're ready to start, apply safety coordinates 010102143079, which are also our destination coordinates."

"Virginia's birthsol," Korbin said and typed in the numbers manually.

"Whenever you're ready, turn on the torrid thrusters, and we will be on our way," Amos said.

"What's going to happen when I turn on the thrusters?"

"Well, I don't really know, but when the vehicle stops, we're gonna feel dizzy. Maybe vomit," Amos replied in an unconcerned way.

"Amos?" Korbin began. "You don't seem nervous or worried at all about this mission, even though your life is on the line. Why?"

He gave a carefree shrug. "There's been a lot of magic happening since the beginning of the Unity Festival, like the Anantas showing up in all the cities, Virginia's grandmother, getting a sponsorship to stay at Nos, my show making a lot of money with sponsorship... Ya know, Korbin, magic like this, well, I've never experienced it. And I just don't believe that with magic like this around anything could go wrong."

Korbin agreed. "Wise man." He gave Amos a confirming nod. "Danny, torrid thrusters on."

"The machine takes you theeeeere!" Grandmother caroled.

Within moments the spacecraft began to move so fast, the boys rattled furiously in their seats and Grandmother's song diminished as the galaxies melted away into the darkness.

Eventually Korbin opened one eye to find the ship had come to a stop in an empty black abyss. "Greaaaat," he mumbled as he peered out the window into the complete darkness, nausea roiling in his stomach.

Soon he opened another eye to look at Amos, who wasn't moving at all. "Hey, Amos! You okay?" he mumbled as loudly as his feeble body could.

Amos stayed silent and still.

He was looking out the windows, waiting for Amos to wake up, when he heard the giddy voice of Grandmother Blane calling his name. Her transmitter was not in the dash cavity where Amos had put it. He searched the spacecraft and finally noticed the purple glow under Amos's seat.

Grandmother pointed her banana stick at Amos. "Your seeing-eye dog." She laughed like it was the best joke ever told. "He'll help. Here comes danger!"

Korbin looked out into the total blackness, his heart speeding up and his core tightening. "What danger? Where, Grandmother Blane?" Waiting for her to say something else. Waiting for Amos to wake up. Waiting for something.

SWOOSH!

The ISV bounced around from a gust of wind. Outside, two glowing white clouds appeared to flap up and down like bird wings, moving away from the vehicle.

"Will someone please tell me what is going on here?" Korbin spoke into the fear that seemed to have replaced the air.

"He is not made of matter." Grandmother laughed.

Amos grunted and mumbled, "What the heck?"

"You gotta get up, man, I don't know what's going on here."

Amos cracked open his eyes, then stared past Korbin. "I'm up, but maybe you should worry less about me and more about that." He pointed out the window at the giant bright white wings flapping.

"Keep moving, boy," Grandmother sang.

Korbin looked at the spacecraft's gauges. "Engines on, Danny. Move forward immediately." He held his breath. "Amos? What happened? What was that cloud of light kinda thing that I saw back there?"

"His only form is fear," Grandmother chimed in.

"What is she talking about?" Korbin was panicking.

"He doesn't have a solid form. You can fly right through him," Amos explained. "That's what Virginia did."

"I didn't even tell my mother goodbye," Korbin whispered and continued to steer the ISV around the pair of white wings that became brighter as he drew closer. "Why did Grandmother say 'he'?"

"He is the Dutch. You know, that winged hologram you visited inside the Love Counseling Booth?"

"What? I thought he was AI, programmed by a Truth Bearer with a hyperinflated ego. What's he doing out here? With us?" Korbin asked while steering away from the white cloud of wings.

"He's stuck here. Until he can end enough Royal Unions—or better yet, Legendary Unions."

"So he's really a bad guy?"

"Yeah. A *really* bad guy. For now though, just fly through even if we get rattled. He wants to keep us out of that gate," Amos said, pointing to the white glowing pin-sized dot ahead.

Korbin steered the spacecraft around and flew directly into the wings of light, watching them dissipate behind them. "Okay, we're still alive. Now where's the gate?"

Amos pointed forward and to the left. "Over there. See? It looks like a star. But hurry. He'll be back, and he'll be angrier than a den of yellow jackets."

At high speed, the spacecraft was there within seconds.

"Wow. It's bright here," Korbin said as they floated in front of the gate that ended the empty darkness. "Danny, UV shields on."

The spacecraft sailed into the gate. "What, am I hallucinating or something right now? I just got chills down my back." He looked to the left and the right at the rows of boxes lit up in various colors. "It looks like really messed-up psychedelic dream."

"Yeah. I think it's people's futures. Their souls. Virginia was inside yours, destroying your future with Jayne, before she got hurt. We have to find Virginia's future box," Amos explained. "Once we find her box, you need to destroy any roads that don't have you on them."

"Her future? You didn't tell me I would be changing her future. Seems like something we should definitely not be doing."

"I get it," Amos said, "but uh, you gotta just know. Believe that you're doing what's right, and hurry up and finish the job so you and Virginia can live happily ever after."

"This is all about me and Virginia being together?"

"Yup."

"But why? I mean, I really like her, but why all this?"

"All you gotta know *right now* is we have to do this to save her life—because she didn't finish the mission. If I told you that you two have Perpetual Love, greater than Royal love, you wouldn't believe me."

Korbin's head was spinning. "Yeah, that's too much for me to process right now. But I want you to explain when we are done with this." He glanced at the time. "Weird. It's still 5:05."

"Maybe time is just space. Now move, man!"

Korbin applied a second layer of UV protection around the spacecraft's windows and cautiously maneuvered down a large aisle that had smaller aisles connected to it at ninety degrees.

Both boys looked down every connecting aisle. "How do I know which way to go?"

"Boys, sense strong," Grandmother sang in the background.

"What's she talking about?" Korbin asked Amos.

"I think you're close."

Korbin turned right, down a smaller aisle, and flew the ISV forward for what seemed like forever. "This one's different," he said, stopping in front of a dimly lit four-sided purple square.

"Hover atop it. Let's check," Amos said, pointing his finger.

They looked down to see a mass of roads layered on top of each other, crossing over each other, running parallel with others. "Now what?" Korbin wondered aloud.

"Turn on the cameras. Let's see if this is Virginia's future box."

Together the boys peered at the screen as the camera traced a dark road until it finally turned bright. "Ah! That's me... leaving Virginia's side in Alcetra's aid station. This is her future box!"

"Well done, cap'n. Now you gotta eliminate all these roads until you find her in her present moment. With the laser cannon or whatever destructive tool you got in here," Amos explained.

Korbin fought his unsurety by rationalizing aloud. "And this is going to save her. Ensure that we are together because we belong together." He touched the camera screen and zoomed in on the first road, which crossed on top of all the others, intersecting at many different points. He carefully followed Virginia around and around on the roads. "She's just in a lab every sol. And alone. Looks like a miserable space to be in." He felt sadness for her as he watched more of Virginia's future. "This makes me believe in what I'm doing now."

"Find where that road starts and—"

Before Amos could finish, Korbin had used the laser cannon to explode the road with that future. He was relieved. "Wow, okay. I can do this, and get this done fast!" Within seconds he had analyzed another road and used the laser cannon to destroy it at its origin.

~Phheeeeeeeww~

A bright white cloud of light whipped past the spacecraft, halting Korbin from continuing. The boys watched it zoom away. "Hurry before he comes back!" Amos shouted.

Korbin's palms were sweating. "Coming back. Great." He focused hard on the box, analyzing the next road on top of many more layers of roads—when just then, the white cloud returned. This time circling around the spacecraft over and over again, entrapping the PPV in its vortex of rage. The ship shook and rattled violently inside the clutch of the energy of the angry Dutch.

"Captain? May I suggest turning the heat shield on?" the calm voice of the computer asked.

"Yes. Heat shield on," Korbin stuttered between the turbulence.

And immediately the white light disappeared and Korbin's unfinished business in the box below became clear again. He aimed the laser cannon beam at the next road and pulled the trigger. Nothing. He pulled the trigger again. Nothing. He tried again, and still nothing.

"Something happened during that crazy spin. The laser cannon isn't working!"

"Use the X-actionator," Amos said.

Korbin's stomach knotted up immediately. "No. I can't."

"Why not?"

"I don't know. Something about it makes me nervous."

"Now's not the time to be nervous, Korbin. That cloud of rage is gonna be back any second—for our lives!"

Korbin's heart raced fast and hard. "Okaaaay!" he yelled and aimed the X-actionator, and the road disappeared.

"I only have like three shots I can take with this thing, and there must be at least twenty-five more roads to look through," he said. He breathed rapidly, worries of never seeing his family again, of failing Virginia and Amos, flashing through his mind.

Through the camera screen, he stared at Virginia's dismal future. "Cutting off more than one road at a time would be better, but it would be a guess. What would happen if I took off too many?" His body was stiff with panic.

"Seven, boys," Grandmother sang.

They looked at each other. "Take off seven roads!" they said simultaneously.

Korbin started counting.

"I'll keep an eye out for the enemy," Amos said.

"Seven!" Korbin exclaimed.

Amos's voice dropped. "He's—" was all he could say before the white wave of light had wrapped itself around the spacecraft and spun them in circles with its mighty wind.

"May I make a suggestion, Captain?"

"Aaah..." Korbin yelled as his head went from up to down and right to left.

"Turning on the torrid thrusters will put some resistance up against this uninvited force of energy," Danny said calmly.

"Yes, Danny! Torrid thrusters on!" Korbin yelled.

The deep hum of the torrid thrusters started, and the spacecraft stopped spinning upside down and returned to a slow rocking, until finally the white light of the Dutch flew away.

"Move!" Grandmother's voice said clearly without a song.

The cloud was back, strangling the spacecraft, leaving no view from the port or starboard, bow or stern windows.

It wasn't shaking the spacecraft or spinning—it was turning red, as red as flames.

"I think it's getting hot in here."

"I think you're right," Amos replied, dumbfounded.

The cloud of now-red light began whirling around the ship, making whispering sounds—leaving the boys only glimpses out the windows.

"Danny, what do we do?" Korbin yelled.

"Both heat shields are up, Captain. We need to leave," Danny replied in his unconcerned AI voice.

"Danny, velocity max forward."

"Captain, our engines are too hot."

"I have waited out here long enough."

"What?" Korbin looked at Amos.

Amos shook his head. "Wasn't me."

"You will not take this from me."

"Uh… that was the Dutch," Amos said.

Korbin unbuckled his seat belt as a sense of resolve came over him. "We don't *all* have to lose our lives to this mission. If I go out there, at least we have a *chance* of finishing this and going home." He dug through the cabin closet until he came out with a jetpack and hastily put it on his back. "Amos, while I'm out there, talk to me on the radio. If you can see anything on the screen, help me figure out how to get this done quicker."

Amos leaned forward and looked at the screen, covered in a cloud of red light. "I'm sure this thing will go after you once he realizes you left the vehicle."

Korbin grabbed the ray guns from under both the captain's and co-captain's chairs. "You're the captain now. Make sure you get yourself home. I will be finishing this mission." He put on his air mask and waited for Amos to put on his before he opened the door, then fell into Virginia's dimly lit box of the future.

"I can see things pretty well from here. I see the road where she is now. I even see you and me. It's a long road." Korbin stopped talking while he used the ray gun to sever the final road.

Amos's voice sounded nervous. "Korbin, I can't see you. Are you okay?"

"It's taking a while. This ray gun is so small. I'm gonna use them both."

"I think he saw you," Amos warned him. "He's unraveling himself slowly from the spacecraft. Thankfully—I thought the ship was going to catch on fire."

"This is a wide road to sever," Korbin said, "but I'm getting it. Don't worry, Amos! We've got this!"

"Right, and all the roads above it will fall off, and we can get the heck outta here," Amos confirmed. "But you better do it quick, because the Dutch isn't on the PPV anymore, and I don't see him either."

"Ugh, I'm almost... Oh no, he's—he—" Korbin sputtered into silence as the cloud of the Dutch rolled toward him.

"Korbin, I see it. He's right above you."

"I'm still cut—" He halted, noticing the strange movements of the red fog above him. The Dutch transformed into a cloud of white light, with large open wings, a chiseled chest, and long wavy locks that blew back from his face. He muffled a laugh, which echoed as he laughed more. "Did you really thhh..." His tongue escaped his mouth and split in two with the syllable. "...ink I would allow you to succeed, boy?" he said in a loud whisper.

Korbin froze. He didn't hear Amos on his radio, attempting to coax him out of his trance.

"I saw you cross my domain into this new body of yours. Did you really think that after 1523 years here that I wouldn't figure out how to escape?" The Dutch opened his wings and moved them like a bird preparing to fly, not even realizing that Korbin had the ray gun on and was severing the road. "Now you and she and the little friend you dragged into..." His tongue revealed the creepy split again. "...this mess can hang out here until you figure out how to keep Legendary Love separated." He threw his head back and laughed, then slowly dissolved, changing again into a shapeless cloud of red light.

"Danny, what's the status of the torrid thrusters?" Amos asked.

Cooled, sir, but there is only nine percent energy left.

"Ugh. Graaaandmoooooother? Where's those backups you promised?" he yelled.

She didn't reply.

"Hey, Korbin," Amos radioed. "He's turned himself into a red cyclone-vortex-type thing right above Virginia's box, and I can't see you. Are you okay?"

Transmission was lost, and Korbin's jet pack couldn't resist the mighty suction of the cyclone. "Korbin, where are you, man? Answer me!" he tried again, watching, waiting for him to zip back to the spacecraft.

Would he find Korbin's body? How would he bring it back? What would Virginia say? Would Charles's soul find her again? No, of course not—the three of them would be stuck in space together forever. His body stiff with fear, he barely breathed.

"Aha! Korbin! There you are, man. I see you!" He watched Korbin whipping around inside the cyclone, but he was moving too fast. "Don't worry, buddy, Danny is coming for you."

"Chrk... wicked... pshthc... too... shich... wind... krick... can't."

"Danny, we have to move. Lock destination on the moving target."

Lights flashed on the dashboard, and the engines started. "Sir, the vortex will require torrid thrusters powered at max to stabilize. We will have three minutes before we have no power and the vortex takes us," Danny said.

"Well, hurry then!" Amos put on his mask, strapped on the other jetpack, and attached himself to the spacecraft's winch.

"Watch magic," Grandmother's voice sang from somewhere.

A flash of light grabbed his attention through the window. He rubbed his eyes and looked again—purple dashes of light. He narrowed his eyes, trying to make sense of the sparks of purple light piercing the red cyclone from above, below, all sides.

Turbulence caught him unexpectedly and threw him back into the captain's chair. "I'm inside the cyclone," Amos whispered. He watched out the window, dumbfounded as the walls of the red cyclone around him transformed to purple.

~Pwooooh~

An explosion vibrated the spacecraft. The cyclone stood still.

"Oh no!" Amos was flushed with sadness, almost certain that he was going to be taken out into space with this crazy thing.

But as the minutes passed, the cyclone began to dissolve, and he was surprised to see Korbin drifting in the distance, almost free of the cyclone, out the starboard window. "I can see you again, buddy. Can you hear me?"

He didn't reply. Amos opened the door, turned on his jet pack, and retrieved Korbin's limp body in the clutch of his arm. With no wind to fight, the two boys safely returned to the spacecraft, where Amos set him in the captain's chair.

"I know you're alright. You have to be," Amos mumbled, two fingers on Korbin's neck, checking for the pulse that was definitely there.

Something was clanging at his foot. He bent down to pick it up. "Hmmm... this is Virginia's magic water that Farro gave her. You are certainly in need of magic. Because you need to come to, like immediately." He tipped the bottle into Korbin's mouth until it dripped down his face.

Korbin coughed.

"I knew you would be okay! Korbin, Korbin, talk to me!"

He remained silent.

"Oxygen. That's what you need," Amos said to his unresponsive friend. He rummaged through the emergency compartment and found oxygen. He put the mask on Korbin's face and watched his breath cloud it.

Leaning into the forward window, he watched what looked like a battle between good and evil. The cloud of purple light overwhelmed the red light of the Dutch, circling it into a smaller and smaller form. "I think I'm watching the Royals defeat the Dutch right now, Korbin," Amos said, not expecting a reply.

The purple became a cyclone and carried the tiny red blob of light to the top of a box that was vacant of any future, pushed it in, and ran a beam of light around all four sides, locking it.

Inside the dark room of the door that didn't close, an hour past the time that the Dutch had scheduled their meeting, he still hadn't shown up.

"Let's get out of here. We got Korbin and Jayne in the booth. Virginia is gone—we don't have anything to worry about. Korbin's gonna Unite with that Dot," a gruff girl's voice said.

"But we don't know if they're gonna Unite as Royals or not. If we're gonna get our powers."

"Well, I guess it doesn't matter!" she snapped. "If the Dutch isn't showing up, he probably ditched us after he spent all season using us."

"Yeah. He's probably gonna keep the powers to himself," another girl said.

On Kobe Bryant's death: "Tragedies like this have a cruel way of reminding us of what's important in life: spending time with our loved ones, and being there for them no matter what."

~ Derek Jeter

CHAPTER 18

During the winter season, Mars temperatures can drop as low as –125°C (–195°F), and it sometimes has carbon dioxide "snow" storms.

Too frightened to open his eyes, moving only his fingers around, Korbin felt the bed underneath him and the blankets on top, searching for something familiar. He listened closely to distant voices, which he determined to be a news station playing in another room. The loud echoes of ladies laughing lowered his apprehension, and he opened his eyes to warm lights in the ceiling above him. He sat up and scanned the room, baffled by which aid station he was in.

He noticed his stiff legs when he got out of the bed and walked to the lavatory sink, pausing to question his disheveled self in the mirror. He pressed his pale and worried face between his hands for several moments, finally releasing himself with a long exhale. He splashed cool water on his face and groomed his hair with the excess water on his hands until a strange alarm sounded. It was loud but not obnoxious at all. Korbin rushed to put on the clean suit that hung on the lavatory door.

"Amos?" he said to the lanky guy, more overdressed than usual, who was standing relaxed, smiling, in the middle of his room. "What is going on—where are we?"

"You look confused, frien'. Take a deep breath," Amos said. "Er... maybe you should take a hundred," he added, seeming to notice the vertical line between Korbin's eyes that was slowly splitting his face in half. "We're in Alcetra. We survived, and you finished the mission, and we're never going back!"

Korbin sighed in relief. "What's that alarm? It almost sounds... uh... friendly?"

"Ah! It does. That's a recording of Earth's nineteenth-century church bells. Alcetra uses them the morning of the final event of the Unity Festival."

"It's the last sol of the Unity Festival? Where's Virginia?" Korbin asked through his panic.

"Yes. And she's a few doors down," Amos replied, dropping his head.

Korbin put on his shoes. "But that means if she doesn't wake up and get United tonight, she will have to go live on another planet." He was nervous, scratching his head and pacing. "I thought you said a Healer saw her—shouldn't she be well by now?"

Amos shrugged. "The aids say she's fine, her brain is just easing its way back, that's all."

"You gotta take me to her," Korbin said, and Amos cheerfully waved for him to follow him out the door.

"So what else happened out there? After I finished cutting off that road in Virginia's future? All I remember was getting sucked into that angry red cyclone," Korbin asked as they walked together.

"I watched that thing whipping you around in circles. You probably went unconscious. Then I noticed that one by one these flashes of purple light showed up, beginning to cover that red cyclone. I believe it was the army of Royals. Wow, Korbin. I wish you'd seen it. It was beautiful, spectacular. It turned into a mass of purple light that engulfed the entire angry cyclone of the Dutch. They turned him into a little red ball of light and stuffed him in one of those boxes and sealed it. I don't think the Dutch will ever find the energy to escape."

Amos opened the door to Virginia's room, where a quirky-looking old woman and a beautiful dark-haired young lady sat next to her. The young woman got up from her seat and looked Korbin up and down with a scowl. "This is all your fault."

"I'm sorry. I... I don't know you, and I don't know what you're talking about," he replied.

"Amos told me the whole story! Virginia wouldn't be in this mess if you had just courted her or told her you weren't interested in her. But no, you said nothing. You confused her, and now she is going to miss her chance to Unite into a good family. A family with me." She held her stance in front of him, tossing her long silky black hair behind her shoulders and crossing her arms.

"Uh, I'm really sorry," Korbin said humbly.

A quiet knock on the door interrupted her gaze of death. The door opened to reveal the gentle presence of an oddly familiar man, tall and strong with a square jaw. He walked over to them, and the young lady abandoned her unyielding posture to melt into his warm embrace. "I came to take you ladies to lunch," he said.

The quirky old woman popped up from her seat. "That would be great! I'm famished," she exclaimed as she shuffled to the door.

The oddly familiar man looked at Korbin, gently bowed his head, and smiled with his eyes. "Korbin, I'm Mr. Bryant. And I'm so glad you're here." He squeezed his shoulder.

Korbin was speechless, unsure of the reason for the chills that went through his body. He returned a smile with a sparkle in his eye.

As Mr. Bryant, the old woman, and the beautiful young woman left the room, Korbin asked Amos, "Should I know all of them or something? And why do I sense that Mr. Bryant is really important to me?"

He laughed. "The older woman is Ms. West, who is like Virginia's family, and the girl is Paden, her best friend. When Virginia wakes up, you should talk to her about Mr. Bryant."

They stood by Virginia's bedside for a while, talking about the events of their mysterious flight to Anywhere. "Let's go get lunch. Surely you're hungry too," Amos suggested.

Korbin shook his head. "I think I just want to stay here and talk to Virginia. Maybe she will wake up and give me those answers about Perpetual Love. Why she's so sure about it, and what would happen if we did Unite tonight."

He sat in the chair that Ms. West abandoned, right next to Virginia, and listened to the quiet in the room, noticing each beep of the machines and the whirring of the fans, sitting silent, enjoying his deep level of consciousness. He heard a sound that was the rhythm of a heartbeat and scanned the room to locate it.

The Unity Festival tablet, on the small round table next to her bed, caught his eye. He looked at the first page and began reading the Unity Creed aloud: "'Remember a perfect Union will provide you a lifetime of peace and contentment, but it is your soul that will lead you to the perfect Union that holds your joy.'

"I was so afraid of you, Virginia," Korbin whispered. "From the moment I saw you stumble through the lab door, I could sense that I had known you for a million years and that you were one big piece to my puzzle. And when you stood next to me at the table in class, I was so excited. But I didn't know why. It didn't make any sense to me. I didn't allow myself to believe you were anyone special. I was so worried about having opportunities in space flight and Uniting into a family for opportunity that I denied the joy of my soul." He looked at her closed eyes, sadness running through his blood. He took a deep breath and leaned back in the chair.

"It was just easier to use the excuse of Uniting with someone else than to face my fear. I mean, really, I'm just a simple scientist turned space enthusiast. I never thought I was worthy of a special love. Of joy. Definitely not Perpetual Love."

He listened to the worries in his head, of the troubles that would come if Virginia didn't Unite tonight—if she didn't Unite with him. He leaned forward to inspect the cream-colored ringlet that rested on the pillow next to her ear. "There was a little voice in my ear that always said, 'I know you.' And now your family and friends are somehow strangely familiar. Please wake up so you can help me figure it out."

He took a deep breath and shook his head. "And I don't know why you and I both took that strange mission, nearly lost our lives, but I'm glad we did. Because whatever happened out there took my fear with it. I'm not afraid to trust my soul now. I don't fear Uniting into a family without privilege or flight opportunity. My only fear is that I may never see you again."

Korbin took her hand and held it between both of his. He pulled their hands to his mouth and whispered, "Will you please seek Unity with me? Tonight? But don't worry—if you don't wake up this sol, I'm gonna go live on Earth with you." He pressed his lips to her fingers, held tightly inside his hands, kissing them until he took a breath. "I'll never let you go again," he whispered.

Hearing a commotion outside, Korbin looked toward the door to see Amos, surrounded by a swarm of female aids, in a heated discussion. As he approached, the ladies fell away one by one.

Amos turned to Korbin to answer the questions written on his face. "They love my latest news drop! I put a few pieces of our little adventure up. It's a huge hit. Don't worry—no one believes it was real. They want to, that's why they follow my news channel, but they really don't believe it. It was all too wild to *really* believe," Amos said before he noticed the pain on Korbin's face. "Korbin, man, you look like you're dying."

I'm worried she's not going to wake up. I can finally hear the voice of my soul, and I know we belong together. We just have to Unite tonight. "I'm just nervous about Virginia not being able to Unite tonight and stay here with her work and her friends."

"Expect good things, frien'!" Amos patted him on the shoulder. "Ms. West and Paden are on their way here to sit with her. You should come with me to the Main Conservatory and get something to eat. Aren't you hungry yet?"

Korbin looked at the time on his wrist. 2:11. "Uh, yeah, I am."

They walked together, Amos greeting his fans along the way and Korbin pondering ideas for how to get Virginia to wake up. "Amos, can you tell me more about what it is about me and Virginia, why it's us that has to be together and why we both needed to take that crazy-dangerous mission?"

He laughed and rolled his eyes. "Ugh! I wish I could. But it's Virginia who's gotta tell you the unbelievable truth."

"If she ever—"

"Enough!" Amos smiled and stomped his foot. "She saw a Healer. She'll be up and at 'em any minute now. You gotta just know."

The Main Conservatory was busy with Uniteds transforming the white tables and chairs into a brilliant celebration of all the Unity colors and piling the tables high with food, all lit by the purple glow of the Ananta high in the center of the conservatory dome.

Pointing in the direction of the band, Amos announced, "I'm gonna do a live broadcast. You'll probably be in it too, when I come back." He disappeared into the crowd.

Korbin ate his lunch wistfully and waited, still and pensive, listening to the band play a full song and then another, checking their sound. Some other Uniteds took their place onstage and fiddled around with outlets and connections on the stage floor. White lights changed to blue, then blue lights changed to red and then purple, green, and yellow as they tested the stage lighting.

Eventually, he looked through the dome and noticed the sun was setting. He glanced at the time: 5:10. *How did so much time pass?*

Korbin circled the conservatory, searching for Amos. When he didn't find him, he decided to return to the aid station and made his way to the Main Hall.

"She's awake!" he heard someone yell.

It was Amos, running toward him on the hyperwalk. "Virginia's awake! She's awake. Back to normal and everything—she's even dressing for the Unity Festival Dinner that starts in... like an hour or something."

Korbin lifted his pinky finger to his mouth and started biting the nail. *Will she want to talk to me? I was so foolish. There's no way I'll be able to convince her to Unite tonight.*

"You look nervous," Amos pointed out. "Now's not the time for that either! Now's your chance, ole sport!"

"That's the thing. I have to ask her, and I haven't exactly been... the kind of man she deserves. She has every right to tell me no, and I expect her to tell me to go away. But I need to try."

"The man she deserves is waiting right outside her room," Amos said from the side of his mouth.

"What do you mean?"

"This really nice kid from Diony has been waiting for her, planning to Unite when she returned from Nos. She broke it off with him, for you, a few weeks ago, but he's here—waiting outside her room."

Korbin's stomach flipped. In that moment he realized how small he'd been. He was embarrassed with himself.

They walked into the aid station, where the same faces that had haunted Korbin the first time were outside her room—plus a few new ones. Amos nudged Korbin with his elbow as they passed a handsome dark-haired boy he didn't recognize. "Handsome fella, isn't he? Too bad he doesn't have your soul," Amos whispered

They sat next to Ms. West. "She's just in there gettin' all gussied up," she explained, and then she leaned forward and peered into Korbin's eyes. "Probably gonna get United tonight." She dropped her voice to a whisper and stuck two of her fingers out and wiggled them up and down. "To one of you two boys."

"Is she talking about that one? The one you told me about?"

Amos pressed his back against his chair and pointed. "Frankie Casmiri. One stand-up guy. Here to save her from an eternity separated from her work and friends."

Korbin sprung up and walked toward Virginia's room. He looked at the door, then peered into Frankie's dark eyes. "Can I talk to you in the hall?"

Frankie didn't hesitate. "Do I know you?" His smile was warm and contagious.

"I don't think so, but we both know Virginia, and we both want to Unite with her tonight."

Frankie held his smile and looked down at his foot, which was tracing the line of the inset bamboo floor.

"I know you care for Virginia," Korbin began. "I'm ashamed of myself for not listening to my senses and courting her when she was in Nos. I always sensed she held the joy of my soul. I was just afraid. You're a better man than me, and she should have the best man. I want you to know, if she chooses me, I will promise to be the best man."

"I always knew I wasn't her first choice. But I thought her first choice had crossed into the next life." Frankie's smile was still warm, kindness glowing through his dark-chocolate eyes. "Then you ask her, and if she says no, then I'll be here for her."

Korbin knocked on the door.

"Yes?" he heard a girl's voice say.

He walked in to see Virginia and Paden laughing at something on the entertainment hologram. "Korbin!" Virginia's face lit up with her smile.

He was surprised she was so happy to see him. And relieved.

She looked at Paden, who flashed her an expression of deep concern before she left the room.

Virginia didn't have a second to ask him any questions before he threw himself to her side. He explored her whole face before he grabbed it in his hand. "I'm sorry, Virginia. For everything. And the worst is, I put you in danger—all because I didn't listen to my soul."

Her face was kind and caring, soft with empathy. "I think if it weren't for my superhuman power of sense and weird clues from my grandmother, I wouldn't have known either. I had a lot more help than you did—more clues and magic to show me. So don't worry. I forgive you."

"There's so many answers I need... about this whole Dutch thing and why I was the only one who could help you... Why do I sense that I know all your friends, and why do I suddenly just know we need to be United?"

Virginia waited for him to continue, but he didn't know what else to say. "Was that supposed to be a proposal?"

Korbin smacked his hand on his knee. "Ugh! I didn't say it right. Well, I did, but you were still sleeping a few hours ago." He bent to one knee in front of her. "The moment you stood next to me in class, I was excited you were there. But it was strange, and I didn't trust my senses. I know now that you are the one for me, and I am the only one for you. Will you please seek Unity with me tonight?"

She replied with a warm smile, nodding her head over and over.

"Is that him?" he heard the woman next to Mr. Bryant whisper.

Korbin pretended he didn't hear Mr. Bryant's reply: "Yes, but he doesn't know yet."

As the line to the Unity Booth took Virginia and Korbin closer to their future, they remained anchored by the smiles of Virginia's friends cheering silently for the couple from the wall.

"Is that woman with Mr. Bryant Mrs. Bryant?"

Virginia looked at him with wonder. "Yes, of course."

"When are you going to tell me how I somehow know them?"

She looked at him from the tops of her eyes, smiling deviously. "I'll tell you later."

A newly United pair exited the booth, jumping up and down, holding hands and waving erratically to their friends and family, who waited for them at the wall. Korbin watched them, thinking about his mother and sisters, how happy they would be to see him exiting the Unity Booth as a United pair with Virginia.

Someone called their names, and they turned around to see Amos grinning and yelling from the side of the rope, "Good luck!" as the couple went forward into the Unity Booth.

Tradition in the city of Alcetra stated that no one talked about what power they were given with their Union, but Amos News caught the whole thing on camera. Documenting the time Virginia and Korbin walked into the Unity Booth, showing moments later a bright orange light exploding from the cracks of the booth, right before the Ananta that hung from the top of the conservatory exploded into orange fireworks. Then fireworks of all Unity colors exploded from everywhere as Korbin and

Virginia walked out of the booth, hand in hand, with puzzled smiles.

"Death is not ***the end,*** *it's merely a change in form."*

~ Grandmother Blane

ACKNOWLEDGMENT

I thank my Father for nurturing my superpower of GRIT, for teaching me to take on big tasks and never give up; for teaching me to think and work hard, and for helping me see that I am bigger than any task put in front of me!

My dearest friends who were with me along this journey, some who held me up in the darkness, others a constant source of encouragement, stability and who were my glimmers of happiness: Victoria, Marita, Corinne, Lee, Judy, Brian, Paulo, Diana, Tara, Rosa, Travis. Never forgetting all the family, friends, acquaintances and clients whose love and kindness and teaching brought me to this journey.

Special thanks to my editor, Kara Aisenbrey, who magically appeared on the last stretch of my writing journey when I was so tired and weak. She read through my mess repeatedly, somehow understanding everything I couldn't say and helped me tell a better story.

For Don, whose life and death brought me to this story, my person, and loving fortress for me and my daughter along our journey, so very long ago. Acknowledging also his mother and father, and sisters, who raised him to be the person for me. I still miss him every day.

To my dogs: Charlie, the best boy– greatest there ever was, love of my life, who walked beside me and sometimes leading me from the dark into the light; and Pearl, the best girl ever who is my future, the soul for whom my heart beats for.

Of course, I am thankful to my grief and sadness, which no longer hides behind anger. I was very sad along this writing journey, and I don't know what this story would look like if the deep sorrow I felt hadn't taken home in every drop of my blood.

www.ingramcontent.com/pod-product-compliance
Lightning Source LLC
LaVergne TN
LVHW010559100826
845148LV00014B/2776
9798218666286